Dance of the Firefly

The Emma Series, Volume 1

Melissa Ann Palmer

Published by Melissa Ann Palmer, 2026.

DANCE OF THE FIREFLY

First edition. January 6, 2026.

Copyright © 2026 Melissa Ann Palmer.

ISBN: 978-1964882048

Written by Melissa Ann Palmer.

Beth,

Your belief in me gave me the courage to put pen to paper and bring this story to life. Thank you for your unwavering support and friendship.

Part 1

Chapter 1

EMMA, TWO YEARS AGO

The pregnancy test clattered into the sink as my knees gave out.

Two lines. Positive.

I sat on the closed toilet lid, staring at those two pink lines that had just rewritten my entire future. The bathroom walls seemed to tilt and close in. My breathing came faster, shallower. The fluorescent light buzzed overhead, too bright, making my head pound.

No. No, no, no.

This was not how my story was supposed to unfold. I was supposed to finish my psychology degree first.

Scott and I were supposed to be stable first. We were supposed to be happy first.

Instead, I was trapped in a relationship that was slowly destroying me, planning a wedding I wasn't sure I wanted, and now, God, now I was pregnant.

My hand pressed against my still-flat stomach. The clinical part of my brain, the part that had spent three years studying human behavior and psychological patterns, supplied the facts with detached precision:

Panic attack. Hyperventilation. Elevated heart rate. Feeling of impending doom.

The feeling was justified.

How did I get here?

The question echoed in the small bathroom, and suddenly I was back there. Three months ago. The company party where everything had started to unravel in a way I could no longer pretend to ignore.

***

The black dress still had the tags on when I pulled it from my closet that December evening. I'd bought it three weeks earlier with Becca, back when Scott first mentioned his company's winter party. Back when I'd been excited about it.

"You're going to look amazing," Becca had said in the dressing room, watching me turn in front of the mirror. Then her voice had shifted to that tone she used when she was about to say something I didn't want to hear.

"Just... be careful, okay? With the drinking."

I'd known what she meant. Scott's drinking had gotten worse over the past few months. Not every night, but enough that I'd started counting his beers, started watching for the signs. The way his jaw would set after the third one. The edge that crept into his voice after the fourth.

"It'll be fine," I'd told her. "It's a work party. He'll keep it together."

She'd given me that look. The one that said she didn't believe me but loved me enough not to push. "If you need me, I'm one phone call away. Any time, Em. I mean it."

I should have listened to her.

Standing in front of the bathroom mirror that night, I studied my reflection. The dress fit perfectly. Knee-length, open back, simple black beads at the neckline.

I'd styled my hair in a chignon because Scott had mentioned once, early on, that he liked it that way.

When he'd still noticed things like that. When he'd still looked at me like I was someone special instead of someone who couldn't do anything right.

Stop. Tonight will be different. It has to be.

Six months ago, Scott had been different too.

Attentive. Supportive. He'd listened when I talked about my psychology classes, about my dreams of graduate school. He'd made me feel seen in a way I'd never experienced before.

"You're going to change lives," he'd said once, his eyes warm with certainty. "You're going to be amazing at this."

I'd believed him. I'd believed in us.

When had that shifted? When had his interest turned into interrogation, his protection into control?

The bathroom door opened and Scott emerged in his charcoal suit, looking sharp and handsome. For a moment, I saw the man I'd fallen for.

"You look beautiful," he said, and something in my chest loosened.

Maybe tonight would remind us both of who we used to be.

***

The hotel ballroom glittered with crystal chandeliers and candlelight. Scott's coworkers welcomed me warmly, asking about my studies at Providence

College, making me feel included. The meal was excellent. Prime rib and roasted vegetables, chocolate mousse for dessert. When Scott led me to the dance floor, I let myself relax into his arms.

This was good. This was what we needed.

But I'd been counting. Three beers before dinner. Two during. Another after dessert.

My stomach tightened each time I saw him reach for a new bottle, each time I caught the looseness creeping into his movements. The flutter of nervousness was familiar now, a constant companion. I'd learned to read the signs: the way his laugh got louder, the way his grip on my waist would tighten just slightly.

Around nine o'clock, an older man approached our table.

"Scott! There you are." Distinguished, silver-haired, expensive suit. "And this must be the lovely Emma you've been telling us about."

Scott stood quickly. "Emma, this is Jim Patterson, my boss."

"It's wonderful to meet you," I said, shaking his hand.

"The pleasure is entirely mine," Jim said. "I hope Scott's been treating you well. He's one of our best. We'd hate to lose him."

"He speaks very highly of the company," I replied carefully.

"Well, I won't monopolize your evening, but I wonder if I might steal you for one dance?" Jim extended his hand. "I promise to return her in one piece, Scott."

I glanced at Scott. His smile didn't quite reach his eyes, but he nodded. "Go ahead. I'll grab another beer."

Another beer. Seven. Or was it eight?

Jim was a proper dancer, old-school, keeping appropriate distance. He asked about my psychology studies, told me about his daughter in social work, was generally charming in a grandfatherly way. I got enthusiastic explaining my research interests, the way I always did when someone actually seemed interested.

Cognitive behavioral therapy. Trauma recovery. The way the brain could rewire itself, create new patterns.

I didn't notice Scott watching us. Didn't see the way his expression had hardened.

As the song ended, Jim bowed slightly and kissed my hand. It was a gesture that felt like something from another era. "Thank you for the dance, my dear. Scott is a lucky man."

I felt myself blush, flustered by the unexpected chivalry. "Thank you."

When I returned to our table, Scott was sitting with another beer, his expression unreadable.

"That was nice of him," I said brightly. "He seems like a good boss."

"Yeah." He took a long drink, not looking at me.

The temperature in the room seemed to drop. I knew that tone. That flatness that meant I'd done something wrong, though I couldn't figure out what.

"Are you okay?" I asked quietly when we danced later, his grip on my waist too tight.

"Fine."

But he wasn't fine. I could feel the anger radiating off him in waves.

***

The elevator ride to our hotel room was silent. My heart hammered against my ribs. What had I done? I replayed the evening, the dance, the conversation with Jim. Had I smiled too much? Said something wrong?

I took my time in the bathroom, removing my makeup slowly, changing into the black silk nightgown I'd bought for tonight. When I'd imagined this moment earlier, I'd pictured romance. Scott's face lighting up, us falling into bed together and forgetting everything except each other.

But when I emerged, the scene was all wrong.

Scott sat on the edge of the bed, tie removed but still dressed, jaw set. The air felt heavy, dangerous.

"The bathroom's free," I said quietly.

"You look nice." His tone was ice-cold.

"Thank you. I hoped you would like it." My voice came out smaller than I intended.

"Really? Were you thinking of me when you bought that?"

The question hit like a slap. "What? What do you mean?"

"I couldn't help but notice how you and Jim looked at each other while dancing." He was still sitting, but everything about his posture screamed danger. "Are you sure you didn't buy that with hopes that he would see you in it?"

"Scott, what are you talking about? I didn't even know Jim until tonight!"

"I don't appreciate you making me look like a fool while you flirt with my boss." His voice rose, cutting.

"How do you think that looked? In front of all my colleagues?"

"It was one dance! I was being polite. He's your boss..."

"Exactly. That's my point exactly." He stood, and I took an instinctive step back toward the bathroom. "So next time, if you're going to start flirting with some guy right next to me, I would appreciate it if you didn't choose my boss!"

"He asked me to dance. What was I supposed to do, refuse?" My voice shook.

"Just don't ever embarrass me like that again."

His fists were clenched at his sides. For a moment, I thought he might...

But he didn't. He stormed past me into the bathroom, slamming the door hard enough to make me flinch.

I stood frozen, trembling. The nightgown I'd been excited about felt wrong now, exposing. I climbed under the covers and pulled them to my chin, turning off the light.

In the darkness, tears slid down my temples into my hair. I kept silent, not wanting him to hear, not wanting to make it worse.

How had this happened?

I replayed the dance. Had I smiled too warmly? Jim had asked about my research and I'd gotten enthusiastic explaining it. Had that looked like flirting?

The hand kiss. That's when I'd blushed. Scott must have seen that.

Maybe I had been too animated. Too friendly.

Scott's ex had cheated on him. He'd told me that much, though he never gave details. Of course, he was sensitive to anything that might look like I was seeking attention from other men. Of course he'd be hypervigilant.

And the nightgown. God, from his perspective it must have looked like I'd dressed up for Jim.

I should have been more careful. More aware.

When Scott emerged from the bathroom, he got into bed without a word, turning his back to me. I stayed perfectly still, barely breathing.

This wasn't abuse. Abuse was violence, broken bones, bruises you had to explain away. This was just jealousy, insecurity. His past trauma making him reactive. Lots of men got jealous when they'd been hurt before.

Even as I thought it, I knew I was lying to myself. I'd studied this. I could draw the cycle of abuse from memory, label each phase, cite the research on escalation patterns. Tension building. Incident. Reconciliation. Calm.

We were in the tension-building phase. And I was already making excuses for him, already blaming myself.

Eventually I fell into fitful sleep, Scott's breathing heavy and even beside me.

***

The morning light felt too bright, too cheerful. Scott was already up, dressed, packing his overnight bag. His movements were sharp, his jaw set.

"Morning," I ventured.

"Morning." Cold. Distant.

I wanted to apologize, to explain, but the danger signals were too strong. I packed in silence, and we drove home without speaking.

The quiet in the car was suffocating. I stared out the window, too anxious to even suggest music.

Finally, halfway home, Scott spoke.

"I'm sorry about last night."

Relief flooded through me. "I'm sorry too. I should have been more careful."

"It just... seeing you with him like that. The way he was looking at you." His voice was softer now, almost vulnerable. "It brought back a lot of stuff with my ex."

His ex. The woman who'd cheated, who'd made him unable to trust. Of course that's what this was about.

"I know," I said gently. "But Scott, I would never do that to you. You have to know that."

"I do know that." He reached over and took my hand.

"It's just hard sometimes. When I see other guys looking at you the way he was."

"He wasn't looking at me like anything. He was just being polite."

"You didn't see it from where I was sitting." His grip tightened slightly. "But I trust you, Em. I just need you to understand how things look sometimes."

"I do understand. And I'll be more careful. I promise."

His hand stayed in mine the rest of the drive, and by the time we got home, the tension had dissolved. Scott kissed me before heading to the living room. I went to unpack.

As I hung up the black dress, I felt that complicated mix of emotions I was getting used to. Relief that we'd worked through it. Guilt that I'd triggered his insecurity. Determination to be more careful next time.

Scott had been badly hurt. It made sense he'd be sensitive. I just needed to be more aware of how my actions might look to someone carrying that kind of pain.

That wasn't unreasonable. That was just being considerate.

We'd worked through it. We'd communicated.

Everything was fine now.

We were fine.

***

Except we weren't fine.

Two weeks later, Scott proposed. I said yes because I loved him, because I believed the good parts of him were real, because I thought marriage would give us a fresh start. Because I was twenty-two years old and didn't know any better.

His family embraced me completely. His mother especially, warm, welcoming, everything I'd hoped for. One afternoon over tea in her living room, she'd said something that lodged itself in my mind like a splinter.

"I hope he can be the husband you deserve."

The words had made me look up sharply, teacup frozen halfway to my lips. But she'd just smiled and poured more tea, and I'd let the moment pass without asking what she meant.

Did she know something? Had she seen the warning signs I'd been so carefully ignoring?

I didn't want to find out.

The months that followed were a careful balance. Scott's drinking persisted, but his outbursts had diminished. He hadn't broken anything in weeks. He hadn't called me names. We'd achieved a kind of peace maintained by my vigilance and his relative calm.

The honeymoon phase of the cycle. I knew that. The calm after the storm, the reconciliation period before tension started building again.

But knowing the theory and accepting it applied to my life remained two separate things.

I threw myself into wedding planning, into making my own dress to save money. I threw myself into my coursework, pushing harder and harder because if I stopped, if I slowed down, I'd have to think.

I'd have to feel.

And then April arrived, and the exhaustion hit. Bone-deep. Unshakeable. The nausea came next, relentless vomiting that left me bedridden.

That's when I knew.

***

Now, sitting on the bathroom floor with a positive pregnancy test in the sink, all of it crashed over me at once.

I was pregnant. Engaged to a man who terrified me. Planning a wedding I wasn't sure I wanted. And I couldn't see a way out.

What kind of father would Scott be? The question surfaced unbidden, and with it came all the research I'd studied, all the statistics I'd memorized. Children who witnessed domestic violence showed increased risk of behavioral problems, anxiety, depression, PTSD. The cycle often continued into the next generation.

Children learned what love looked like from watching their parents.

What would this child learn from watching us?

I thought about Scott's mother's words: *I hope he can be the husband you deserve.*

Would he smash coffee cups when the baby cried?

Would he call me names in front of our child? Would the drinking get worse under the stress of parenthood?

The research on abuse during pregnancy was clear. It often escalated. Having a baby didn't fix relationships. It strained them. And I was already walking on eggshells, already counting his drinks, already measuring every word and gesture to avoid triggering his anger.

For the first time, I allowed myself to think the unthinkable: What if I didn't go through with any of this? What if I just... left?

But even as the thought formed, I felt the weight of expectations crushing down on me. His family who loved me. The dress I was sewing, hours of work already invested. The invitations we'd ordered. The vision I'd had since I was a little girl of what my life would be.

And now, a baby. How could I possibly leave now?

What kind of person would I be? Pregnant women didn't leave. Families stayed together. That's what you did. That's what was right.

Except it wasn't right. Nothing about this was right.

I was trapped.

I thought about calling Becca. But I already knew what she'd say. She'd tell me to leave. She'd tell me none of this was normal. She'd see right through every excuse

I'd built, every rationalization I'd constructed.

So, I didn't call.

I don't know how long I sat there before I finally pulled myself together. Splashed cold water on my face. Looked at the stranger in the mirror and tried to recognize her.

I hid the pregnancy test in the back of a drawer, wrapped in toilet paper like a terrible secret.

I had to tell Scott. But not yet. Not today. I needed time to figure out what this meant, what I was going to do.

I needed time to figure out how to breathe again.

But somewhere in the back of my mind, I already knew the truth. I knew what the research said about abuse during pregnancy. I knew the statistics on escalation. I knew that having a baby wouldn't fix us, wouldn't make him stop drinking, wouldn't make him stop hurting me.

I knew all of this with perfect clarity.

And I still didn't know how to leave.

Chapter 2

I t felt so overwhelming to have to tell Scott about this secret. To be completely honest, I wanted to wish this news away. I lay awake at night imagining different scenarios: that I'd made a mistake, that the test was faulty, that I'd wake up and my period would start and this would all be a bad dream.

But I knew that wasn't possible. The nausea was too real, too persistent. My body was changing whether I wanted it to or not.

I avoided him for two days, carrying this secret like a stone in my chest. Every time I opened my mouth to tell him, fear sealed my throat shut. What would he do? Would he explode again? Would he blame me?

Part of me knew that telling him would make it real, would close off any escape routes I'd been unconsciously mapping.

Several mornings later, I steeled myself and approached him while he was drinking coffee at the kitchen table. The morning light was pale and watery. He was scrolling through his phone, still in his undershirt and boxers, his hair rumpled from sleep.

"Um, Scott, do you have a minute?" My voice came out thin, anxiety threading through every syllable. My hands were clammy. My pulse fluttered in my throat like a trapped bird.

"Yeah, babe, what's up?" He didn't look up from his phone.

I took a breath. "Um, I'm not sure how to tell you this." Just say it. Just get it over with. "I'm pregnant."

I handed him the test stick, the plastic warm from my sweaty palm. My heart pounded so hard I thought he might hear it.

He finally looked up. His eyes moved from my face to the test in his hand. Heavy silence hung in the air as he processed the news. Minutes felt like hours. I watched emotions flicker across his face. Shock, confusion, something that might have been anger or fear or both.

The refrigerator hummed. A car drove past outside. Time stretched.

Finally, he spoke. "Are you sure? Can we trust these things?" His voice trembled. His hand holding the test shook slightly.

"Well, I suppose I could take another one, but I think they're pretty accurate." I wrapped my arms around myself. I felt exposed, vulnerable, like I'd confessed to something shameful.

"No, you should see a doctor. That's the only way to know for sure." An air of finality in his tone. He set the test down face-down on the table, as if he couldn't bear to look at those two pink lines.

"Okay. I'll make an appointment."

He stood abruptly, his chair scraping against the floor. He ran both hands through his hair. It was a gesture I'd come to recognize as his tell when he was struggling to maintain control. Then he walked toward the bathroom without another word, without touching me, without offering any reassurance.

I noted this distantly. The complete absence of concern for how I was feeling. The way he'd made this entirely about him. Classic narcissistic response pattern: external locus of control, inability to regulate emotion, displacement of responsibility. I could write a textbook example of what was happening here.

But knowing the clinical terms didn't make it hurt less.

A few minutes later, I heard the water running in the shower. Then Scott's emotions erupted behind the closed bathroom door. "Son of a bitch!" His frustration echoed through the house. Something slammed, his fist against the wall, maybe. I flinched at the sound.

I stood frozen in the kitchen, still holding myself, wishing I hadn't had to break this news to him. Wishing I could take it back. Wishing I could rewind time to before any of this happened.

He was just shocked, I told myself. He needed time to process. This was a lot for both of us.

But that small voice in my head, the one that sounded like my abnormal psychology professor, whispered: He didn't ask if you were okay. He didn't ask how you felt. He made your pregnancy about his frustration. Those are red flags.

I called my doctor from the bedroom, keeping my voice low even though the shower was still running. I was fortunate to secure an appointment later that day. The receptionist's cheerful tone made me want to cry.

During the visit, Dr. Wilson probed about my symptoms. Her office smelled like antiseptic and the lavender oil she kept in a diffuser. I'd been coming here since I was a kid. The same ocean-scene print on the wall, the same crinkly paper on the exam table. The familiarity made me feel both comforted and terrified.

"So, have you been tired lately?"

"Exhausted. Like I can barely keep my eyes open past six."

"And you've been vomiting and experiencing nausea?"

"Yes, to both. Mostly mornings, but sometimes all day."

"Any constipation issues?"

"Very much so." My cheeks heated with embarrassment even though she was a doctor, even though this was clinical.

She took my blood for a pregnancy test, the needle pinching as it slid into my arm. I watched my blood fill the vial, dark red and warm. "The urine tests are almost 100% accurate," she assured me, "but I'll do this to put your mind at ease."

But my mind wasn't at ease. My mind was screaming.

As I waited for the results in the small exam room, anxiety gnawed at me. I studied my hands, picked at my cuticles until one started to bleed. The clock on the wall ticked loudly.

What was I going to do? How was I going to finish school? How was I going to afford this?

And underneath all those practical concerns was the deeper, more terrifying question: How am I going to raise a child with Scott?

The research on domestic violence during pregnancy was unequivocal. Abuse often escalated when women became pregnant. The violence became more frequent, more severe. Pregnant women in abusive relationships faced increased risk of miscarriage, preterm labor, low birth weight, even homicide.

Homicide. The leading cause of death for pregnant women wasn't complications from pregnancy. It was homicide. Usually by an intimate partner.

I knew these statistics. I'd studied them. And now I was living them.

The blood test confirmed what I already knew. Dr. Wilson returned with a smile I couldn't return. She asked whether I preferred to work with an OB/GYN or have her handle my prenatal care and delivery.

Because she treated my whole family, I worried about confidentiality. The thought of my mother finding out before I was ready made my stomach clench. "I'd love for you to deliver the baby," I said, my voice steadier than I felt. "But can we keep this between us for now? I'm not ready to share this with my family."

"Of course, Emma. This is your news to share when you're ready. You're the patient, not them." Her hand was warm on my shoulder.

I nodded, grateful, blinking back tears. Her kindness was almost harder to bear than Scott's anger.

I walked outside to find Scott waiting in the car, engine running. He was staring straight ahead, jaw tight, hands gripping the steering wheel.

I slid into the passenger seat, the vinyl cold against my legs. The pine air freshener hanging from the rearview mirror smelled artificial and cloying.

"So," I began tentatively.

"Yeah, I know." A heavy sigh. "I figured you'd have been out here sooner if it was negative."

His voice was flat. Defeated. He still wouldn't look at me.

When he finally glanced my way, I saw distress in his eyes, red-rimmed, like he'd been crying. The anger from this morning had given way to something worse. Resignation. Despair.

"I'm sorry, Scott," I murmured.

The apology was automatic. Even though I knew, logically, that this wasn't just my fault. It took two people. But somehow, I still felt the need to apologize, to shoulder the blame, to make him feel better.

This was another pattern. Another textbook example. The victim apologizing to the abuser. Taking responsibility for situations beyond their control. Trying to manage the abuser's emotions to prevent the next explosion.

"Yeah," he whispered, his voice fraught with emotion. "Me too."

He put the car in drive. We pulled out of the parking lot in silence. I watched the medical building recede in the side mirror, watched the normal world going about its day. People walking dogs, a mother pushing a stroller, someone getting coffee at the Dunkin' Donuts drive-through. All these ordinary moments happening while my life was falling apart.

I pressed my hand against my stomach, still flat, still showing no signs of the life growing inside. A baby. Our baby.

The words didn't feel real.

Scott turned on the radio, loud classic rock that made conversation impossible, and we drove home without speaking.

Back at the apartment, he went straight to the TV room. I heard the clink of a bottle opening before I even made it to the bedroom.

Of course. Of course that's how he'd cope with this.

I sat on the edge of our bed, doctor's pamphlets about prenatal vitamins and first-trimester care clutched in my hands. The walls felt like they were closing in. The wedding dress hung on the back of the closet door, white lace mocking me. The fabric I'd so carefully chosen, the pattern I'd modified, the hours of work I'd poured into it. All of it suddenly seemed like evidence of my own delusion.

I was going to marry him. I was going to have his baby. And I had never felt more alone in my life.

Somewhere in my psychology textbooks was a chapter on learned helplessness. About how repeated exposure to inescapable stress teaches people to stop trying to escape even when escape becomes possible. The famous experiments with dogs receiving electric shocks. After enough trials where they couldn't escape, the dogs stopped trying even when the barrier was removed. They just lay down and took the shocks.

Was that what I was doing? Lying down and taking it?

I thought about the pregnancy statistics again. The escalation patterns. The cycle that would likely intensify now. I thought about my textbooks, my professors, everything I'd learned about abuse and trauma and the psychological factors that kept women trapped.

I had all the information I needed to understand my situation perfectly. I could diagnose it, analyze it, predict where it was heading with reasonable accuracy.

What I didn't have was the strength to do anything about it.

The thought was too big, too frightening. I pushed it away and focused on the practical. I needed to take my prenatal vitamin. I needed to eat something. I needed to keep functioning.

One foot in front of the other. That's all I could do.

Just keep moving forward, even if I wasn't sure where I was going anymore.

Even if some part of me suspected I was walking deeper into a trap.

***

The following days were fraught with an eerie tension that clung to the air like thick fog. We moved around each other carefully, like dancers who'd forgotten the steps. Afraid of touching. Afraid of speaking. We talked about groceries and bills and whether it would rain.

We didn't talk about the baby. We didn't talk about us.

I was preparing dinner one afternoon in April, chopping vegetables with mechanical precision, when Scott entered the kitchen. The late afternoon sun cast long shadows across the floor. I heard him before I saw him. Heavy, deliberate footsteps.

"So, we should probably move up the wedding if we're going to have a baby. You can't walk down the aisle at eight months pregnant."

The knife stilled in my hand. I set it down carefully on the cutting board, my fingers trembling slightly. "Yeah, I guess so."

Not *should we still get married?* Not *how are we going to make this work?* Just *you can't be visibly pregnant in the wedding photos.*

"Do you want to call your parents?" I kept my voice neutral, my eyes on the half-chopped carrots.

"Yes, I suppose so. I thought we'd do it in a couple months. Like June?"

He leaned against the counter, arms crossed.

"Yeah, that sounds good."

The words felt empty, devoid of the excitement that should accompany wedding planning. June. Two months away. I'd have to finish the dress faster. We'd have to tell everyone we'd moved it up. What would we say? That we couldn't wait?

It was as if we were navigating through motions we were expected to perform, rather than choices made from love and desire. Check the boxes: engagement, wedding, baby. The order was wrong, but we could fix that with a revised timeline.

Scott left the kitchen without another word. I heard the refrigerator in the TV room open, heard the now-familiar sound of a bottle cap twisting off.

I resumed chopping, the rhythmic sound of the knife against the board the only noise in the apartment.

***

The idea that a tiny life was growing inside me felt surreal, like it was happening to someone else. Some other Emma in some parallel universe. My body was changing in ways I couldn't see yet. Cells dividing, a heart forming, beginning to beat.

And I felt... nothing. Or maybe I felt too much and had gone numb from the overload.

Dissociation. A defense mechanism where the mind disconnects from reality to cope with overwhelming stress. I was watching my own life like a movie, observing from a safe distance because being fully present was unbearable.

I tried my best to embrace the idea of motherhood, to feel what I was supposed to feel. I signed up for countless email newsletters from parenting websites, their cheerful subject lines mocking me: "Your baby this week!" and "Get ready for parenthood!" I scrolled through baby products online and smiled when people asked how I was feeling. I offered the expected responses about being tired but excited.

I played the part. Yet the empty feeling persisted, gnawing at me from within like a dull, constant ache.

Finally, we decided to share the news with our families. Scott's parents were thrilled. His mother held my hands and told me I'd be a wonderful mother, and I had to look away so she wouldn't see the doubt in my eyes.

My own family's reaction was more subdued but no less congratulatory. My mother's smile didn't quite reach her eyes. She knew me too well, could read the tension in my shoulders, the strain in my voice. But she said all the right things and didn't voice whatever concerns lurked beneath her careful pleasantry.

Behind all the smiles and well-wishes, my heart ached. I felt like a fraud, accepting congratulations for something that felt more like a trap than a blessing.

Chapter 3

One evening in late April, I returned home after a late class to find Scott sitting in the TV room, a nearly empty vodka bottle by his side. The sight made my stomach drop. Not because he was drinking, that was routine now. But because of how much he'd consumed. The bottle had been full this morning.

His mood was noticeably off, and his eyes bore an unsettling look. Glassy, unfocused, but also somehow hyper-focused on me as I walked in. Predatory.

The room was dark except for the television's flickering blue light. I could smell the alcohol from the doorway.

"Hey, I'm home." Cautious. My eyes darted to the bottle, calculating how drunk he was, assessing the danger level. My backpack still hung from my shoulder; my keys clutched in my hand like a potential weapon.

"Hey." His voice laced with tension and something darker. Not quite slurring, but slower than normal. More deliberate.

"Is everything okay?"

My heart pounded. Every instinct told me to turn around, to leave, to get out. But where would I go? This was my home. My stuff was here. And I was so tired of running, of being afraid in my own apartment.

"No. No, everything's not okay. We are not okay. This is not okay."

Each word enunciated with chilling precision, like he'd been rehearsing this, building up to it all day. He set the bottle down on the side table with exaggerated care.

A shiver ran down my spine. "So, do you want to talk about it?"

My voice came out smaller than I intended.

He stood up, and I took an involuntary step backward. "You can't have this baby."

His voice a cold blade slicing through the air.

The words didn't make sense at first. "What do you mean?"

My breath caught in my throat. My hand moved unconsciously to my stomach, protective.

"You know what I mean, Emma. You can't have this baby. We can't have this baby."

He took a step toward me.

Dread washed over me, cold and nauseating. "Scott, I know the timing isn't great, but I just can't have an abortion. It's not something I could ever do."

My voice shaking now. My legs unsteady.

"No, Emma. You need to do it. We can't have this baby. I'm not ready to be a dad. This is not what I wanted."

Another step toward me.

The clinical part of my brain noted this for what it was: coercive control. Reproductive coercion. The deliberate interference with pregnancy decisions. The use of threats or intimidation to force reproductive choices. It was a form of intimate partner violence, a predictor of escalation to physical abuse.

I was living the textbook definition. Again.

"I'm sorry, Scott." Feeling the tension and fear rise within me like bile. My back was against the wall now. Literally. When had I backed up that far? "It's not what I wanted for us either, but I'm not going to end my baby's life."

"Emma, you don't have a choice." Chilling finality. He was close enough now that I could see the veins in his eyes, red from alcohol and rage.

"What are you saying, Scott?"

My voice quaking.

"I'm saying you will put an end to this. Immediately."

His words dripping with venom. He wasn't yelling. Somehow that was worse, that eerie control, that cold deliberation.

A surge of fear coursed through me, primal and consuming. Fight or flight response. Amygdala hijack. My hands were shaking. My vision narrowed. My body knew the danger even as my mind scrambled to process it.

He's threatening your baby. He's threatening you. Get out. Get out now.

But my mouth said, "Okay."

The word came out automatically, a survival response. Appeasement. Fawn response, the lesser-known fourth option when fight, flight, and freeze aren't available.

"Okay, I will." My voice barely above a whisper.

I hated myself the moment I said it. Hated how small I'd become, how easily I capitulated, how I'd learned that agreement, even false agreement, was the fastest way to safety.

"Good."

Something in his expression shifted. Satisfaction replacing rage. He'd gotten what he wanted. He'd won.

I retreated from the room, desperate to escape his presence, my legs shaky as I climbed the stairs. I went straight to the bathroom and locked the door. The only room in the apartment with a lock. I took a long, solitary shower, turning the water as hot as I could stand it, letting it mask the tears streaming down my face, letting the sound drown out my sobs.

I scrubbed at my skin until it was red, trying to wash off the feeling of his words, his proximity, his threat.

The steam filled the small bathroom, making it hard to breathe. Or maybe that was just the panic. I slid down the shower wall and sat on the floor of the tub, water pounding on my head, and let myself fall apart where no one could see.

I didn't know how long I stayed there. Long enough that the water started to run cool. Long enough that my fingers pruned. Long enough to cry out the worst of it.

Afterward, I changed into warm pajamas. Soft flannel that felt like armor, like comfort, like safety even though I knew it was just fabric. I checked that he was occupied in front of the TV before climbing into bed. Then I cried myself to sleep, quieter this time, my face pressed into the pillow so he wouldn't hear if he came upstairs.

The weight of my choices bore heavily upon my heart.

The nightmare was here, and I was living in it, and I'd just promised to do something I couldn't do, wouldn't do, to appease a man who'd threatened me and my unborn child.

I knew what this was. I could name every element: the escalation pattern, the reproductive coercion, the threat of violence, the survival response of compliance. I could cite studies on pregnant women in abusive relationships, statistics on violence escalation, research on the effectiveness of safety planning.

I had all the knowledge. All the clinical terminology. All the theoretical understanding.

What I didn't have was a way out.

In the darkness, my hand found my stomach again, still flat, still showing nothing. "I'm sorry," I whispered to the tiny life inside me. "I'm so sorry."

I didn't know what I was apologizing for. For bringing them into this, for not being stronger, for not leaving sooner, for making promises I couldn't keep. Maybe all of it.

Maybe I was apologizing for not being the mother they deserved, the way Scott's mother had hoped he'd be the husband I deserved. We were all hoping for people we'd never be, trapped in roles we didn't know how to play.

I fell asleep with tears still wet on my face, with fear still tight in my chest, with no idea what I was going to do tomorrow, or the day after, or the day after that.

One day at a time, I told myself. Just survive one day at a time.

It was the only plan I had.

***

The morning after our tense conversation, Scott seemed to be in a markedly better mood. Perhaps due to my reluctant agreement with his plan. He was almost cheerful as he made coffee, humming under his breath, a sound I hadn't heard in months.

It made my skin crawl.

As we sat together at the kitchen table, his demeanor suddenly shifted, his face taking on a serious expression. I tensed, my hands wrapping around my coffee mug.

"So, you need to make a phone call this morning to make arrangements." His eyes bored into me over the rim of his cup.

My throat felt tight. "Yeah, I will." My voice heavy with the weight of the lie I was telling. Because I knew, even as I said it, that I wasn't going to go through with it. I couldn't. But I needed him to believe I would.

He slid a piece of paper across the table. The name and phone number of a local Planned Parenthood office. His handwriting, deliberate and neat. He'd looked this up. Planned this. Written it down like a to-do list item.

"Scott, I said I would call." A flash of irritation breaking through my fear.

"Good, see to it that this gets taken care of soon." His tone unwavering. Businesslike. As if we were discussing getting the oil changed in the car.

"I hope you're planning on going with me." My voice tinged with fear and desperation. "Because I'm scared, Scott. That's the least you can do."

He reluctantly agreed. "Okay, I'll go with you." But his expression showed no empathy, no comfort. Just satisfaction that I was falling in line.

I made the call right there, while he watched, his arms crossed. My hands shook as I dialed. The clinic staff was kind, professional, explaining the process in a gentle voice that made me want to cry.

I secured an appointment for the following Tuesday. Scott visibly exhaled in relief when I hung up, his whole body relaxing. He smiled at me, actually smiled, and reached across the table to squeeze my hand. "See? That wasn't so hard. Everything's going to be fine now."

I had five days to figure out what I was really going to do.

***

That evening, we decided to grab dinner at one of our favorite local restaurants. His suggestion, his attempt to celebrate that he'd gotten his way. The atmosphere was cozy, with dimmed lights and soft jazz. It could have been romantic. Once upon a time, it would have been.

Scott confidently ordered the sirloin, complete with mashed potatoes and carrots, and, of course, a Budweiser.

His first drink of the evening. I noted it. Catalogued it. Began my mental calculations.

I chose a mushroom burger, crispy fries, and a Diet Coke.

Scott shot me a questioning look, his eyes narrowing.

"Don't you want a glass of wine?" His gaze steady while the waitress stood ready, her pen poised.

Something in his tone set off alarm bells. "No, I'd rather have the Diet Coke, thanks." Keeping my voice light.

The waitress left, and Scott launched into a conversation I dreaded. "Why aren't you drinking all of a sudden?" His voice tinged with concern that felt more like suspicion.

"I'm just not in the mood." Hoping to brush off the topic. My heart was starting to beat faster.

"Are you sure it's not because you're pregnant?" His voice had an edge now, sharp and cutting. "I mean, you agreed to get the procedure. You're getting the procedure, right? There's no reason not to have a glass of wine." He leaned forward across the table.

"Scott, I'm just not in the mood to drink. Do I have to have a reason?" My hands twisted the napkin in my lap.

It was evident he was concerned about my commitment to the appointment. He didn't trust me. Maybe he shouldn't.

"Yes, I just think if you're having the procedure, then there's no reason why you shouldn't have a simple glass of wine." His voice progressively louder. People at nearby tables were starting to glance over.

"Scott, please, let's drop this." My voice low and urgent. "I just want the Diet Coke."

He didn't mention the wine again, but the atmosphere was ruined. When our food arrived, we ate quickly, mechanically, barely tasting it. I forced down my burger even though my stomach was in knots.

On our way home, Scott stopped at the liquor store and picked up an 18-pack of beer. I watched him carry it to the car and felt dread settle over me like a heavy blanket.

When we got home, I grabbed a book and retreated to the bedroom, closing the door softly behind me. Scott took the beer into the TV room and settled in for a solo drinking session. I could hear the television, the hiss of bottles opening, one after another.

I tried to read but couldn't focus. I kept listening to the sounds from downstairs, counting the bottles in my head. One. Two. Three. By the time I got to eight, my anxiety was through the roof.

Finally, I gave up and turned off the light. I changed into pajamas, brushed my teeth, got into bed. The apartment had gone quiet. Too quiet. I lay there in the darkness, listening, my body tense.

Several hours later, Scott stormed into the room and flipped on the light, jarring me abruptly from fitful sleep. The sudden brightness felt like an assault.

"Emma, get up. We need to talk." He pulled the covers back. His words were slurred, his movements uncoordinated but aggressive.

Startled, I blinked in confusion, my heart immediately racing. "Scott, what time is it? Can't this wait until morning?" The clock on the nightstand read 2:47 AM.

"No, this is important. Get up." He tugged at the blankets, pulling them completely off me.

"Okay, what's so important that you had to wake me?" My voice laced with irritation and fear. I was sitting up now, fully awake, adrenaline flooding my system.

"I just wanted to make sure you plan on keeping your end of our agreement." His tone ominous. He was swaying slightly, his eyes unfocused but fixed on me with an intensity that made my blood run cold.

"What are you talking about?" Struggling to keep my voice steady. I knew exactly what he was talking about.

"You know what I'm talking about. And I don't know what you were trying to pull tonight at the restaurant, but if you have any ideas about not going through with it, you'd better think again. Trust me, you will regret it." His voice dripping with menace. He took a step closer to the bed.

Something in me snapped. "Are you threatening me? I don't need to take this from you! Who do you think you are?" I shouted, my fear giving way to anger, to months of suppressed rage finally breaking free.

Ignoring my protests, he lunged forward and grabbed my arm, his fingers digging into my flesh, and pulled me close. I could smell the beer on his breath, sour and overwhelming. "Don't make me repeat myself. You will get that procedure done on Tuesday, or you will regret it for the rest of your life." He whispered into my ear, his grip on my arm tightening.

I attempted to pull away, twisting in his grasp. "Cut it out! You can't talk to me like that!" I screamed, struggling to free myself, my bare feet scrambling for purchase on the floor.

He dragged me toward the door. I realized we were at the top of the stairs. He still had one hand tightly clutching my arm. He took his other hand and seized my hair in his fist, yanking my head back. Pain exploded across my scalp. And then, suddenly, he attempted to push me toward the stairs.

Time seemed to slow down. I saw the opening of the stairwell, saw the darkness below, understood with perfect, terrible clarity what he intended to do.

He was trying to throw me down the stairs. He was trying to kill my baby. He was trying to kill me.

"Scott, no! STOP!" I screamed, the sound ripping from my throat, primal and terrified.

Despite his inebriation, he was much stronger than me, and for several harrowing minutes, we were locked in a fierce standoff. He was trying to push me with his body weight behind it. And I was desperately clinging to the railing, my fingers wrapped around the wooden banister so tightly I thought they might break.

Fear coursed through me like electricity. I believed, with absolute certainty, that he would kill me if he could.

My psychology training kicked in even through the terror: This is attempted feticide. Falls down stairs, plausible deniability. You're in immediate danger. Fight. Fight.

I managed to grip the railing with my entire arm, wrapping it around the post, holding on with everything I had. My muscles screamed in protest. My shoulder felt like it might dislocate. But I held on.

He was pulling at me, trying to break my grip. His fingers were digging into my ribs, my waist, anywhere he could grab. In a desperate attempt to save myself, I summoned every ounce of willpower and bit his arm with all the force I could muster. Bit down hard, tasting blood, feeling skin break between my teeth.

He immediately let go, howling in pain, stumbling backward. "You fucking bitch!"

Recognizing my chance, I ran. Down the stairs, my feet barely touching each step, convinced he was right behind me. Into the kitchen, near the door, my hand reaching for the knob, ready to escape into the night in my pajamas. I was barefoot, not caring about anything except getting away.

But Scott followed me down and stopped suddenly at the bottom, sinking into a chair at the kitchen table and breaking down in tears. It was a shocking turn. The instant transformation from violent attacker to weeping victim.

But I knew this pattern. I'd studied it. The cycle of abuse: tension building, acute violence, reconciliation and calm. Here was the reconciliation phase, right on schedule. Where he makes promises to change. Where the victim's empathy is weaponized against her.

And I knew, standing there with my hand on the doorknob, my chest heaving, my whole body shaking, that I had an opportunity. An opportunity to make him think everything was okay. To buy myself time. To survive until morning.

This was strategic compliance. Survival mode.

"Scott, honey, please, let's not fight." Gently, my voice not my own. Soft, soothing. I was watching his reaction closely, calculating my next move.

He remained silent but looked up at me, tears streaming down his face.

"Everything is going to be okay. I'm going to get the procedure done on Tuesday. This will be over soon, and then we can go back to normal. Just you and me. Happy." I spoke soothingly, even as inside I was screaming.

He seemed to be responding, his breathing slowing, his shoulders dropping. I moved closer. Each step was deliberate, cautious, ready to bolt if he lunged again.

"Scott, I love you. You know that. We love each other. And everything is going to be okay. There's nothing for us to fight about. It will all be over on Tuesday."

The lies came easily now, survival instinct overriding everything else. Still standing over him, I leaned in to hug him, my whole body tense.

He put his head on my chest and cried, his tears soaking through my pajama top. His arms wrapped around my waist, and I stood there, one hand mechanically stroking his hair, the other poised to push him away if needed.

Then I took his hand and led him back upstairs to bed. "Come on, honey, let's go to bed." We passed the railing where, minutes before, he'd tried to throw me to my death.

He obediently followed, docile now, the rage burned out. Within minutes of laying down, he succumbed to slumber. His breathing deepened, became rhythmic. He was out.

I lay there beside him, keeping one eye open for the rest of the night. Every creak made me jump. Every time he shifted, my body tensed, ready to flee. I watched the darkness slowly give way to gray dawn light.

My arm ached where he'd grabbed me. My scalp throbbed where he'd pulled my hair. My shoulder was stiff from clinging to the railing. But I was alive. We were alive.

I spent those dark hours planning. I couldn't stay here. I'd almost died tonight. He'd tried to murder me.

The clinical terms marched through my mind: Attempted feticide. Most dangerous time is when the victim tries to leave or when she's pregnant. And I was both. Leaving and pregnant.

But knowing the terms didn't tell me what to do. I had no money. My car was on its last leg. I had nowhere to go in the middle of the night. I was pregnant and exhausted and terrified.

So, I lay there next to my would-be murderer and waited for morning, making lists in my head. What I needed to do. Who I could call. How I could get out.

The appointment was Tuesday. Today was Thursday. I had five days.

Chapter 4

T he next morning, I woke up with a heavy heart, knowing I needed to plan my escape. The bruises on my arm had darkened overnight. Deep purple and yellow, the clear outline of his fingers. I pulled my sleeve down to cover them.

The events of the previous evening had revealed a darker side of Scott that I had never imagined. Or maybe that I'd been willfully ignoring for months. I felt unsafe around him. The word seemed too mild. Unsafe suggested you might trip and fall, not that someone might throw you down the stairs and kill you. I was in danger. I was living with someone who had tried to murder me and our unborn child.

I was resolute in my decision: I couldn't marry him, live with him, or bear his child. Not his child. Not now. Not ever.

My top priority was to end this pregnancy and distance myself from him without arousing suspicion. The decision settled over me with a strange, cold clarity. This wasn't what Scott wanted. This was what I needed to survive. To escape. I couldn't run while pregnant, couldn't start over with a baby tying me to him forever.

The psychology was clear on this. Shared custody would mean contact with him for eighteen years minimum. Court dates. Drop-offs and pick-ups. Holidays negotiated. Endless opportunities for him to hurt me, to manipulate me, to use the child as leverage. The research on post-separation abuse was unequivocal. Children became weapons, custody battles became warfare, and women ended up trapped in a different way.

This was my choice, made for my own reasons, and I would carry that knowledge forward even as I let him believe he'd won.

Over the next three days leading up to my scheduled appointment, I put on an act, pretending to be the sweet and loving girlfriend I once was. The performance was exhausting. I smiled when he came home from work. I made his favorite dinners. I asked about his day. I assured Scott that we would soon return to a carefree, simple existence, just the two of us, like it used to be.

He seemed visibly relieved by my reassurances. His whole demeanor was lighter. He stopped drinking as much. He was almost tender with me.

It made me sick.

I was engaged in a form of strategic deception, a survival mechanism documented extensively in domestic violence literature. I was performing compliance to ensure my safety long enough to escape. I knew what I was doing. I knew why I was doing it. And I felt no shame about it.

I maintained the charade until the fateful Tuesday morning arrived. I'd barely slept the night before, my mind racing through logistics, through what came next, through how I was going to get out. Scott drove me to the appointment, his demeanor lighter than it had been in a while. He held my hand in the car. Turned on the radio to a station I liked. Asked if I wanted to stop for coffee after.

"Sure," I said. "That sounds nice."

At the clinic, the building was nondescript, set back from the street. A few protesters stood on the sidewalk with signs, but they were quiet this early in the morning. Scott squeezed my hand as we walked past them. Inside, the waiting room was painted in soothing beiges and blues, with magazines fanned across side tables and a television playing morning news on mute.

I checked in, and the receptionist, a middle-aged woman with kind eyes, swiftly led me to the back, while Scott sat nervously in the waiting room. I glanced back once and saw him settling into a chair, pulling out his phone. He looked almost normal. Like any concerned boyfriend waiting for his girlfriend.

In a large, eerily quiet room, I sat among eight other women, all clutching clipboards with our intake paperwork. The chairs were arranged in rows, and no one made eye contact. Unspoken tension filled the air as we waited for our names to be called. Some women looked young, maybe eighteen or nineteen. Others looked older, maybe in their thirties. One woman's hands shook as she filled out her forms. Another stared straight ahead, expressionless.

How many of them were here for the same reason I was? How many were escaping? How many had someone waiting in that lobby who'd hurt them? The statistics suggested I wasn't alone. One in four women experienced intimate partner violence. Reproductive coercion affected up to 15% of women. I looked around the room and wondered which ones were like me, sitting here making an impossible choice to save their own lives.

The nurse called another name every fifteen minutes, and each woman would stand and follow her through a door, disappearing. It took nearly forty-five minutes until it was finally my turn.

"Emma?" A friendly nurse with graying hair and scrubs covered in butterflies appeared in the doorway.

I stood, my legs feeling unsteady, and followed her.

The friendly nurse led me to a small office, where she briefly reviewed my paperwork before stating that she wanted to "have a little chat." The office was small but warm, with a desk and two chairs facing each other. Tissues on the desk. Pamphlets about birth control and counseling services.

She inquired about my reasons for being there and how I had arrived at my decision. I wisely chose not to mention the horrifying incident with Scott a couple of nights ago or my plans to escape him after the procedure. Those words stayed locked inside. Instead, I told her I was focused on finishing my education and wanted to provide a stable life for my future child when the time was right. The words came easily, sounding reasonable and mature.

She nodded approvingly, making notes on her clipboard.

She asked if anyone had influenced my decision, watching my face carefully. I knew what she was really asking: Is someone forcing you to do this?

I met her eyes steadily. "It was entirely my choice." And it was. Not for the reasons she might think, but it was my choice. "My boyfriend is sitting in the waiting area to make sure I get home safely. He's been very supportive."

Another lie, smooth and practiced. But what else could I say? That he'd tried to kill me and now I was performing compliance to stay alive long enough to escape? That I was terminating a pregnancy I might have wanted in different circumstances because it was my only path to freedom? That this procedure was my ticket out of an abusive relationship but I couldn't tell anyone because he was sitting in the waiting room?

The system wasn't designed for women like me. The screening questions assumed coercion meant being forced to terminate, not being forced to carry. They didn't account for the complexity of reproductive coercion that worked in both directions.

She seemed satisfied with my response and proceeded with her questions. Medical history, allergies, last menstrual period, any previous pregnancies.

After a series of routine queries, she declared that she believed the procedure was in my best interest. She handed me a hospital gown, the fabric thin and papery. "Get undressed and put this on, opening in the front. You can leave your clothes in the stall. Each girl gets a stall. Once you've changed, someone will assist you."

I took the gown and headed to the changing stalls. The stall was small, with a bench and hooks on the wall. I undressed slowly, folding my jeans, my sweater, leaving them in a neat pile. Standing there in my underwear, I caught my reflection in the small mirror. Pale, thin, bruises still visible on my arm. I pulled the gown on and tied it loosely.

After changing, I left my clothes in the stall as instructed. As I emerged, a young woman fastened a paper identification bracelet around my wrist. My name and a number.

"You can go straight through those doors and take a seat," she said, pointing to a set of double doors.

I walked into a room where about a dozen women sat in rows of chairs, each facing a screen on the wall. We sat for an eternity as more women arrived and took their seats. Still, no one spoke. Still, no one looked at each other. We were all here for the same reason, but we were each completely alone.

Finally, a video began to play, explaining the procedure in great detail. It showed diagrams, used clinical terms. Dilation, suction, cervix. It emphasized the emotional aspects, suggesting that speaking with someone about our feelings afterward could be helpful. Some women might feel relief. Some might feel sadness. Some might feel both. All feelings were valid.

I appreciated that. The validation that I could feel multiple things at once. Relief and grief. Freedom and loss. Both could be true.

The video lasted about forty-five minutes, and afterward, we sat in silence again. I tried to process what I'd just watched, tried to prepare myself.

After a few more minutes, the nurse returned and explained that there were three "procedure rooms" and that three women would undergo the procedure simultaneously, each taking approximately fifteen minutes.

For the next hour, I sat among the other women, waiting anxiously for my name to be called. The room seemed to echo with silence, broken only by the occasional call of three names. Three women would stand, follow the nurse through the doors, and disappear. Then we'd wait. Then three more names.

Finally, my name was called along with that of two other women. We followed a nurse through another set of doors, and I realized the facility was laid out in a circular pattern. Slowly, I made my way around this disconcerting circle, deeper into the building, further from Scott, from the waiting room, from any possibility of turning back.

The three of us were led to separate small procedure rooms. They were small, windowless, clinical, and contained only a table for me to lie on with stirrups at the end. Medical instruments on a tray, covered with a cloth. A blood pressure cuff on the wall.

The nurse directed me to hop up on the table. The paper crinkled beneath me. She informed me that the doctor would be with me shortly, and once again, I found myself waiting. My legs in the stirrups. The gown barely covering me. The fluorescent lights too bright above.

I thought about the baby. The cluster of cells, the potential life. I felt a pang of grief, sharp and unexpected. Not for what was, but for what could have been. In another life, with another man, this could have been a joyful moment. A wanted pregnancy. A celebration.

Instead, I was here, making an impossible choice in an impossible situation.

I'm sorry, I thought. I'm so sorry. Not for this choice. But for the circumstances that made it necessary.

The doctor, a man with a reassuring smile and gentle eyes, entered the room and introduced himself. Dr. Williams. He was probably in his fifties, with gray at his temples. He explained that I would receive anesthesia, that I wouldn't remember anything, that it would be over quickly. His voice was kind, professional.

A younger man, likely an anesthesiologist, entered the room and prepared a mask. The nurse returned once more, and within moments, the mask was placed over my face. Plastic and oxygen and a slightly sweet smell. "Count backward from ten," someone said.

Ten. Nine. Eight. Sev...

Darkness.

***

I woke up in a different room and felt disoriented, my mind foggy, my body heavy. The lights were dimmer here, softer. Another gentle nurse stood over me, her hand on my shoulder. "Emma? How are you feeling?"

"Um, I'm okay." Mumbling, still struggling to shake off the effects of anesthesia. My mouth was dry. My body felt strange, disconnected.

"The procedure is complete, and everything went well." She reassured me with a kind smile. "You did great. I'll let you rest a bit longer, and then you'll be free to go."

"So," I asked, my voice still groggy, needing to hear it confirmed, "I'm not pregnant anymore?"

"No, you're no longer pregnant."

An immense wave of relief washed over me. Relief and grief and exhaustion all tangled together. The tie was severed. I wasn't bound to Scott forever anymore. I could leave. I could escape. The relief was so overwhelming it brought tears to my eyes.

"It's okay," the nurse said softly, misunderstanding my tears. "A lot of women feel emotional after. It's completely normal."

I nodded, unable to speak. She couldn't know that these were tears of freedom, tears of grief, tears of survival all at once.

I drifted back into a semi-conscious state.

When I woke again, maybe twenty minutes later, the nurse helped me off the table. My legs were unsteady, and I felt cramping in my abdomen. Dull and persistent. Another young woman in scrubs assisted me in walking back to the changing stall, one hand under my elbow, supporting me.

"Okay, Emma, you can get changed now, and then you'll be on your way. You did great today."

I managed to change into the clothes I had worn to the appointment, although I still felt incredibly groggy. Everything took twice as long as it should. My fingers fumbled with buttons and zippers. They led me back to the waiting room, gave me a folder with aftercare instructions and a prescription for antibiotics.

Scott stood as soon as he saw me, his face concerned. "Hey, how are you feeling?" He crossed to me quickly, his hand gentle on my back.

I wondered how he had spent his day, as it was already three o'clock. Five hours I'd been here. "I'm okay. Just tired."

He spoke gently on the way to the car, solicitous, reminding me of the person he was when we first met. Or the person I thought he was. "Take it easy. I'll take care of everything at home. You just rest."

Briefly, I felt the comfort of the past, the ghost of what we'd been. But I quickly snapped myself back to the present and recent events. The stairs, his hands in my hair, his threat. I couldn't let my guard down. This tenderness was temporary, conditional on my compliance. The honeymoon phase. I knew how this cycle worked.

Scott drove us back to the apartment, and I wasted no time heading straight to bed. The cramping was getting worse, and I felt exhausted in a way that went beyond physical. I was sore, drained, and needed to recover. Scott hovered around me, bringing me water, crackers, the heating pad, tending to my needs like he was making amends. I appreciated the reprieve from his recent erratic behavior, but I knew I couldn't be lulled into complacency. This version of Scott wouldn't last. It never did.

Chapter 5

In the following days, I was surprised by the level of pain I experienced. The clinic had warned me, but the reality was worse than I'd expected. I had planned to return to classes but soon realized I was in no condition. I was sore and experienced vaginal bleeding that required me to change pads constantly. My body felt like it had been through a trauma, which of course it had.

I moped around the house and maintained the façade that everything was wonderful for us now. I pretended that we'd turned a corner, that this had been the right decision for "us." Scott seemed lighter, happier, like a weight had been lifted. He drank less. He was affectionate. He talked about our wedding in June, about our future, about how things would be different now.

And I nodded and smiled and agreed, all while secretly continuing to plan my escape.

I couldn't leave immediately. I was still recovering, still bleeding, still in pain. But I used those days to think, to plan. I called Becca when Scott was at work, told her everything in a whispered rush. She was horrified, furious, ready to help however I needed.

"I need a few more days," I told her. "I need to be stronger. I need to figure out the logistics."

I started gathering important documents. My birth certificate, social security card, passport. I hid them in my backpack. I withdrew small amounts of cash from the ATM, amounts Scott wouldn't notice, and hid the bills in different places. Twenty dollars here, forty there.

I made a list of what I absolutely needed to take with me and what I could leave behind.

This was safety planning, the term from my domestic violence class. The most dangerous time for a victim is when she's leaving or has just left. Lethality increases exponentially. I needed to be smart. I needed to be strategic. I needed to survive.

The wedding dress still hung in the closet, white lace mocking me. All those hours of work, all that hope stitched into fabric. I would leave it behind. I would leave most things behind. I just needed to get out alive.

One week after the procedure, I felt strong enough. The bleeding had slowed to spotting. The cramping was manageable. I could move without wincing.

It was time.

I waited until Scott left for work on a Monday morning. Kissed him goodbye. Told him I loved him. Watched him drive away.

Then I moved fast.

I threw essentials into two duffel bags. Clothes, toiletries, my laptop, textbooks, the hidden documents and cash. I took one last look around the apartment. At the kitchen where he'd proposed moving up the wedding. At the stairs where he'd tried to kill me. At the wedding dress hanging in the closet.

I left a note on the kitchen counter. Brief. To the point.

I carried my bags to my car, threw them in the trunk, and got behind the wheel. My hands shook as I started the engine. I half expected him to come roaring back, to have known somehow, to stop me.

But the street was quiet. The morning was ordinary. No one was coming.

I called Becca as I pulled away from the curb. "I'm out. I'm leaving now. Can I come to your place?"

"Yes. God, yes. Drive carefully. I'll be waiting."

I had closed the gap between knowing and doing. Finally. I was choosing action over paralysis, survival over compliance, escape over entrapment.

I knew all the statistics about what happened to women who left. I knew the dangers I was walking into. I knew this wasn't the end, just the beginning of a different kind of battle.

But for the first time in months, I also knew something else. I was going to survive this.

I was going to get out.

And I was never, ever going back.

***

The first few days of freedom were unbelievably peaceful. I woke up each morning without that familiar knot of dread in my stomach, without having to assess the emotional weather before getting out of bed. I felt a bit of sadness over the loss of what I had hoped could have been between Scott and me. Of the fantasy I'd clung to for so long, the fairy tale that had never really existed. But mostly, I felt profound relief that spread through my body like warmth after being cold for too long.

No drunken rages. No guessing what mood he would come home in. No walking on eggshells. No calculating bottle counts or planning escape routes. No bracing for impact every time I heard footsteps.

Two weeks after leaving, I found my own place. It was a studio in the historic district near campus. Small, safe, mine. I'd furnished it simply with my thrift store finds. The futon was lumpy but mine. The dishes were mismatched but mine. Everything in this small space was mine, chosen by me, controlled by me. I could leave a glass on the counter overnight without someone yelling about it. I could go to bed when I wanted. I could breathe.

This newfound peace couldn't have come at a better time because I was nearing finals at school. I spent long days at the library completing term papers and studying for final exams. Abnormal psychology, developmental theory, research methods. My psychology courses felt different now, less academic and more personal. I recognized patterns I'd lived through. I saw myself in the case studies. It was both validating and painful.

By evening, I was exhausted, but it was a good exhaustion. It was the kind that came from productive work, not from constant vigilance.

One Sunday evening, after a particularly brutal study session, I planned an outing with my friend Colleen, feeling I had earned a night out. We met at a casual restaurant for drinks and dinner, nothing fancy, just margaritas and nachos and conversation that didn't revolve around my disaster of a relationship.

Colleen asked how I was doing, really doing, and I told her the truth. That I was scared sometimes, but mostly relieved. That I was starting to feel like myself again. She raised her glass and toasted to new beginnings, and I felt something I hadn't felt in a long time: hopeful.

I returned to my apartment at about 10:30 p.m., the walk from where I'd parked feeling safe in a way it wouldn't have felt a few weeks ago. No one was waiting to interrogate me about where I'd been or who I'd been with. No one would smell my breath for alcohol or accuse me of flirting. I climbed the stairs to my studio, unlocked my door, and stepped into my peaceful space.

I changed into comfy pajamas, soft flannel pants and an old t-shirt, the kind of comfortable clothes I could never wear around Scott because he'd made comments about me "letting myself go." I made a cup of chamomile tea in my tiny kitchenette and snuggled under the covers on my futon with a novel I'd been reading, some light romance that was easy and escapist.

Several minutes later, my phone rang. The sound made me jump, my heart immediately accelerating. I glanced at the screen and saw Scott's name. My stomach dropped. It was late, almost 11 p.m., and I couldn't imagine why he would call at this hour.

This couldn't be good. Every muscle in my body tensed, that familiar anxiety flooding back instantly. So much for feeling safe.

I considered not answering, but some part of me worried that ignoring him would make things worse. That he'd show up here. That silence would escalate the situation. I answered on the fourth ring.

"Hey, Scott. What's up?" My voice tinged with exhaustion and wariness.

"Emma, sweetheart. How are you doing?" He slurred, clearly intoxicated. I could hear it immediately in the elongated vowels, the slight thickness of his words.

My heart sank. Here we go. "I'm good, but tired, Scott. I just got into bed." Hoping he would catch the hint, hoping this would be brief.

"I miss you, Emma. I just... I wanted to see how you were doing." Something in his voice. Sadness? Manipulation? Both? I couldn't tell anymore, and maybe it didn't matter.

"Scott, I'm good. But it's late. I need to get some sleep." Keeping my voice neutral, calm. Not wanting to provoke him, but also not wanting to encourage this conversation.

"Well, I was thinking about you, and I noticed that you didn't take the vacuum cleaner when you left, and I thought you might need it. You know, for your new place."

I hesitated, my mind immediately recognizing this for what it was. This was a classic manipulation tactic. He offered something helpful, something practical, as a pretext for contact. The vacuum cleaner was an excuse. It was a reason to see me, to come to my apartment, to find out exactly where I lived. I'd read about this. The helpful ex. The one who just wants to make sure you're okay. The one who uses benevolence as a pathway to renewed control.

I could use a vacuum cleaner. My thrift store shopping hadn't included one, but I also knew accepting this offer was dangerous.

"Um, that's okay. I'll just pick up another one. You keep that one." Trying to sound casual, appreciative but firm.

"No, Emma, that's silly. Why would you spend money on something you don't need to buy?" His voice had an edge now, irritation creeping in. "My mom already said she has an extra one I can take. So, it doesn't make sense for you to buy another one. I'll drop this one off to you. Is it too late now?"

My chest tightened. He wanted my address. He wanted to come here, to see my space, to know exactly where I slept. To reclaim territory. To reestablish presence. "Yes, it's too late now. I'm already in bed, Scott."

"Oh, right. Okay, well, how about tomorrow then? After you're done with classes?"

He was pressing, persistent, not taking no for an answer. Classic Scott. Classic abuser behavior, persistence disguised as care. Boundary violation disguised as helpfulness.

I considered my options quickly. If I said no outright, he'd push harder, maybe get angry. I needed to redirect this and give him something so he'd back off. "Why don't I pop by your place tomorrow and grab it?"

Keeping my voice light, as if this were the most reasonable solution in the world.

He hesitated, and I could almost hear him trying to think through his alcohol-fogged brain. "Well, I have to work tomorrow."

Perfect. An opening. "That's okay. I can just swing by on my way to school."

"Okay, that's fine." Resignation in his voice. He'd lost this round, and we both knew it.

"Okay, Scott, have a good night." Already moving to end the call.

"Emma, wait..." His voice caught. "I love you."

The words hung in the air. Once, they would have made my heart soar. Now they just made me sad and anxious and tired. "Good night, Scott." I replied, deliberately not returning the sentiment, and I hung up.

I sat there in bed, my tea growing cold on the nightstand, my book forgotten in my lap. My hands were shaking slightly. The peaceful evening I'd been enjoying felt shattered, replaced by that familiar knot of anxiety in my stomach.

He'd been drinking. He was missing me, or missing having control over me, more likely. And he'd tried to get my address under the guise of being helpful.

I should have felt proud of myself for redirecting him, for not giving him what he wanted. And I did, sort of. But I also felt afraid.

This was escalation. Not the dramatic kind. No threats, no yelling, but escalation nonetheless. Increased contact. Persistence. Boundary testing. I'd studied the patterns of post-separation stalking. It often started like this. Small intrusions disguised as normalcy. Testing to see what they could get away with. Seeing if the victim would let them back in, even just a little.

The research was clear: if you gave an inch, they took a mile. Every small boundary violation paved the way for bigger ones. Every time you answered the phone, every time you agreed to see them "just this once," you reinforced the idea that persistence paid off.

I knew this. I could cite the studies. I could draw the escalation curve. And I'd still answered the phone. I'd still agreed to go to the apartment tomorrow. Because what else could I do? Ignore him and risk him showing up here? Block his number and risk him escalating to physical contact?

There were no good options. Just less bad ones.

This wasn't over. I'd known it wouldn't be, but having it confirmed made everything feel more real. More dangerous. The calm had been temporary. Now the storm was starting to gather.

I got up and double-checked that my door was locked, then checked the windows. I was on the second floor, but still. I pulled the curtains closed more tightly, blocking out the streetlight that had felt cozy earlier. Then I got back into bed, but I couldn't focus on my book anymore.

I lay there in the dark, listening to every creak of the old building. Every footstep in the hallway, every car that passed on the street below. Hypervigilance. Another symptom of trauma, another thing I could label but couldn't stop experiencing.

Tomorrow I'd go get the vacuum. I'd sever one more tie. And then maybe, maybe, he'd leave me alone.

But I didn't really believe that. Men like Scott didn't just let go. I'd learned that in my classes, seen it in the statistics, read it in the case studies. The most dangerous time for a woman leaving an abusive relationship is after she leaves. Post-separation violence. Stalking. Homicide. The numbers were stark and frightening.

I was in the most dangerous time. And Scott's phone call had just reminded me of that.

I knew what I should do. I should document this call. Write down the time, what he said, his attempts to get my address. I should start building a paper trail in case I needed a restraining order later. I should call a domestic violence hotline and talk to an advocate about safety planning.

I knew all of this. But I was so tired. Tired of being afraid. Tired of analyzing every interaction. Tired of living in survival mode. I just wanted to feel safe in my own apartment, to read my book, to drink my tea, to be a normal twenty-something college student preparing for finals.

But that wasn't my reality. My reality was lying here with my phone clutched in my hand, 911 pre-dialed and ready, just in case.

I finally fell asleep sometime after 2 a.m., and I dreamed of locks that wouldn't hold and doors that wouldn't close and footsteps coming up stairs that never ended.

***

The next day, with only one class in the morning, I headed to Scott's place at around 11 a.m. I'd timed it carefully. He should be at work, safely away, giving me plenty of time to get in and out without seeing him. I parked in my 'old' spot, the same space I'd pulled into hundreds of times before. The familiarity of it made my chest tight. I sat in the car for a moment, steeling myself, then grabbed my keys and walked to the door.

I let myself into the apartment, and immediately, it was eerie walking into the space that had been our shared home. The air felt different. Stale and heavy. This place where I'd lived, where I'd been attacked, where I'd planned my escape. It didn't feel like home anymore. It felt like a crime scene.

My initial goal was to retrieve the vacuum cleaner and nothing more. Get in, get out, sever another tie. But as I walked through the rooms, something felt amiss beyond just the emotional weight of being here. The apartment was a mess. And not just normal mess, but disaster-level mess. It appeared that Scott hadn't done any cleaning in the two weeks since I had left.

There were piles of dirty dishes in the sink, plates with dried food crusted on them. Empty take-out containers were strewn across the counter. Pizza boxes, Chinese food containers, beer bottles everywhere. The trash was overflowing. A general sense of disarray permeated every surface. The place smelled of spoiled food and something else I couldn't quite place. Unwashed laundry, maybe. Or just the smell of depression and decay.

Things had fallen apart in my absence. Or maybe they'd been falling apart before I left, and I'd been too busy managing his moods and walking on eggshells to notice. Had I been the one holding everything together? The thought made me feel used and angry.

I continued my inspection, drawn by morbid curiosity, heading upstairs to the bedroom. Each step on the stairs made my heart beat faster. These were the same stairs where he'd tried to throw me down. I gripped the railing, remembering. The bedroom was a disaster zone. Dirty clothes were scattered all over the floor. His work clothes were mixed with pajamas, mixed with towels. The bed was unmade, sheets twisted and stained. It looked like he'd been sleeping on top of the covers, not even bothering to get under them.

This was more than just a messy apartment. These were classic signs of severe depression. Poor hygiene, inability to maintain basic functioning, environmental neglect. My clinical training supplied the observations automatically. Major depressive episode. Possible substance abuse disorder. I was looking at someone in psychological crisis.

A pile of unopened mail lay haphazardly on Scott's dresser. There were bills and official-looking envelopes, mixed with junk mail and magazines. I figured I'd better check the mail, as some might be addressed to me. I'd changed my address at the post office, but some things might have slipped through. I sorted through the pile quickly, spotted a couple of pieces bearing my name, a credit card statement, something from my school. I slipped them into my handbag.

As I glanced around the room, something on the floor caught my attention near the bed. It was a crumpled piece of paper, partially hidden under a dirty shirt. Something official-looking. I picked it up and began to read. My hands started to shake as I processed the words.

It was a certified letter from Scott's employer, notifying him of his termination due to not showing up for work for six consecutive weeks without notice or explanation. Six weeks! The date on the letter was from early April. I did the math quickly in my head. That meant he hadn't been working during the last month we'd been together, maybe longer. During the pregnancy. During his worst drinking. During the attack.

My mind raced, questions tumbling over each other. Where had he been going every morning when I assumed he was at work? Had he been sitting in bars? Driving around? Just pretending? How had I not known? And more importantly, how had he been paying his half of the rent?

The answer hit me with sickening clarity: he hadn't been. That's why he kept asking me to cover it. That's why he'd taken money from my account. He'd been unemployed and lying to me, letting me support us both while pretending everything was fine.

Financial abuse. The term surfaced immediately. It hadn't just been about the engagement ring or covering rent occasionally. He'd systematically deceived me about his financial situation. He'd allowed me to support him under false pretenses and stolen from me to maintain the lie. This was exploitation, not just poor money management.

I felt fear wash over me. If he could lie about this, what else had he lied about? It was unsettling, disorienting. It was like finding out the person you thought you knew had never really existed at all.

And if he wasn't working now, where was he? The thought made my blood run cold. I checked my watch. 11:20. I needed to hurry up and leave before Scott returned. If he wasn't at work, he could be anywhere. He could be on his way here right now.

I practically ran back downstairs, my heart pounding. I located the vacuum cleaner in the hall closet, right where it had always been, and grabbed it. I took one last look around the apartment, this place that had been my prison, and then I left, pulling the door shut behind me firmly.

I loaded the vacuum into my trunk and got in my car, locking the doors immediately. Only then did I allow myself to breathe. I sat there for a moment, gripping the steering wheel, before starting the engine and pulling away. I watched the apartment building recede in my rearview mirror, half expecting to see Scott's car pull in as I left.

I couldn't stop thinking about those last weeks as I drove home, replaying memories through this new lens. Why had he stopped going to work? Had he been fired, or had he just stopped showing up? I'd noticed his unstable moods, the increased drinking, the volatile behavior. But I hadn't realized how deeply his life had unraveled. I'd thought it was just our relationship falling apart, but it was everything. His job, his stability, his grip on reality.

And it had continued to worsen in my absence. That apartment was evidence of a man spiraling. The mess, the unopened mail, the filth. Those were signs of someone giving up, falling apart.

Part of me felt a pang of something that might have been pity or concern. But the larger part of me felt validated in my decision to leave and deeply afraid of what a man with nothing left to lose might be capable of.

The research on lethality risk factors was running through my mind like a checklist: Recent separation from intimate partner. Check. Job loss or major financial stress. Check. Substance abuse. Check. History of violence. Check. Depression. Check. Access to victim. He was trying to get that. Every single risk factor was present. I was looking at a textbook high-lethality situation.

I thought about calling someone to tell them what I'd found. But who would I call? What would I say? That my ex-boyfriend's apartment was a mess? That he'd lost his job? Neither of those things was a crime. Neither gave me grounds for a restraining order or police protection.

But they were warning signs. Red flags that Scott was in a dangerous place mentally and emotionally. And men in dangerous places did dangerous things.

I knew the statistics. I'd studied them. The majority of intimate partner homicides happen within two months of separation. The victim often reports increased contact, surveillance, or threats in the weeks leading up to the murder. Stalking is one of the strongest predictors of lethal violence.

I was living inside those statistics now. I could see the pattern unfolding, could track where this was headed. But knowing the pattern didn't give me the power to stop it.

When I got back to my apartment, I brought the vacuum upstairs and immediately locked my door behind me, sliding the chain lock into place for extra security. I set the vacuum in the corner and sat down on my futon, still shaking slightly from adrenaline.

I pulled out my phone and texted Becca: *Went to get the vacuum. Scott's apartment is a disaster. Found a letter. He got fired 6 weeks ago. He's been lying about everything.*

Her response came quickly: *Holy shit. Are you okay? Want me to come over?*

I'm okay. Just shaken. Can you come by later?

Yes. I'll be there at 6. Lock your doors.

I looked around my small studio. It was neat, clean, organized. Mine. The contrast to Scott's apartment couldn't have been starker. He was falling apart without me, and that should have made me feel guilty.

Instead, it terrified me.

Because a man who'd lost everything had nothing left to lose. And people with nothing to lose were the most dangerous kind. That wasn't just intuition. That was documented fact. Loss of employment and loss of relationship were two of the top precipitating factors in intimate partner homicide.

I was in danger. Real, quantifiable, statistically significant danger.

I got up and checked the lock on my door again, then checked the windows. Then I sat back down and tried to focus on my studying. But the termination letter kept flashing through my mind.

Six weeks. He'd been lying for six weeks. And I hadn't known.

What else didn't I know? What else was he hiding? What was he planning?

I opened my abnormal psychology textbook, tried to focus on the chapter about mood disorders, but my eyes kept drifting to my phone.

Should I call the police? And tell them what? That my ex-boyfriend lost his job and his apartment is messy? They wouldn't do anything. There was no crime here. No threat. Nothing actionable.

But there would be. I knew there would be. The question was when, and whether I'd see it coming in time.

I pulled out a notebook and started writing down everything I knew, everything I'd observed. The phone call last night. The state of the apartment. The termination letter. The timeline of his lies. I was building documentation, creating a paper trail, doing what I should have done weeks ago.

Because I had all this knowledge about domestic violence, all this clinical training, all these statistics and risk factors memorized. And maybe, just maybe, if I documented everything carefully enough, if I was vigilant enough, if I made all the right moves, maybe I could survive this.

Or maybe all my knowledge was just going to let me see it coming when he killed me.

I pushed that thought away, but it didn't go far. It sat at the edge of my consciousness, waiting, like Scott himself was waiting.

And I knew, with the terrible certainty that comes from expertise and lived experience both, that this wasn't over.

It was barely even beginning.

Chapter 6

The calls had started the night after I got the vacuum. Then they came every night. Sometimes drunk, sometimes sober, always insistent. He missed me. He loved me. We needed to talk. Why was I doing this to him? I'd documented each one in my notebook, timestamps and what he'd said, building my paper trail.

The voicemails piled up over the following weeks. Some nights I deleted them without listening. Other nights, I played them on the lowest volume, trying to gauge his state of mind, some part of me still believing I needed to monitor the threat level.

***

It was one such night, when I actually managed to fall asleep to some mindless reality show, the kind of noise that filled the apartment without requiring thought. I woke to darkness and the sound of fists against wood.

The red numbers on my alarm clock read 2:32.

My body understood before my mind caught up. My heart was already hammering, my breath already shallow. The banging came again, harder.

Scott.

I pressed myself against the headboard, blanket clutched to my chest like it could protect me from anything. The banging continued, rhythmic and demanding. Then his voice, muffled through the door but unmistakable.

"Emma! Emma, I know you're in there!"

My hands shook as I reached for my phone. What would I even say if I called 911? He wasn't breaking in. He was just knocking. Just calling my name. Just standing outside my door at 2:30 in the morning, and wasn't that what boyfriends did?

Except he wasn't my boyfriend anymore. Except this wasn't okay. Except I knew, somewhere beneath the fear and the guilt and the exhaustion, that none of this had ever been okay.

This was stalking. The word surfaced clearly despite my panic. Showing up at someone's home uninvited in the middle of the night, refusing to leave when asked, this met the legal definition. But knowing the term didn't make my fingers dial 911. Knowing the term didn't stop the voice in my head that whispered *maybe he just needs to talk, maybe you're overreacting, maybe this is your fault for blocking his calls.*

I crept to the living room on unsteady legs, staying low, and eased the curtain back just enough to see.

Scott stood under the porch light, one hand braced against my door. Even from this angle, I could see the tension in his shoulders, the way he swayed slightly. He pounded on the door again.

"Emma! Don't do this! Just talk to me!"

I let the curtain fall and backed away from the window, my breath coming too fast. In some distant corner of my mind, the psychology student in me recognized this as fight, flight, or freeze, and my body had chosen freeze. I was a textbook case. The thought would have been funny if I could remember how to breathe properly.

The banging stopped.

I waited, counting the seconds, afraid to move. Afraid the floor would creak. Afraid he'd hear me breathing. I heard his footsteps on the concrete, growing fainter. An engine started. I stayed frozen by the window until the sound of his car disappeared down the street.

Only then did I let myself slide down the wall to the floor.

The tears came hard and fast, two years' worth of fear I'd been holding behind a dam that finally cracked. My whole body shook with it. I'd left him. I'd done the hard thing, the impossible thing. I'd walked away.

So why did it feel like I was still trapped?

I pulled my knees to my chest and pressed my forehead against them, trying to make myself smaller, trying to remember what safety felt like. The image flashed through my mind unbidden: Scott's face twisted with rage at the top of the stairs, his hand reaching for me, the moment before I'd bitten down on his arm and pulled myself free.

His anger had been just like this then. Consuming. Relentless.

What if he came back? What if next time he didn't just knock? What if he broke the door down, or waited for me to leave for class, or...

I couldn't finish the thought, but my training finished it for me. Escalation patterns. Increased contact frequency. Violation of boundaries. These were all predictors of violence. I'd studied the research. I knew what came next in the pattern.

But knowing didn't tell me how to stop it.

I stayed on the floor until the sky began to lighten, until my legs went numb and the tears finally stopped. I couldn't shake the thought that had lodged itself in my chest like a splinter; he would keep coming back. He would keep calling, keep showing up, keep demanding until I gave him what he wanted.

Or until something worse happened. That's what the statistics said. That stalking behavior escalated in 75% of cases. That the majority of intimate partner homicides were preceded by stalking. That I should document everything, call the police, get a restraining order.

But I just sat there on the floor, too tired to move, too scared to act.

I didn't know what scared me more, that he wouldn't stop, or that some small part of me worried he was right to be angry. That leaving him had been cruel, that I owed him an explanation he would actually accept.

The guilt was irrational. I knew that. Trauma bonding, my therapist would call it. The psychological attachment that forms between abuser and victim, the way the victim learns to empathize with the abuser's pain, to prioritize the abuser's needs, to feel responsible for the abuser's actions.

I could name it. I could explain the neurological mechanisms behind it, the way fear and intermittent reinforcement create powerful emotional bonds that override rational thinking.

But I couldn't make it stop.

***

When my phone buzzed with Becca's morning text, my hands were still shaking from the night before. *Coffee?*

Can we do lunch instead? Federal Hill?

Her response came immediately. *Of course. Usual spot. Noon.*

I needed to tell her what happened. I needed to file a police report. I needed to do all the things I'd learned about in my classes, all the steps that might keep me safe.

But first, I needed to get off this floor.

Chapter 7

The café on Federal Hill was already busy when I arrived, filled with the lunch crowd and the comfortable hum of conversation. Becca was at our corner table, cappuccino already in hand, and the moment she saw my face, her smile faltered.

"Em." She half-stood. "What happened?"

I slid into the chair across from her. The words stuck in my throat until the server left with my order. Then they came tumbling out.

"He came to my apartment. Last night. Two thirty in the morning, banging on my door."

"Jesus Christ." Becca's voice dropped to that low, controlled register that meant she was furious. "For how long?"

"I don't know. Ten minutes? Twenty?" I wrapped my hands around the water glass. "I hid and watched through the window until he left. He was drunk, I think. Or maybe just angry."

"Emma, you need to go to the police."

I'd known she would say it. "I don't know if they can do anything. He didn't threaten me. He didn't break anything. He just knocked on my door."

"At two thirty in the morning. After weeks of harassing phone calls." Becca leaned forward, her voice gentle but firm. "Em, this is escalating. You know it is."

I did know. The psychology student in me could see the pattern clearly. Increased frequency of contact. Boundary violations. Showing up at my home when other methods failed. Classic stalking behavior, textbook escalation.

But knowing it academically and accepting it emotionally were two different things.

"I feel like I'm overreacting," I said quietly. "Like I'm being dramatic. He's my ex-boyfriend. We were together for two years. Maybe he does deserve a chance to talk. Maybe I owe him—"

"Stop." Becca's hand shot across the table and grabbed mine. "You don't owe him anything. Not after what he did to you. And you're not overreacting. Your gut is telling you something's wrong because something is wrong."

"I'm scared," I admitted. "I'm scared if I go to the police, it'll make him angrier. I'm scared they won't take me seriously. I'm scared..." My voice cracked. "I'm scared I'm not strong enough to do this."

"Then I'll be strong enough for both of us." Becca squeezed my hand. "We'll go together. Right after lunch. I'll drive, I'll sit with you. You're not doing this alone."

The tears came before I could stop them. Becca handed me a napkin without comment.

"What if they can't help?" I whispered.

"Then we'll figure out the next step. But Emma, you can't keep living like this. You deserve to feel safe in your own home."

I thought about last night. The sound of his fists on my door. The way I'd curled up on the floor afterward, shaking. The hours I'd spent staring at the ceiling, afraid to sleep, afraid he'd come back.

"Okay," I said. My voice sounded steadier than I felt. "Okay. Let's go to the police."

***

The station was busier than I expected. Officers moved through the lobby with purpose, their radios crackling. People sat in plastic chairs along the wall. I wondered what their stories were. If they felt as small as I did.

The receptionist behind the plexiglass looked up as we approached. When she took in my face, whatever she saw there, her expression softened.

"Can I help you, hon?"

"I need to speak to an officer. I'm being harassed by my ex-boyfriend."

She picked up her phone. "Officer Turner? I've got a young woman here who needs to file a harassment report." A pause. "Emma. Emma Price."

She gestured to the row of chairs. "Have a seat. He'll be right out."

Becca squeezed my shoulder as we sat. I focused on my breathing and tried not to think about Scott's face when he found out I'd done this.

Officer Turner appeared a few minutes later. Tall, broad-shouldered, probably in his forties, with a gentle voice that didn't match his presence.

"Emma? I'm Officer Turner. Why don't you come with me."

Becca started to stand with me, but Officer Turner shook his head. "I'll need to speak with her alone first. You can wait here."

"I'll be right here," Becca said.

I followed Officer Turner down a narrow corridor that smelled like burnt coffee and industrial cleaner. The interview room was small and windowless, with a metal table bolted to the floor. A camera blinked red in the corner.

"Have a seat." Officer Turner settled into the chair across from me and pulled out a notebook. "Take your time. Tell me what's been going on."

"My ex-boyfriend has been calling me," I said. "Late at night. Sometimes multiple times. I blocked his number, but then he showed up at my apartment two nights ago. At two thirty in the morning. He was banging on my door, yelling my name."

Officer Turner's pen moved across the paper. "How long were you two together?"

"Two years."

"And when did you break up?"

"About two months ago."

"What's his full name?"

"Scott Martin."

"These calls, how often are they happening?"

"Almost every night. Sometimes twice in one night. He leaves voicemails, drunk usually, saying he just wants to talk. That I owe him a conversation."

Officer Turner looked up from his notes. "Did he threaten you?"

I hesitated. "Not directly. But he was angry. And he wouldn't leave. I watched through my window until he finally went back to his car."

"Has he been violent with you in the past?"

The stairs flashed through my mind. His hand in my hair, the rage in his eyes, the moment of pure terror before I grabbed the railing.

"Yes," I said quietly. "He tried to push me down the stairs. When I was pregnant."

Officer Turner's pen stilled. "When was this?"

"Three months ago. I had an abortion a week later. Not because of the fall, I didn't fall. But because I knew I had to get away from him, and I couldn't do that if I was tied to him through a child."

I'd never said that out loud before. Not even to Becca. The words felt like they'd been pulled from somewhere deep inside me.

"I'm sorry that happened to you," Officer Turner said. "Did you report the incident with the stairs?"

I shook my head. "I was afraid. He said it was the stress of everything that we'd been going through. He'd been drinking. A lot."

Officer Turner wrote for a long moment. "What about property damage? Has he destroyed anything of yours?"

"He stole four thousand dollars from my bank account. Said he needed it for my engagement ring."

"Did you press charges?"

I shook my head.

The officer looked surprised. I wanted to say that it had never occurred to me. That I was still in love with the person, I thought he was. Because I was terrified. Because I kept thinking if I could just be better, calmer, more understanding, he would go back to being the man I'd met.

"I guess it seems silly now," I said instead.

Officer Turner closed his notebook and leaned back. "Here's what I'm going to do. I'm going to pay Scott a visit. Sometimes just having an officer show up is enough to make them realize they need to back off. I'll make it clear that his behavior constitutes harassment and that if it continues, you'll be pursuing a restraining order."

"Will that work?"

"Sometimes." His honesty was both refreshing and terrifying. "But Emma, if he contacts you again after I talk to him, you need to call us immediately. Don't engage with him, don't respond to his messages, don't open the door if he shows up. Document everything."

I nodded.

"If the harassment continues, we'll help you file for a restraining order. That's a legal document that prohibits him from contacting you or coming within a certain distance of your home or workplace. If he violates it, he can be arrested."

"And if he does it anyway?" The question came out before I could stop it.

Officer Turner met my eyes. "Then we'll arrest him. But Emma, most of the time, people back off once they realize there are legal consequences. You've done the right thing by coming here."

I wanted to believe him. But all I felt was exposed, like I'd opened a door I couldn't close again.

"Thank you," I managed.

"Do you have somewhere safe to stay? Someone who can be with you?"

"My best friend. She's waiting outside."

"Good. Don't stay alone for the next few days if you can help it." He stood. "I'll be in touch after I speak with Scott. In the meantime, here's my card. Call me if anything happens."

I took the card, the paper feeling both insubstantial and impossibly heavy.

Becca jumped up the moment I emerged into the lobby. "How'd it go?"

"He's going to talk to Scott. Tell him to back off."

"And if that doesn't work?"

"Then I file for a restraining order."

Becca pulled me into a hug, right there in the middle of the police station. "You were so brave."

I didn't feel brave. I felt exhausted and scared and angry that I had to do this at all.

But I'd done it. I'd walked into that station and said the words out loud, made it official. There was no taking it back now.

As we walked to the parking lot, the morning sun felt too bright, the world too normal for everything that had just shifted inside me. Somewhere across town, Scott was going about his day, unaware that a police officer would soon be knocking on his door.

I wondered how he would react. If he would be scared, or angry, or if he would finally understand that I was serious about being done.

Part of me knew the answer. Sometimes abusers backed off when victims sought help. But sometimes they escalated. They saw it as a challenge, a betrayal, proof that the victim was trying to destroy them.

I'd just rolled the dice on which kind Scott would turn out to be.

I hoped Officer Turner was right, that a police visit would be enough. But I couldn't shake the feeling that I'd just lit a fuse, and now all I could do was wait to see if it would burn out or explode.

***

The morning sun slanted through my apartment windows, catching dust motes in its path. I was reaching for my keys when my phone rang, an unfamiliar number. My hand froze halfway to my purse.

Scott uses different numbers sometimes.

But it was Officer Turner's voice that came through, steady and professional. "Hello, Emma. I wanted to update you on our conversation with Scott."

I pressed the phone tighter to my ear. My training supplied the term automatically: obsessive relational intrusion. Scott's behavior lately had fit the clinical definition perfectly. unwanted pursuit, repeated contact attempts, boundary violations. A single police visit didn't break those patterns. The research said it could take multiple interventions, or none at all, depending on the perpetrator's level of investment in maintaining control.

"He seemed genuinely surprised when I showed up," Officer Turner continued. "I made it clear that his behavior constitutes harassment. He agreed to stop contacting you."

He agreed. The words should have brought relief. Instead, I felt my chest tighten in that familiar way, the one that came before panic attacks. My body knew something my mind was still trying to rationalize.

"Thank you," I managed. "I really appreciate you doing that."

"If he contacts you again, call me immediately. We'll take further action if needed."

After we hung up, I stood in the middle of my living room, keys dangling from my fingers. The apartment felt too quiet.

Scott had agreed. But Scott had agreed to a lot of things over the years. He'd agreed to cut back on drinking. He'd agreed to stop checking my phone. He'd agreed we were equals in the relationship. He'd agreed to pay his half of the rent.

Agreements meant nothing when someone's sense of entitlement outweighed their capacity for honesty.

I forced myself to breathe. In for four, hold for seven, out for eight. The 4-7-8 technique, designed to activate the parasympathetic nervous system, to override the fight-or-flight response. The one I'd found online, the one that sometimes worked when my thoughts started spiraling.

This is different, I told myself. A police officer showing up at his door, that's real consequences. Real external intervention, not just my own boundaries he could steamroll.

But even as I thought it, I knew the counterargument. I'd read the studies on intervention effectiveness. Police warnings reduced stalking behavior in some cases, but in others, particularly when the stalker had a history of intimate partner violence, it could trigger what researchers called "rage at rejection." The intervention could be perceived as humiliation, as the victim turning others against them, as justification for escalation.

I didn't know which category Scott fell into. I didn't know if today would be the beginning of peace or the beginning of something worse.

My hand was shaking as I locked the door behind me, and I caught myself checking over my shoulder twice before I reached my car. Then once more after I got in. Then again in the rearview mirror as I pulled out of my parking spot.

Hypervigilance. I was doing it again. Scanning for threats that might not even be there.

Except the threats had been there. Were still there, potentially. My nervous system wasn't wrong to stay alert. It was doing exactly what it had learned to do to keep me alive.

I just didn't know how to tell it that maybe, possibly, I might be safe now.

Or if that was even true.

***

The next few nights passed without incident. No calls. No unexpected knocks at my door. No shadow of Scott's car on my street when I came home from campus.

By Sunday afternoon, I'd almost convinced myself it was over.

I pulled my favorite blanket around my shoulders and settled onto the couch with my phone. My mom's voice was tight with worry when she answered.

"Emma, honey, if you need to come home..."

"I know, Mom. But I think it's actually okay now." I tried to sound more confident than I felt. "The police visit worked. Scott hasn't contacted me since."

"Your room is always ready. Your father and I just want you safe."

After we hung up, I tried to let the evening's quiet seep into my bones. Hot cocoa. The mystery novel I'd been saving. A long shower that turned my bathroom into a steam room. Clean leggings and my softest t-shirt.

I curled up on the couch and let the story pull me away from my own life. Somewhere after eleven, my eyes grew heavy, and the book slipped from my hands.

The phone's shrill ring jolted me awake, my heart already hammering before I was fully conscious.

Unknown number.

My thumb hovered over the decline button. But something, exhaustion, curiosity, the stubborn part of me that refused to live in fear, made me answer.

"Hey Em, how are you?"

Scott's voice. But wrong somehow. Strained and rough.

My entire body went cold. "Scott, you can't call me. The police told you..."

"Em, please don't hang up. It's important."

I should have ended the call. My psychology professors would have told me to end the call. Every domestic violence pamphlet I'd ever read said to maintain no contact. Officer Turner had been explicit: *Don't engage.*

"What is it?" The words came out sharp, irritated.

"I tried to kill myself."

The room tilted slightly. "What are you talking about?"

"I tied a noose. I tried to hang myself." His voice was barely above a whisper, and that hoarseness, it could be real. Ligature marks on the neck affected the vocal cords. I knew that from my abnormal psychology coursework. Strangulation injuries, attempted hanging, the physical signs.

"Then why aren't you dead?" The cruelty in my own voice startled me, but exhaustion had burned through my patience.

"I just couldn't imagine never seeing your face again."

Classic manipulation, some clinical part of my brain observed. Suicide threats to regain control. Make the victim feel responsible for the abuser's life, for their mental state, for their continued existence. It was textbook. I'd written a paper on coercive control tactics that had included an entire section on suicide threats as manipulation.

But his voice. That raspiness wasn't fake. Or was it? Could someone manufacture that sound? Was I analyzing or rationalizing?

"Scott, if you actually did this, you need to call 911. You need a hospital, not me."

"Please, Em. I just need..."

"This is serious. You need psychiatric help." My hands were shaking now, adrenaline flooding my system. Fight or flight. My body couldn't tell the difference between danger and this phone call. Couldn't distinguish between a real threat and an emotional one.

He made a sound, a sob or a gasp, I couldn't tell.

And then I heard myself say, "I'm coming over. Thirty minutes."

The words hung in the air after I said them. Wrong. They were wrong. Every instinct screamed at me that this was exactly what he wanted, that I was walking back into his orbit, that the police warning and my freedom and these few peaceful nights were about to evaporate.

But what if he was telling the truth? What if I hung up and he died and I had to live with that?

The what-ifs multiplied in my head: What if he tried again after I hung up? What if he succeeded? What if his mother blamed me? What if I could have prevented it?

My psych textbooks called it trauma bonding. The person who hurt you becomes the person you're compelled to save. The abuser weaponizes your empathy, your caretaking instincts, your fear of being responsible for harm. They train you to prioritize their wellbeing over your own safety.

I knew the theory. I could recite the mechanism. I could explain the neurological pathways that made this response automatic, the way intermittent reinforcement created bonds stronger than consistent affection ever could.

I just couldn't seem to stop myself from living it.

This was a mistake. I knew it was a mistake. Every piece of knowledge I'd accumulated over two years of psychology coursework, every case study I'd read, every warning I'd received from Officer Turner, all of it was screaming that this was dangerous. That I was about to undo everything I'd worked for.

But I was already reaching for my shoes. Already grabbing my keys. Already walking toward the door like my body was on autopilot, overriding every rational objection my mind could produce.

I paused with my hand on the doorknob. Pulled out my phone and texted Becca: *Scott called. Says he tried to kill himself. I'm going to check on him. His apartment. If you don't hear from me in an hour, call the police.*

Her response came within seconds: *EMMA NO. Don't go. Call 911 for him. Don't go there.*

She was right. I knew she was right.

I went anyway.

Because that's what trauma bonding did. It made you walk back into danger even when you could see it clearly, even when you knew better, even when every part of you understood you were making the wrong choice.

Knowledge wasn't the same as power. Understanding the trap didn't mean you could escape it.

I was living proof of that.

Chapter 8

The drive to Scott's apartment felt surreal, like watching myself from outside my body. I kept both hands locked on the steering wheel to stop them from shaking.

You shouldn't be doing this. Turn around. Call Officer Turner instead.

But what if he was dying right now? What if I turned around and tomorrow I found out...

The door was unlocked. Of course it was. He'd been expecting me.

The apartment was dim, just one lamp casting long shadows across the living room. Scott sat on the floor beside the fireplace, and my breath caught when I saw what he was looking at.

My wedding dress.

He'd kept it. After everything. After I'd left, after the police visit, he'd kept my wedding dress and now he had it displayed like some kind of shrine. Like evidence of what we were supposed to be. Like a relic he was worshipping.

My stomach twisted. This was wrong. Everything about this was wrong. The staging of it. The symbolism. This wasn't just depression; this was obsession.

Then he turned his head, and I saw his neck. An angry red mark circled his throat, the skin abraded and raw.

"So where did you try to hang yourself?" My voice came out flat, clinical. Somewhere in my mind, I was already cataloging symptoms, assessing risk, doing what my professors had trained me to do instead of feeling what I should be feeling.

"In the basement." He barely whispered it.

I moved toward the basement stairs like a sleepwalker. Each step down felt heavier than the last.

The rope hung from a beam near the washer and dryer. It was a simple loop, not even tied correctly. Not the slipknot that would tighten under weight. Either he didn't know how to tie a proper noose, or he'd deliberately tied it wrong.

I stared at that rope, and something crystallized in my chest. The mark on his neck was real. The attempt was real. But this, this performance, the unlocked door, my dress on display, the convenient timing after the police visit...

This was manipulation. Calculated or desperate, I couldn't tell, but manipulation nonetheless. Suicide attempts could be genuine cries for help *and* coercive tactics at the same time. The research said both things could be true. He could genuinely want to die *and* be using that pain as a weapon to pull me back.

He's sick, I thought. *And I can't fix him.*

The realization should have freed me. Instead, I felt myself sliding back into old patterns, old responsibilities. The caretaker role. The fixer. The one who managed the crisis.

"Scott, you need to talk to someone." I climbed the stairs, my voice steady even as my heart hammered. "Get your things. I'm taking you to get help."

He didn't argue. He changed clothes mechanically, grabbed his wallet and keys.

"Health insurance card," I reminded him, and hated myself for it. For still being the one who managed things, who took care of details, who made sure he had what he needed. This was exactly what trauma bonding looked like. I could observe myself doing it, name it in real time, and still couldn't stop.

I didn't tell him where we were going. I just drove, my hands white-knuckled on the wheel, while he sat silent in the passenger seat. The psychiatric hospital's lights were harsh against the dark sky.

"Come on." I took his hand and led him inside. *Why am I holding his hand?*

The admissions desk. The explanation. The nurse appearing immediately at the word "suicide." Scott remained passive, letting me guide him, speak for him, translate his crisis into the language of intake forms and assessment criteria. I was good at this. Too good. I'd practiced it too many times.

We sat in the waiting area, and he said, "Maybe after this we can grab breakfast on the way home."

I stared at him. He genuinely didn't understand. He thought this was like an emergency room visit for a sprained ankle. In and out. Back to normal. Back to *us*.

I said nothing.

When the nurse called us back, Scott wanted me present for the interview. Of course he did. I followed them into a small, sterile room and sat in a plastic chair that squeaked against the linoleum.

"Tell me what brings you here tonight," the nurse began.

Scott's version of events was careful, curated. He talked about feeling depressed, about the attempt, about recent stress. He made it sound like a mental health crisis that appeared out of nowhere. A chemical imbalance. Bad luck. Nothing to do with losing his job, losing his girlfriend, losing control.

The words came out of my mouth before I could stop them: "Scott, you should probably mention that you've been drinking daily. That your alcohol use is contributing to how you're feeling."

Why am I still advocating for his treatment? Why am I still trying to help him get better care?

He shot me a look I couldn't quite read. Gratitude? Resentment? "Well, yeah, maybe I've been drinking more than I should."

The nurse continued her assessment with professional efficiency. When she finished, she recommended their dual diagnosis program. Inpatient. Several days minimum. Psychiatrist. Medication. Treatment groups for both depression and alcohol use.

"That sounds good," Scott said, and he actually looked relieved.

"I didn't bring any clothes or anything," he added, looking at me expectantly.

And there it was. The next expectation. The next way I'd be pulled back in. The next task that would require me to maintain contact, to return to his apartment, to stay engaged in his life.

"I can drop things off tomorrow," I heard myself say.

No. No. Say no. This isn't your responsibility. You're not his girlfriend anymore. You're not anything to him.

But the words were already out.

More paperwork. Scott being led away down a locked corridor. His house key pressed into my palm so I could gather his belongings like I was still his person, still his caretaker, still responsible for making sure he had clean underwear and his phone charger.

I walked out to my car in a daze.

The drive home should have felt like victory. He was in a locked facility. He literally could not call me, couldn't show up at my door, couldn't manipulate or threaten or plead. For the first time in weeks, I was physically safe from him.

So why did I feel hollow?

I let myself into my apartment and locked the door behind me. One lock, two locks, the chain. The wedding dress was still at his apartment. I'd have to go back tomorrow to get his things. Which meant seeing it again. Which meant stepping back into that space he'd made into a museum of our failed future.

I sank onto my couch, pulled my knees to chest, and waited for relief that wouldn't come.

Scott was getting help. That was good. That was what he needed.

But I'd just spent three hours caretaking my abuser, holding his hand, advocating for his treatment, promising to bring him fresh clothes. I'd driven him to the hospital like a concerned girlfriend instead of calling 911 like a survivor protecting her boundaries.

The clinical part of my brain supplied the analysis: I'd just reinforced every behavior I needed him to stop. By responding to his suicide threat, by rushing to his aid, I'd taught him that this tactic worked. That threatening self-harm would bring me back. That no matter what boundaries I set, no matter what the police said, he could override them by escalating the crisis.

Operant conditioning. Variable ratio reinforcement schedule. I was rewarding the exact behaviors I needed to extinguish.

I knew this. I could explain the learning theory behind it. And I'd done it anyway.

He was a good person, I tried to tell myself. *Just not the person I thought he was.*

But good people didn't steal four thousand dollars. Good people didn't try to throw their pregnant girlfriends down stairs. Good people didn't use suicide attempts to bypass police warnings and pull you back into their orbit.

Good people didn't keep your wedding dress on display like a trophy or a threat.

My phone sat on the coffee table, dark and silent.

I should call Officer Turner. Tell him what happened. But what would I say? *Scott threatened suicide so I spent the evening taking care of him and I'm going back to his apartment tomorrow?*

I'd violated everything Turner told me to do. I'd engaged. I'd responded. I'd maintained contact.

I'd undone everything. One phone call, and I'd walked right back into the role he needed me to play.

The apartment was quiet. Safe. Empty.

And I'd never felt more trapped.

Because the trap wasn't just Scott's behavior. The trap was inside me. It was the trained response to prioritize his needs, the guilt that made me responsible for his wellbeing, the caretaker role so deeply ingrained I couldn't shed it even when I could see exactly what it was costing me.

I understood the psychology of it. Could cite the research on trauma bonds and learned helplessness and the difficulty of breaking patterns even with full conscious awareness.

But understanding didn't equal freedom.

I was proof of that.

Tomorrow I'd go back to his apartment. I'd pack his bag like a good ex-girlfriend. And with every item I folded, every kindness I extended, I'd be tightening the bonds that kept me attached to someone who'd tried to destroy me.

I knew all of this.

And I didn't know how to stop.

***

I didn't sleep well. Every time I drifted off, I jolted awake with the image of that rope burned into my vision, the wedding dress hanging like something preserved in formaldehyde.

The next morning, my phone rang before I'd finished my coffee. A social worker named Tia from the hospital.

"I understand you're bringing some items for Scott today?"

"Yes, this afternoon." My voice came out mechanical. Professional.

"Would you mind stopping by my office when you arrive? Just ask the receptionist to page me."

After we hung up, I stared at Scott's house key on my kitchen counter. The logical part of my brain, the part that had memorized every textbook definition of healthy boundaries, knew exactly what I should do. Mail the key back. Let the receptionist know that he's have to find someone else to help. Cut contact completely.

Instead, I picked up the key and drove to his apartment.

***

The key turned easily in the lock. He'd never changed it, even after I'd moved out. Some distant part of me registered this as significant, another way he'd kept me tethered, kept the possibility of my return alive in his mind.

Inside, the apartment looked the same but felt evacuated. Stale air thick with the smell of old takeout and spilled beer. Dishes crusted in the sink. And there in the living room, my wedding dress still hanging like an exhibit in a museum of things that would never happen.

I moved quickly to the bedroom, muscle memory guiding me to his dresser. I grabbed clothes without looking too closely, shirts, jeans, socks. I let the routine task occupy my hands so my mind couldn't catch up with what I was doing. The clinical term floated up: *avoidance behavior*. I pushed it away.

On my way out, something on the entry table caught my eye. An envelope, official-looking, already torn open.

I picked it up. My hands knew what they were doing even as my brain tried to stop them.

EVICTION NOTICE.

The words swam. I had to read them twice before they solidified into meaning. Three months unpaid rent. Final notice. Thirty days to vacate.

Three months.

I'd given him my half of the rent every single month. Five hundred dollars, handed over like clockwork because we were building a life together, because that's what couples did. Fifteen hundred dollars he'd just, what? Spent on Jim Beam? Pocketed while I believed we were covering our expenses?

My chest constricted. The four thousand dollars he'd stolen for the "engagement ring" had felt like an isolated incident, a desperate mistake. But this was a pattern. A systematic dismantling of trust, so gradual I hadn't seen it happening.

The notice was dated a week ago. Right before Officer Turner's visit. Right before the rope.

The connection clicked into place with awful clarity. He was losing control. Of the apartment, of me, of the carefully constructed narrative where I was his salvation and he was my protector. And when control slipped through his fingers, he'd found the one method guaranteed to bring me back.

I dropped the notice and left; the duffel bag suddenly unbearable in my hand.

***

The hospital receptionist paged Tia, and within minutes I was sitting in a cramped office that smelled like burnt coffee and anxiety. Tia had kind eyes behind wire-rimmed glasses, the sort of eyes that had seen every version of human pain and learned not to flinch.

"Emma, thank you for meeting with me." She gestured to a chair. "Scott mentioned you're his fiancée and primary support person."

The air left my lungs. "No. We broke up. We were engaged, but I ended it."

Something shifted in Tia's expression, not surprise exactly, but confirmation of a suspicion. "I see. Can you tell me more about that?"

So I did. The story spilled out in fragments I'd been trying to keep contained. The control, the manipulation, the money, the pregnancy I hadn't meant to share but suddenly couldn't hold back. Things I hadn't told my mother, hadn't fully admitted to Becca. Tia listened without interrupting, occasionally making notes, and I watched myself from somewhere outside my body. *Dissociation*, the textbook term whispered. *A defensive response to overwhelming emotion.*

"I wondered if I was getting the full picture," Tia said when I finished. "This helps clarify the situation considerably."

"He's been harassing me." My voice was shaking now, the clinical distance I'd tried to maintain crumbling. "Calling constantly, showing up at my apartment. I was terrified. That's why I went to the police."

"And then he called you with the suicide threat."

"Yes."

Tia leaned forward, her voice steady and clear. "Emma, I'm going to be direct with you. Based on what you've told me, I believe Scott's suicide attempt was another form of manipulation. A way to regain control when other methods stopped working."

I'd known it. Some part of me had known it the moment I heard his voice on the phone. But hearing Tia say it, a professional naming what I'd been afraid to name, made the knowledge real in a way it hadn't been before.

"I know," I whispered. "I knew that's what it was. But I came anyway."

"You came because you're a compassionate person who didn't want someone to die, even someone who hurt you." Tia's voice softened without losing its firmness. "That says something good about your character. But Emma, you cannot fix this. Scott needs professional intervention that you are not qualified to provide. More than that, your continued presence in his life is actually preventing him from accepting reality and doing the work he needs to do."

I nodded, tears blurring the edges of Tia's face.

"I'm going to make it very clear to Scott and the entire treatment team that this relationship is over. You've done more than enough by bringing him here safely. Now I strongly recommend complete disengagement. If he contacts you again after discharge, don't hesitate, file for a restraining order immediately."

"I really hoped it wouldn't come to that." The words came out small.

"I know. But sometimes protecting yourself requires legal intervention." She paused, and I saw something like recognition in her expression. "You deserve to move forward with your life. Scott's recovery is his responsibility, not yours. It never was."

I thanked her and handed over the duffel bag I'd been clutching. My hands felt strange without its weight, lighter but unsteady, like I'd been holding something so long I'd forgotten what empty felt like.

***

Outside, the afternoon sun hit me like a physical thing. I stood on the sidewalk, blinking against the brightness, and felt something vast and shapeless settle over me. Not the sharp grief of loss, but something more complicated. The weight of every version of us I'd imagined colliding with every version of us that had actually existed. The man I'd thought I was saving and the man who'd been slowly dismantling me. The life I'd tried to build and the life I'd been living without seeing it clearly.

I got in my car and sat there, hands resting on the steering wheel. Through the windshield, I could see the psychiatric wing where Scott was somewhere behind those locked doors. I knew with absolute certainty I'd never see him again.

The knowing felt both like relief and like grief, and I didn't have the energy to parse which feeling was stronger.

I started the engine and drove home, the empty passenger seat beside me somehow louder than any conversation we'd ever had.

***

I was home maybe an hour when my phone rang again. Scott's mother.

My stomach dropped. For a moment I just stared at her name on the screen, my thumb hovering over the decline button. But I answered.

"Emma? What's going on with Scott? He called and said he's at Arbor Fuller Hospital. What happened?"

The question pinned me in place. We weren't together anymore. His mental health wasn't mine to explain, wasn't my responsibility to manage or translate or make palatable for anyone else. But Mrs. Martin's voice carried something I recognized, the particular terror of a mother who knows her child is in danger but not how or why.

"Emma, he's my son. Please."

"He tried to kill himself." The words came out flat, clinical. Saying them a second time made them feel more like fact than trauma. "He called me last night. I took him to the hospital."

The sound that came through the phone was barely recognizable as language. Then, "Oh God. Oh God, no." Her breath hitched and caught. "How did he...how did he try?"

I didn't want to say it. Didn't want to give it shape again.

"He tried to hang himself."

The noise she made was raw and animal, grief without any civilized veneer. I heard her crying, gasping for air, and felt my own throat tighten in response. Some mirror neuron firing that made me want to cry with her even as I stayed locked in that numb, distant place.

"I'm so sorry, Mrs. Martin." My voice sounded like it was coming from someone else. "The social worker said he'll be there for several days. They have a dual diagnosis program for the depression and the drinking."

"Emma." She was trying to steady herself, I could hear it. "This isn't the first time."

The words didn't register at first. Then they did, and my whole body went still.

"What?"

"This isn't the first time Scott's been hospitalized for mental health issues."

The room shifted. I sat down hard on my couch, the leather cold against the back of my legs.

"He didn't tell you." Not a question. Her voice carried something that sounded like guilt and resignation tangled together. "Oh, Emma. I should have said something. You two seemed so happy at first, and I thought, I hoped, that you were good for him. That maybe this time would be different."

"This time?" The words felt foreign in my mouth.

"He tried to kill himself in college. Pills. And there was another hospitalization his senior year of high school." She paused, and I heard her exhale shakily. "I thought he'd gotten better. I thought the therapy and medication were working."

Each sentence landed with physical weight. Our entire relationship reconfigured itself in my mind. Every moment I'd thought I was helping him, saving him, being the person who finally understood him. But I'd just been the latest in a line of people trying to fix something that had been broken long before I existed in his life. And he'd let me believe I was special, that my love could be the difference, when he'd known all along it wouldn't be enough because it never had been.

"Emma, I'm going to say something that's very hard for me." Mrs. Martin's voice steadied, took on a different quality. Resolved. "You need to move on. You need to leave my son and build your own life."

The bluntness of it shocked me.

"You're young," she continued. "You have so much ahead of you. Scott is sick, and I don't know if he's ever going to get better. Maybe he won't. You would have been a wonderful daughter-in-law, but you deserve better than this. You deserve better than him."

His own mother. Telling me to leave him. Releasing me from whatever obligation I'd felt, whatever guilt had wrapped itself around my lungs since the moment he'd called me with that rope.

"I wanted a good life for Scott." Her voice was quieter now, sadder. "But I want a good life for you too. And those two things, they're not the same anymore. Maybe they never were."

I was crying openly now, tears dripping off my chin onto my shirt. "I'm so sorry. I wish things were different."

"Me too, sweetheart. Me too."

After we hung up, I sat there on my couch in the late afternoon light, phone still in my hand. I thought about all the versions of Scott I'd known, the charming one who'd seemed like a knight in shining armor, the controlling one who'd slowly tightened his grip, the desperate one on the phone last night. And now this new version, the one with a history I'd never been allowed to see. A pattern that predated me and would likely outlast me.

I'd been engaged to someone I didn't actually know. Someone who'd hidden hospitalizations, suicide attempts, an entire history that explained so much but that he'd never trusted me enough to share. He'd let me move in with him, plan a wedding, get pregnant, all while keeping me in the dark about the fundamental reality of who he was. Not just flaws or struggles, but the architecture of his mental illness, the pattern that had been there long before I'd arrived thinking I could be different.

The guilt surfaced first, insistent. Guilt for the relief I felt at being out. Guilt for not being able to save him when maybe if I'd known sooner, if I'd understood better, if I'd been more patient or more careful or just more. Guilt for the anger burning underneath the sadness, hot and accusatory.

But Mrs. Martin's words cut through: *You deserve better than him.*

Even his mother knew. Even the person who loved him most in the world had looked at the situation clearly and told me to go.

I thought about my wedding dress, still hanging in his living room like a relic. The idea of going back for it made my stomach turn. That dress represented a fantasy I'd constructed—a man who didn't exist, a future that was never real. I'd been so busy trying to save him that I'd never stopped to ask if the person I was saving was actually the person standing in front of me.

I pulled my knees to my chest, making myself small on the couch, and let the tears come. Not the sharp, shocked tears from earlier, but something deeper. I wasn't crying for what I'd lost. I was crying for what I'd never actually had.

I'd thought I was the person who could save him. His mother had thought I might be too.

We'd both been wrong.

Chapter 9

Several weeks passed. No calls. No visits. No messages slipped under my door.

At first I'd checked my phone compulsively, my body tensing every time it buzzed, bracing for his name to appear. But as September arrived and the leaves started their slow turn toward gold, the vigilance began to ease. Maybe Tia had gotten through to him. Maybe the hospitalization had been the turning point he needed. Maybe I could actually believe it was over.

I registered for fall semester classes. Abnormal Psychology, Research Methods, Cognitive Development. The irony of studying abnormal psychology while living through my own case study wasn't lost on me, but I pushed the thought away. This was a fresh start. My final year at Providence College, and this time I'd be able to focus on my studies instead of managing Scott's crises or parsing his moods or walking on eggshells through my own life.

One afternoon, Becca called, her voice bright with the kind of excitement that made me smile before she'd even explained. "Em, I need your help. Date tomorrow night with that guy from the climbing gym, and I have absolutely nothing to wear."

"You have an entire closet full of clothes."

"Nothing that says 'I like you but I'm not trying too hard,' you know?" She paused, and I heard the genuine nervousness underneath her theatrical tone. "Em, I really like this guy. It has to be perfect."

The ordinariness of it made my chest ache in a good way. This was what normal looked like, helping your best friend pick an outfit, worrying about date clothes instead of police reports.

"Meet you at two tomorrow. We'll find something."

After we hung up, I pulled up a workout video on YouTube, grateful for the mundane rhythm of my afternoon. Shopping trips with Becca. Classes starting next week. A future that felt like it might actually belong to me instead of being held hostage by someone else's instability.

My phone rang again. Probably Becca remembering something else she needed, another shoe option to consider.

But the screen showed Officer Turner's name.

Everything stopped. My breath, my heartbeat, the cheerful instructor on my laptop counting down jumping jacks. He wouldn't call unless something had happened. Unless Scott had violated the hospital's discharge plan, unless he'd done something wrong, unless...

"Hello, Emma. It's Officer Turner."

"Hi." My voice came out thin, reedy.

He was quiet for a moment. In that pause, something in my body already knew. Some animal part of my brain that could read silence, that understood the weight of what was coming.

"I'm about to break protocol here, but I think you should hear this from me rather than through other channels." He took a breath. "We found Scott Martin's body early this morning. He died by suicide last night."

The words hit me in the wrong order. Body. Scott. Suicide. My brain tried to rearrange them into something that made sense, but they stayed fractured, refusing to cohere.

My legs gave out. I was on the floor suddenly, phone pressed to my ear, the workout video still playing on my laptop, some relentlessly cheerful instructor counting down burpees like the world hadn't just tilted sideways.

"Emma? Are you there?"

"Yes." The word barely made it out. "I'm here."

"I'm sorry to break this news over the phone. Are you alone? Is there someone who can come be with you?"

Am I alone? I looked around my apartment like I might find the answer written on the walls, in the afternoon light slanting through the blinds. The question felt existential. I'd been alone for weeks now. Months, really. Since the moment I'd walked out of his apartment and decided to save myself instead of him.

"His family," I heard myself say. "Does his family know?"

The clinical part of my brain had taken over, asking about notification procedures, about protocol. A psychology student observing proper channels even while sitting on the floor of her apartment, trying to process that someone she'd loved, someone she'd been terrified of, was dead.

"His mother couldn't reach him yesterday. She went to his apartment this morning." Officer Turner's voice was gentle. "She found him, Emma."

The image slammed into me. Mrs. Martin walking into her son's apartment, calling his name maybe, looking for him. Finding him. The same woman who'd told me I deserved better, who'd released me from the obligation of saving him, now carrying the weight of discovering he couldn't be saved at all.

I pressed my hand over my mouth. I was crying, I realized. Tears running down my face, dripping off my chin. When had that started?

"The coroner will perform an autopsy, follow all the legal procedures." Officer Turner's voice felt far away. "But we know what happened."

"Okay." What else was there to say? What response existed for this?

"Emma, if you need anything, if there's anything I can do..."

"Thank you." My voice had gone flat, mechanical. "Thank you for telling me."

"Emma?" He paused, and I could hear him choosing his words carefully. "None of this is your fault. You know that, right?"

None of this is your fault.

The words hung there, waiting for me to accept them. I nodded even though he couldn't see me, the motion automatic. "I know."

But I didn't know. Sitting there on my floor with my workout video still playing and my best friend's date outfit waiting to be chosen and my fall semester classes queued up like promises of a normal life. I didn't know anything anymore.

After we hung up, I stayed on the floor. The instructor finished her routine, the video ended, and the silence that followed felt cavernous. I thought about calling Becca, but I couldn't make my hand move toward the phone. I thought about the wedding dress still hanging in Scott's apartment. Did Mrs. Martin find that too? Would she have to pack up the evidence of all his fantasies along with everything else?

I thought about the last time I'd seen him, holding his hand in that hospital room, and how I'd known with certainty I'd never see him again. I'd been right, but not in the way I'd imagined.

He was gone. Actually gone. Not just out of my life but out of life entirely, and I was sitting here crying but also feeling something else underneath the tears. Something I couldn't name yet but that felt uncomfortably like relief, and that made me cry harder because what kind of person felt relieved when someone died?

The kind of person who'd been trying to survive, some distant voice answered. The kind of person who'd been living in fear.

But that didn't make it feel any less wrong.

***

After we hung up, I stayed on the floor, phone still in my hand.

Scott was dead.

Scott had killed himself.

Scott had successfully done what he'd threatened that night with the rope. What he'd attempted with a noose that wasn't tied right. What maybe he'd been planning all along.

The apartment was too quiet. I could hear my own breathing, ragged and uneven, and the relentless cheerfulness of the workout instructor of the next video that had started automatically.

He's never going to call again. The thought arrived with strange clarity. And then, immediately behind it: I should feel relieved.

But relief wasn't what I felt. I felt like I was falling through multiple realities at once. The one where I'd escaped, the one where I'd failed to save him, the one where none of my choices had mattered because this was always how it would end.

I'd wanted him out of my life. I'd reported him to the police, ended our engagement, moved out, blocked his number. I'd followed every piece of advice from every pamphlet and hotline and domestic violence advocate. I'd done everything right.

And now he was dead.

This is what he wanted, some clinical part of my mind observed. *He wanted you to feel responsible. This is the ultimate control, making you carry this forever.*

But he was still dead. And understanding the manipulation didn't make the weight of it any lighter.

My phone buzzed. Becca, texting about tomorrow's shopping trip, about her date outfit, about which shoes to wear. I stared at the message, at the jarring normalcy of it. She didn't know yet. Nobody knew except me and Officer Turner and Scott's mother, who'd walked into her son's apartment this morning looking for him and found something else entirely.

I thought about calling her. Offering condolences, the way you're supposed to when someone dies. But what would I say? *I'm sorry your son killed himself after I left him and reported him to the police?* She'd told me to move on, to build a good life. She'd known, somehow, that it might end like this. Maybe she'd always known.

I pulled my knees to my chest and let the sobs come. Ugly, gasping cries that hurt my throat and made my ribs ache. I cried for Scott, for whatever version of him had existed before the alcohol and the rage and the mental illness consumed everything else. I cried for Mrs. Martin, who'd lost her son and would carry the image of finding him for the rest of her life. I cried for myself, for the two years I'd given to someone who'd been drowning and who'd tried to pull me under with him.

But mostly I cried because I didn't know how to feel. The relief and the guilt and the grief were all tangled together, knotted so tightly I couldn't separate one strand from another. My psychology textbooks had entire chapters on complicated grief, on trauma responses, on survivor's guilt. I'd highlighted passages about supporting clients through loss, written papers on the stages of grief and the neurobiology of trauma. But none of it had prepared me for this; for the way your hands shake when you learn your abuser has died, for the way your first thought is *I should have done more* even though you know, intellectually, that there was nothing more you could have done. That doing more would have meant sacrificing yourself.

The silence pressed in. No workout video, no phone calls, just the sound of my own breathing slowly steadying.

I thought about the wedding dress still hanging in his apartment. The police would clear out his belongings eventually. His mother would have to sort through his things, decide what to keep and what to throw away. Would she find the dress? Would she understand what it meant that he'd kept it displayed like that, like a shrine to a future that was never going to happen? Like if he just held on tight enough, he could make me come back?

He did come back, I realized. Not literally, but he'd been in my head all along; in every phone call I screened, every time I checked my locks twice before bed, every nightmare that jolted me awake at 3 a.m. He'd made a home in my anxiety, carved out a space in my hypervigilance. And now he'd be there forever, not as a threat but as a ghost. The complicated grief of mourning someone who hurt you, the impossible mathematics of losing someone you'd had to lose in order to survive.

The autumn light was fading, my apartment growing dim around me. I should turn on a lamp. Should call Becca. Should get up off the floor and do something, anything, other than sit here with my thoughts spiraling.

But I couldn't move yet. My body felt heavy, anchored to the floor by something I couldn't name.

Tomorrow there would be practicalities. Tomorrow I might see an obituary, hear whispers around campus, face questions from people who'd known we were together. Tomorrow I'd have to figure out whether to go to a funeral, whether to reach out to his family, whether to tell people what had really happened or let them believe whatever story felt easier.

Tomorrow I'd have to be a survivor again, put on that identity like armor.

But tonight I could just be a person who'd lost someone they'd once loved, someone they'd once promised to marry. Tonight I could mourn the version of Scott I'd invented when I was young and naive and believed that love could save people. That my love, specifically, could be the difference.

I stayed on the floor until the room went completely dark, until my tears ran out and left only a hollow ache behind. Until I could sit with the terrible, complicated truth:

He was gone, and I was free.

And somehow those two things felt exactly the same.

Part 2

Chapter 10

It had been a long day, the kind that left me feeling wrung out and hollow. The moment I stepped into my apartment, I kicked off my shoes and reached behind my back to unhook my bra, sliding it off through my sleeve with the practiced ease of someone who'd performed this ritual a thousand times. Small freedoms mattered when so much else felt constrained.

I grabbed a family-sized bag of M&M's from the pantry and collapsed onto my couch, pulling my laptop onto my knees. The apartment was quiet. Safe. Mine. After two years, I still felt a small surge of relief every time I walked through the door and locked it behind me.

My phone pinged.

Becca: *Stopping by in ten.*

I felt the familiar mixture of affection and mild dread. Becca's visits were rarely low-key affairs.

Emma: *k*

I scrolled through my inbox with mechanical indifference while I waited. Electric bill. Delete. Sale at H&M. Maybe later. "Embark on an Adventure of a Lifetime: Hike the Appalachian Trail." Delete.

Moments later, Becca burst through the door like a tornado in designer jeans, her energy filling the small apartment instantly. She'd been doing this for two years now. Showing up. Refusing to let me disappear completely into my fear.

"Okay, clear that busy calendar of yours." She made a beeline for the kitchen, grabbing a Diet Coke from my fridge with the casual entitlement of eighteen years of friendship. "We need to talk about your birthday."

"My birthday isn't for three months," I said.

"Exactly. Which gives us time to plan something amazing." She dropped into the chair across from me, eyes already gleaming with whatever scheme she'd concocted. "I'm thinking we do something big. Something to celebrate you turning twenty-five. Something that gets you out of this apartment."

My chest tightened. "I go out."

"We went to watch my niece's play two weeks ago."

"Exactly. I go out."

"Em, watching third graders pretend to be bumblebees doesn't count."

I looked away. The truth sat between us like a third presence in the room. I hadn't really gone out. Not in any meaningful way. Not since Scott. Since the police. Since Officer Turner's phone call. Since the funeral I hadn't attended. Since the complicated grief that still sometimes caught me off guard in the frozen food aisle or while brushing my teeth.

Becca's expression softened. "Look, I'm not trying to push you into anything you're not ready for. But Em, you can't let the past hold you back forever. You deserve happiness just as much as anyone else."

Do I? The question rose unbidden. Some days I wasn't so sure. Some days I felt like something broken that couldn't quite be glued back together properly, all the cracks still visible no matter how hard I tried to hide them.

"I know you're not ready for dating," Becca continued. "I get that. But what about something else? Something that's just for you?"

Her gaze landed on my laptop, still open on the table, and her face lit up. "Em, this is it!" She turned the screen toward herself. "'Embark on an Adventure of a Lifetime: Hike the Appalachian Trail.' This is perfect. We can hike the Appalachian Trail!"

"What?" I stared at her. "Are you kidding me?"

"I'm serious! Just nature. Fresh air. You and me. You love to hike."

"No," I corrected, "*you* love to hike. I love to sit on my couch."

The distinction felt important. I'd spent two years learning to distinguish between what I actually wanted and what other people wanted for me. It was harder than it sounded, especially with Becca, who genuinely believed she was helping.

"Come on, Em! You're turning twenty-five. What better way to celebrate than by challenging yourself?"

I managed a halfhearted smile. "You know me, Bec. I'm not exactly the adventurous type. I'm more of a 'stay within my comfort zone' person."

And my comfort zone is very small these days. About the size of this apartment.

"That's exactly why you should do this!" Becca grabbed a handful of M&M's, my M&M's, and leaned forward with that earnest look that had been convincing me to do things since second grade. "Look, I'm not saying you need to jump into a relationship or become a different person. I'm saying you need to remember who you were before Scott. You used to be fun, Em. You used to say yes to things."

The words landed with physical weight. I had been different before. Lighter. More willing to take risks, to be spontaneous. Scott hadn't just broken my heart. He'd stolen something essential. My ability to trust. My belief that good things could happen without a terrible price attached. My conviction that I could trust my own judgment about people.

I'd loved him. I'd thought I was saving him. And then he'd died, and I'd been left holding all of it. The grief, the guilt, the relief, the shame of feeling relieved. The impossible tangle of mourning someone who'd hurt you while simultaneously feeling free of them.

"Just promise me you'll think about it," Becca said softly.

I looked at my best friend. The person who'd been by her side through everything. Who'd held me when I sobbed on my bathroom floor after Officer Turner's call. Who'd helped me change the locks. Who refused to let me disappear completely.

Maybe Becca was right. Not about finding myself or having some transformative experience. But about getting out. About doing something that scared me for reasons that had nothing to do with Scott. The hiking itself didn't appeal to me. The thought of being that exposed, that vulnerable, that far from the safety of my apartment made me anxious.

But maybe that was exactly why I should do it. Not because Becca wanted me to, but because I was tired of being afraid. Tired of letting Scott's ghost dictate every choice.

Or maybe I was just too exhausted to keep saying no.

"I promise I'll think about it," I finally said.

The words felt heavier than they should, like I was agreeing to more than just considering a hike.

Becca's face broke into a triumphant smile, and I felt the familiar mix of affection and resignation wash over her.

What am I getting myself into?

But even as the thought crossed my mind, something else stirred. Something small and stubborn that Becca had somehow kept alive all these years. Not hope exactly, but maybe the memory of what hope used to feel like.

I wasn't sure I believed anything would change. But I wanted to. And after two years of just surviving, maybe wanting was enough to start.

***

The Uber dropped us at Sky Meadows State Park just after nine. My legs felt unsteady as we climbed out, whether from the drive or nerves

I couldn't say. The visitor center rose before us, all wooden beams and stone that seemed to grow from the landscape itself. Beautiful. Completely intimidating.

Through the trees, I could see our group already gathering. My stomach lurched.

"Ready?" Becca shouldered her pack with the ease of someone who actually knew what they were doing.

I hoisted my own pack, felt the weight settle onto my hips like a declaration. No turning back now.

Our trail guide was exactly what Emma had pictured: weathered skin, lean frame, the kind of easy movement that came from thousands of miles on the trail. He had to be in his fifties but moved like someone half his age, which only made my twenty-four-year-old body feel more inadequate.

"You must be Emma and Becca." His smile was warm, genuine. "I'm Tony. Welcome."

The others were already there. A middle-aged woman with sun-kissed skin introduced herself as Carol, a nurse from Pennsylvania, doing this for her fiftieth birthday. A young guy named Jake, fresh out of college, who looked like he'd actually hiked before. A couple in their thirties, Liam and Sophia, celebrating their anniversary in what Sophia called "the worst romantic getaway ever." And Elijah, an older solo hiker with an enigmatic smile who offered nothing beyond his name.

Everyone looked ready. Everyone except me.

Tony unfolded a topographical map, and the group leaned in. "You're starting at roughly the halfway point of the entire AT," he said. "Over the next few weeks, we'll tackle this first leg together, though you'll each be hiking your own pace. Some of you are headed to New Hampshire. Others are determined to make it to Maine."

I tried to focus on his words, but my mind kept wandering to worst-case scenarios. What if I twisted my ankle on day one? What if I couldn't keep up? What if...

"The most important thing to remember," Tony continued, "is that this isn't a race. Establish a comfortable pace. Don't try to keep up with someone faster, and don't feel guilty if you're ahead. Starting as a group provides security and support, but you're each on your own journey."

He pointed to the map. "It should take about two days to reach Bear's Den. There are designated camping spots along the way; use them. And watch for the white blazes on the trees. Those mark the trail. As long as you keep seeing white blazes, you're going the right way. If you haven't seen one in a while, stop and backtrack."

The idea of getting lost sent a spike of fear through my chest.

"The terrain is rocky," Tony said. "Filled with roots and obstacles. Most injuries happen because people aren't watching where they step. Stay alert." He folded the map partway, his expression warming. "And remember Leave No Trace. Pack out everything you pack in. Respect this place. We don't want to go pissing off the wildlife; they were here first."

The group laughed. I managed a weak smile.

As Tony concluded, everyone seemed to settle into easy camaraderie. Carol was already chatting with Elijah about something. David and Sarah stood hand in hand, grinning at each other like this was the best idea they'd ever had. Jake adjusted his pack straps with practiced confidence.

And I stood there trying not to throw up.

Becca caught my eye and squeezed my hand. I squeezed back, drawing strength from my best friend's certainty even as my own crumbled.

With final preparations complete and a chorus of "good lucks" echoing around us, the group began to disperse toward the trailhead. Some moved quickly, eager. Others lingered, checking gear one last time.

Becca and I stood at the threshold, the literal edge where pavement met trail, where civilization gave way to wilderness.

I stared at the path disappearing into the trees. This ribbon of packed earth that would be our home for months. No more preparing. No more planning. Just walking.

My chest tightened. All those years of psychology training, all those textbooks about anxiety and trauma responses and cognitive behavioral techniques; none of it made this moment less terrifying. I could name what was happening in my body (hypervigilance, threat response, catastrophic thinking) but naming it didn't stop it.

You've done hard things before, I reminded myself. *You called the police. You left. You survived.*

But this felt different. Those things had been about survival. This was a choice. A choice I still wasn't sure I'd actually made or if it had been made for me.

"Ready?" Becca's voice was soft.

No. I would never be ready.

But I nodded anyway.

I took the first step. Felt the give of dirt beneath my boots, so different from pavement. The weight of the pack pulled at my shoulders.

Then another step.

And another.

Behind us, the parking lot faded. Ahead, the Appalachian Trail stretched out, over a thousand miles of uncertainty.

I kept walking.

Because ready or not, the journey had begun.

***

The first hour wasn't terrible. My pack felt heavy but manageable, and the trail wound gently through forest that smelled like pine and earth and possibility. Becca chattered beside me, pointing out trail markers and wildflowers, taking photos of everything. The group had already dispersed. Jake was somewhere ahead, Carol and Elijah behind them, David and Sarah stopping every few minutes to take couple selfies.

"See?" Becca said. "This isn't so bad. You were worried for nothing."

I adjusted my pack straps for the third time. "We've barely gone a mile."

"Details! We're doing it. We're actually hiking the Appalachian Trail!" Becca threw her arms out dramatically. "We're basically the Thelma and Louise of the AT. Except, you know, with a better ending. Hopefully."

Despite myself, I laughed. That was Becca; always ready with a joke, always able to lighten the mood even when my mind was circling what-ifs.

By the second hour, my feet had started to ache. Not terrible. Just a dull throb that I tried to ignore. The pack felt heavier now, the straps digging into my shoulders no matter how I adjusted them. My shirt was damp with sweat despite the shade.

You can do this. It's just walking. You know how to walk.

By the third hour, something was definitely wrong with my right heel. A hot, burning sensation that had been building for the past thirty minutes. I didn't say anything. We were making good time. I didn't want to slow Becca down.

The psychology student in me recognized what I was doing; minimizing, pushing through pain, that familiar pattern of not wanting to be a burden. Interesting how I could observe my own maladaptive coping mechanisms even as I engaged in them.

"You're thinking too much," Becca called from ahead. "I can hear your brain working from here."

"How do you do that?"

"Eighteen years of friendship, babe. I'm basically psychic at this point."

When Becca finally suggested a break, relief flooded through me. I sat on a fallen log and took off her boot with a grimace. Her heel was bright red and oozing. The skin had torn off, raw and angry-looking.

"Just give me a second," I said quietly, reaching for my first aid kit.

"Let me see." Becca crouched beside her, then let out a low whistle. "Em, that's not 'just a second' level bad. That's a legitimate blister situation. Why didn't you say something?"

"It's fine. I can handle it."

"Uh-huh. And by 'handle it,' you mean ignore it until you can't walk anymore?" Becca fixed me with a knowing look. "Don't do that thing where you pretend you're fine when you're clearly not."

I felt my cheeks flush. "I didn't want to slow us down."

"Emma." Becca's voice was gentle but firm. "We're not in a race. And your feet are kind of important for, you know, the remaining seven hundred miles. Let's actually take care of this, okay?"

I nodded, feeling a wave of gratitude for my friend. Becca always saw through my deflections, always called me out when I needed it. While I tended to the blister with antibiotic ointment and moleskin, Becca disappeared behind a tree to pee. We each chugged a bottle of water, then kept moving.

The afternoon stretched long. The trail climbed steadily now, and my legs burned with each step. The initial excitement had worn off completely, replaced by the simple, grinding reality of putting one foot in front of the other. My pack felt like it had doubled in weight. My shoulders ached. The moleskin on my heel helped, but I could still feel every step.

This is what the next few months will be like, I realized. Not the excitement of starting something new. Just this. Walking until your body screams at you to stop, then walking anyway.

The thought should have been devastating. Instead, it felt oddly grounding. No more anticipation. No more what-ifs. Just the physical reality of movement and pain and breath.

When we finally stumbled into Rod Hollow just after four, I wanted to collapse right there on the trail. Other tents were already scattered around the clearing, proof that we'd made it, that we hadn't been the slowest ones.

"We did it!" Becca's voice was triumphant despite her obvious exhaustion. "Seven miles, Em. On our first day!"

Seven miles. It didn't sound like much. It felt like a marathon.

Setting up the tents took forever. My fingers fumbled with poles and stakes, my brain too tired to remember which piece went where. Becca wasn't much better, wrestling with billowing nylon and muttering under her breath.

"I thought you said you watched all those YouTube tutorials," I said, jamming a stake into the hard ground.

"I did! But apparently that guy with the soothing voice who kept talking about 'becoming one with nature' skipped some important steps."

"Oh my God, I know exactly who you're talking about!" I struck a dramatic pose despite my exhaustion, dropping my voice to a breathy whisper. "'The tent is not separate from you. You are the tent.'"

We dissolved into tired giggles, the kind that came from exhaustion and relief in equal measure.

By the time both tents stood, mine leaning slightly to the left but standing nonetheless, every muscle in my body was screaming. I removed my boots carefully and sank onto my sleeping pad with a groan.

We ate protein bars and dried fruit, too tired for anything more complicated. I had imagined leisurely evenings on the trail, reading, journaling, feeling zen and contemplative. Instead, I could barely keep my eyes open.

"Day one down," Becca's voice came from the tent next to mine, muffled but triumphant.

"Day one down," I echoed.

And despite the aching feet and the exhaustion and the doubts that still lurked in the corners of my mind, I felt something else too. Something small but persistent.

Pride.

Maybe I could actually do this.

Within minutes, sleep claimed me, pulling me under like a wave.

***

I woke to the smell of campfire smoke and something cooking, and for a confused moment couldn't remember where I was. Then my body reminded me, every muscle aching, my feet throbbing, my shoulders stiff from the pack.

Rod Hollow. Second morning. First night in a tent.

Yesterday had been harder than I thought it would be. It left me limping by the end. But I'd survived the night, even if sleep had been elusive on the uneven ground.

I pulled on whatever clean clothes I could find. Well, cleaner clothes anyway. A slightly less sweaty tank top and the hiking pants I'd tried to air out overnight. My hair was a disaster, tangled and greasy, pulled back in a messy ponytail. I ran my fingers through it halfheartedly and gave up. No point in trying when I'd just sweat through everything in an hour anyway.

I crawled out of my tent and shuffled toward the communal fire pit where the smell of coffee and breakfast hit me full force. Someone had gotten a good fire going, and several hikers were clustered around it with their camp stoves and mess kits.

Becca was already there, cradling a metal mug, her eyes bright despite the early hour and her own rumpled appearance.

"Morning, sunshine," Becca said with a grin.

I glanced at who else was there: Tony, looking impossibly awake; Sophia and Liam, disgustingly cheerful despite their wrinkled clothes; Elijah with his quiet presence...

And someone new.

My breath caught.

He had deep brown eyes that met mine as I approached, and something in my chest tightened. Not butterflies exactly. More like warning bells. His smile was warm, open, the kind that should have been disarming but instead made my walls snap into place.

No. Absolutely not.

"Emma, this is Noah," Becca said, and there was something knowing in her voice that made me want to kick her. "Noah, meet my hiking partner, Emma."

"Nice to meet you, Emma." He extended his hand, and I took it briefly. His grip was warm, firm. I pulled back quickly.

"You too," I managed, finding a spot on a log and focusing very intently on digging out my instant coffee.

"Noah just graduated from Brown," Becca continued. "Medical school."

"You're from Providence?" Despite myself, I looked up. That was safe. Geographic proximity. Neutral territory.

"Well, Indiana originally, but yeah. Just finished at Brown." His smile was easy, but I noticed something underneath it. A tension around his eyes. A careful quality to his expression, like he was holding something back.

"It's too bad we never met before this," I said, then immediately regretted it. Did that sound like I was interested? I wasn't interested. I was absolutely not interested.

Becca was watching me with barely concealed amusement, and I resisted the urge to glare.

"We didn't see you last night," Becca mentioned to Noah. "You must have pitched your tent on the other side of the clearing."

"Yeah, got in around dusk. Could barely see to set up. Glad I didn't miss meeting you all, though." His eyes settled on me for just a moment longer than necessary, and I felt heat rise to my cheeks.

Stop it. You don't know him. And the last time you trusted your judgment about a man...

Elijah passed around a pot of oatmeal he'd made, and we all dug in. The conversation flowed around me: trail stories, plans for the day, complaints about blisters. I was acutely aware of Noah across the fire, the way he laughed at Becca's jokes, the way his hands moved when he talked.

"So what brings you out here?" Sophia asked Noah. "Most medical students spend their summers doing research or something."

For just a moment, something flickered across his face. A tightness, a shadow. "Just needed some time to think," he said, his voice still light. "Clear my head. Figured a solo hike would be good for that."

Solo hike. My psychology training kicked in before I could stop it. People didn't usually choose solo adventures to celebrate good things. They chose them to escape or process or heal.

What are you running from?

And why do you care? You don't care. You're not doing this again.

"That's brave," Liam said. "Going solo takes guts."

"Or stupidity." Noah's laugh was self-deprecating. "The jury's still out."

We discussed the day's plans. Gathland State Park to refill water, then another half mile to Crampton Gap Shelter. Sophia and Liam would head out with Becca and me. Noah and Elijah were leaving later. Noah wanted to check his map; Elijah needed to adjust his pack.

I told myself the small stab of disappointment was relief. That's what it was. Relief. I didn't want him hiking with us anyway.

As we shouldered our packs at the edge of camp, Noah appeared beside the fire pit. "Hey," he called out, and my heart did something stupid. "I'll see you on the trail."

His eyes were on me when he said it, and I felt Becca elbow me in the ribs.

"Yeah," I replied, trying for casual. "See you out there."

As we started down the trail, Becca leaned in close. "So. Noah seems nice."

"Don't."

"Don't what? I'm just saying..."

"Becca."

"He's clearly interested. Did you see..."

"I'm not doing this." I adjusted my pack straps harder than necessary. "I came here to hike. Not to... whatever you're thinking."

"I'm not thinking anything," Becca said, but her grin was wicked. "I'm just observing that a very attractive, very intelligent man seemed very interested in talking to you."

"Well, you can un-observe it. I'm not interested."

Even as I said it, I knew it was a lie. But saying it out loud made it feel more solid. I could control this. I could shut it down before it became anything.

I had to.

Because the alternative (opening myself up again, trusting my judgment again, risking that kind of pain again) was unthinkable.

Sophia glanced back with a knowing smile. "For what it's worth, Noah seems like a good guy. Liam and I talked to him this morning. He's got good energy."

"See?" Becca crowed.

I groaned and picked up my pace, trying to outrun both the conversation and the feeling in my chest that refused to go away.

Behind us, somewhere at the campsite, Noah and Elijah were packing up to follow.

And despite everything I told myself, despite every wall I'd carefully constructed, I couldn't help but hope that maybe (just maybe) he'd catch up sooner rather than later.

Chapter 11

The next eight miles stretched north through Virginia, mercifully flat after yesterday's climbs. Becca and I fell into rhythm with Liam and Sophia, the couple's easy affection both charming and unsettling.

"We met on the trail," Sophia shared, reaching for Liam's hand. "Liam was hiking solo, and I was on a section hike with friends. Our paths crossed, and well, the rest is history."

"There was a little more to it than that," Liam chuckled. "Sophia had gotten separated from her group. I came to her rescue."

"Yes, he was my knight in shining armor," Sophia teased.

The phrase hit me like a physical blow.

Knight in shining armor.

I kept walking, kept my face neutral, but my mind was suddenly somewhere else. Somewhere dark. My old apartment. The sound of gunfire. Scott's arms around me, later, when I told him about the shooting. His voice, steady and certain: *I just want to keep you safe. I couldn't live with myself if something happened to you.*

At the time, it had felt like love. Like being cherished.

Now, with two years of distance and hard-won understanding, I could see it differently. He hadn't been protecting me; he'd been using my fear. The shooting had been terrible, but it had also been convenient. An opportunity to bind me closer, to make me dependent, to position himself as the only person who could keep me safe in a dangerous world.

How had I not seen it?

"So has the distance been hard?" Becca was asking. "Iowa and New Hampshire, that can't be easy."

"It's tough, but we make it work," Liam said. "We're partners, you know? We figure it out together."

Partners. Together.

The words felt hollow to me. Or maybe just foreign. I'd thought Scott and I were partners too, once.

As the trail led us deeper into the woods, a massive fallen tree blocked our path, remnants of a recent storm.

"Let's toss our packs over first, then climb over," Liam suggested.

I hoisted my pack over the trunk, wincing as the movement pulled at my shoulders. My whole body ached, deep, bone-tired exhaustion that seeped into my marrow. The blisters on my feet burned with each step, and I could feel moisture in my boots that was probably blood.

But I kept walking. Because that's what I did. Push through the pain. Prove I could handle it. Never complain, never show weakness, never be a burden.

Over the next mile, the group staggered with Liam and Sophia pulling ahead and Becca and I trailing behind. I was grateful for the distance. I didn't want anyone to see how much I was struggling.

"Hey." Becca's voice was soft. "Penny for your thoughts."

"Just enjoying the scenery," I said automatically.

"Emma." Becca's tone sharpened. "Don't do that. Not with me."

I kept her eyes on the trail. "Do what?"

"Pretend you're fine when you're clearly not. You've been quiet since Liam told that story about meeting Sophia. What's going on?"

For a long moment, I said nothing. Then, quietly: "He called himself her knight in shining armor."

"Yeah, it was sweet."

"Was it?" My voice cracked. "Or is that just what we tell ourselves when someone sweeps in during a vulnerable moment and makes themselves indispensable?"

Becca stopped walking. "You're thinking about Scott."

I nodded, feeling the burn of tears I refused to shed. "He rescued me too, remember? After the shooting. I was so scared, and he was so... there. So certain that he knew what I needed. And I just... I let him take over because I was terrified. And he used that. He knew I was vulnerable, and he used it."

"Hey." Becca's voice was gentle. "Ready for a break?"

We found a boulder and dropped our packs. The relief was instant. I devoured a small bag of cashews while Becca was quiet beside me, giving me space.

Finally, Becca spoke. "You know you're not that person anymore, right?"

I looked at her, surprised.

"The girl who let Scott control her, who was too scared to see what was happening," Becca continued. "That's not who you are now. You're out here hiking the Appalachian Trail. You're facing challenges head-on. You're stronger than you think."

"I don't feel very strong." I gestured to my battered feet, my exhausted body.

"Are you kidding? Look at what you're doing. You're in pain, you're exhausted, and you're still going. That's strength." Becca paused. "Although, maybe ease up a little? You've been limping since yesterday, your blisters are clearly getting worse, and you haven't complained once. You're pushing yourself too hard."

The words landed like a punch. Because Becca was right.

"I don't know how to do it differently," I whispered.

"I know," Becca said gently. "But maybe this hike is your chance to learn. You can be strong and take care of yourself. Those things aren't mutually exclusive."

We sat in silence, drinking water. The humidity clung to our skin, mosquitoes buzzing around us.

Then a gentle rustling nearby made us turn.

A mother deer stood in the dappled sunlight, two delicate fawns beside her.

My breath caught. Time seemed to slow as we shared a quiet moment with these woodland creatures.

"Look," I breathed, nudging Becca.

The mother deer stood protectively beside her young, their innocence striking against the backdrop of the wild. She took a few cautious steps closer, as if acknowledging our presence, accepting it.

For a full minute, we watched in reverent silence. I felt something inside me shift, a softening, a release of tension I hadn't realized I'd been holding.

The deer finally turned away, her fawns following, and they retreated gracefully into the woods.

"That was beautiful," I said quietly.

"Yeah," Becca agreed. "It was."

As we stood to continue, I heard voices approaching from behind. I turned to see Noah and Elijah making their way up the trail.

My heart did that stupid flutter thing again.

Noah's face broke into a smile when he saw us. "Hey! We were hoping we'd catch up with you."

We, he said. But his eyes were on me.

"Couldn't handle the slow pace?" Becca teased.

"Something like that," Elijah said, adjusting his pack.

Noah fell into step beside me as we started walking, and I was acutely aware of his presence. The easy confidence in his stride, the way he kept glancing over as if checking I was okay.

We walked for maybe ten minutes before Noah spoke. "Hey, can we slow down a bit?"

I looked at him, surprised. I'd been trying to keep up with Becca's pace, ignoring the way my lungs burned. "I'm okay."

"Maybe, but I'm not," Noah said with a self-deprecating smile. "Medical school doesn't exactly prepare you for this kind of workout."

It was clearly a lie. He was barely winded. But something about the way he said it made my throat tight. It was gentle, without judgment, giving me permission to slow down without admitting I needed to.

"Okay," I said softly. "We can slow down."

As we eased into a more manageable pace, I felt my breathing regulate, my muscles relax. Becca dropped back to walk with Elijah, leaving Noah and I side by side.

"Thanks," I said after a moment.

"For what?"

"For being thoughtful."

Noah glanced at me, his expression warm but with that hint of sadness I'd noticed at breakfast. "It's just walking, Emma. No need to thank me."

But it wasn't just walking. It was noticing. It was caring without controlling. It was offering help without making me feel weak.

It was different.

He was different.

And that scared me almost as much as it intrigued me.

As we continued through the Virginia woods, I found myself acutely aware of Noah beside me. The comfortable silence between us, the occasional brush of our arms on the narrow trail, the way he pointed out a hawk circling overhead without expecting me to respond.

I didn't know what to do with this feeling. This tentative, fragile hope that maybe, just maybe, not all rescues were traps. That sometimes thoughtfulness was just thoughtfulness. That someone could be kind without expecting something in return.

It was too soon to trust it. Too soon to trust him. Too soon to trust myself.

But as we walked together through the dappled forest light, I let myself imagine, just for a moment, what it might be like to try.

***

By late afternoon on our third day, we crossed into Maryland. My feet screamed with every step, but Noah had been hiking with us since catching up yesterday morning, and somehow that made the pain slightly more bearable.

"Your first time through didn't convince you this was worth it?" Becca asked him as they climbed another incline.

"Oh, that." Noah's expression shifted, not quite a shadow, but a flicker of something. "That was different. I hiked this trail once before, right after my senior year of high school. With my dad. Sort of a coming-of-age thing." He laughed, but it didn't reach his eyes.

I caught it, that subtle change when he mentioned his father. The same sadness I'd glimpsed at breakfast. "That sounds like it could have been really special," I said carefully. "Or... maybe not?"

Noah glanced at me, surprised I'd noticed. For a moment, I thought he might deflect. Then he shrugged. "Let's just say my dad and I have a complicated relationship. That trip was more about what he wanted than what either of us needed."

"I'm sorry," I said softly.

"It's okay." I could see him consciously lightening his tone. "This time is different. This time it's just for me."

Something about the way he said it, the quiet determination, the hint of defiance, made my chest tighten. I understood that. Doing something just for yourself when you'd spent so long doing things for everyone else.

The conversation shifted as we walked. We talked about Providence, comparing favorite restaurants, neighborhoods we'd explored.

"Have you been to Federal Hill yet?" I asked.

"Yeah, a few times. Incredible pasta."

"There are some amazing places around there," I said, surprising myself with my enthusiasm. "I could show you around sometime. Have you seen the Water Fire displays?"

"No, but I've heard they're incredible." Noah's smile widened. "I'd love that. It's always better to explore with a local expert."

As soon as the words left my mouth, I felt it, a flutter in my chest that was equal parts panic and excitement. I'd just made plans to see him again. After the hike. Back in Providence.

What exactly did that mean?

Becca shot me a look that said *I heard that*, and I felt my cheeks flush.

With each ascent, the trail led us higher until we reached a breathtaking overlook. The world stretched beneath us, rolling hills in every shade of green, fading to blue in the distance.

"Wow," I breathed, my aching feet momentarily forgotten.

Noah stood beside me, close enough that I could feel the warmth radiating from him. "This," he said quietly, "is why people do this."

"Yeah," I murmured, acutely aware of his presence. "It's beautiful."

Becca pulled out her phone to take photos, then caught my eye with one of those unmistakable *I'm giving you two some space* looks.

"I'm going to get some shots from over there," Becca announced, gesturing to an outcropping twenty yards away. "The light's better."

My face heated as Becca wandered off with a knowing smirk. But beneath the embarrassment, there was something else, a secret happiness that fluttered in my chest.

"So," Noah said, turning to face the view. "Tell me something. What made you decide to do this hike?"

The question caught me off guard. I opened my mouth, then closed it. How did I explain? That Becca had signed me without asking? That I'd been too worn down to say no? That I'd spent two years hiding in my apartment and needed to prove I could still do something hard?

"My best friend is very persuasive," I finally said.

Noah laughed. "That's the diplomatic answer. What's the real one?"

I glanced at him. His expression was open, genuinely curious, with no pressure behind the question. Just... interest. In me. In me answer.

"I needed to prove something to myself," I said quietly. "That I could do something that scared me."

Noah nodded slowly, his eyes on the distant hills. "I get that."

We stood in comfortable silence for a moment. I was hyperaware of how close we were standing, close enough to see the gold flecks in his brown eyes, close enough to notice how his hair curled slightly at his temples. His hand rested on the rock barrier, inches from mine.

"Emma, I..." Noah started, then stopped. He turned to face me more fully, and suddenly the space between us felt charged with something I couldn't name.

My breath caught.

Noah was looking at me with an expression that was warm and intent and maybe a little uncertain. I found myself wondering what would happen if I just moved my hand slightly, if our fingers touched...

"You guys ready to keep moving?"

I jumped slightly as Elijah's voice cut through the moment. He'd appeared on the trail behind us, adjusting his pack.

"Yeah," Noah said, his voice slightly strained. When I glanced at him, I thought I saw disappointment flicker across his face.

Or maybe I was just projecting.

As we rejoined the group and continued hiking, Becca fell into step beside me, wiggling her eyebrows suggestively. I elbowed her in the ribs.

But as we walked, I couldn't help glancing back at Noah, who kept looking over at me. When our eyes met, he smiled, that warm, genuine smile that made my stomach flip.

I'd offered to show him around Providence. I'd stood close enough to count his eyelashes. I'd wanted him to move closer.

And God help me, despite every wall I'd built, despite every promise I'd made to myself, I was starting to think maybe, just maybe, I wanted to see where this could go.

Even if the thought terrified me.

Chapter 12

We'd fallen into a comfortable rhythm, the four of us. Becca and I and Noah and Elijah. The conversation flowed naturally between stories and silences, punctuated by the crunch of leaves beneath our boots.

As we rounded a bend, we encountered a day hiker coming from the opposite direction. He was a middle-aged man wearing a faded North Central Panthers t-shirt.

"Afternoon," he greeted cheerfully.

"Hey," we chorused back.

I noticed Noah's expression shift as he watched the man disappear. Something had changed in his eyes. A tightening, a shadow.

"You okay?" I asked.

Noah blinked. "Yeah, sorry. That shirt just... brought back memories. North Central. They were our rivals in high school. Football rivals."

"Oh, you played football?" I asked, trying to picture him in pads and a helmet. It wasn't hard; he had the build for it.

"Yeah. All four years. I was even captain my senior year." Noah's voice was quiet, almost distant.

"That's impressive," Becca said. "You must have been pretty good."

Noah let out a laugh that held no humor. "I hated it."

I stopped walking. "Wait, what?"

"I hated football," Noah repeated, louder this time, testing the words. "I hated everything about it. The practices, the games, the pressure."

"But... you played for four years?" I couldn't wrap my mind around it. "And you were captain?"

"Yeah." Noah started walking again, his jaw tight. "My father always said his sons would play football. Except I was the only boy."

I felt something twist in my chest.

"You played for four years just to please your father?" The edge in my own voice surprised me.

Noah's hands gripped his pack straps tighter. "I wanted to make him proud. It was the only way I knew how." His voice cracked. "But it wasn't what I wanted. It was never what I wanted."

"What did you want?" I asked softly.

Noah glanced at me, vulnerable and unguarded. "I don't know. That's the thing. I spent so much time doing what he wanted that I never figured out what I wanted. Music, maybe. Art. Literally anything that wasn't football or medicine or whatever my father decided was the right path."

I felt it like a physical blow. The recognition, the terrible familiarity. I knew that feeling. Molding yourself into what someone else wanted, losing pieces of yourself so gradually you didn't notice until there was almost nothing left.

"I get that," I heard myself say. "The doing things for someone else part."

Noah looked at me. Really looked at me.

"My ex," I continued, the words coming before I could stop them, "he had this very specific idea of how I should look. He liked my hair long, so I grew it out even though I'd always preferred it shorter. He thought I looked better in dresses, so I stopped wearing jeans. Little things, you know? Except they weren't little. They were me disappearing, piece by piece."

I caught Becca's look, surprise mixed with concern. I rarely brought Scott up myself, especially not with someone I'd just met.

"I'm sorry," Noah said quietly, and something in his tone told me he understood.

"Yeah, well." I tried to laugh it off, suddenly uncomfortable with how much I'd revealed. "We all do stupid things, right?"

But even as I said it, I felt it, the realization crystallizing. I'd spent two years playing Scott's game. Making myself smaller. Pretending his needs were more important than mine.

Just like Noah had learned to play a sport he hated for four years.

We were the same, Noah and me. Both so good at disappearing for other people.

"It's weird, isn't it?" I said. "How you can spend so much time trying to be what someone else wants that you forget who you actually are."

Noah nodded slowly. "Yeah. And then you wake up one day and realize you don't even recognize yourself anymore."

"Did something happen?" I asked. "That made you realize?"

Noah's expression darkened. "Let's just say I learned the hard way that sacrificing yourself for someone doesn't guarantee they'll appreciate it. Or stay."

I heard the pain beneath his words. Fresh pain. Whatever had happened, it hadn't been that long ago.

"I'm sorry," I said.

"Don't be. I needed to learn it." Noah's smile was sad but genuine. "This hike, it's about figuring out who I am when I'm not trying to be what everyone else wants."

I felt my throat tighten. "That's kind of why I'm here too."

We walked in silence for a moment. I was acutely aware of how much I'd just shared. It was more than I'd shared with anyone except Becca in two years.

It scared me. Understanding led to trust, and trust led to vulnerability, and vulnerability was how you got hurt.

But it also felt right.

"My dad's a podiatrist," Noah said suddenly. "Very successful. He has this whole plan mapped out. I'll finish medical school, do my residency, take over his practice. He's been planning my life since I was born."

"And you don't want that," I said. Not a question.

"I don't know what I want," Noah admitted. "But I know I don't want to wake up in twenty years and realize I'm still living his dream instead of mine."

I felt something shift in my chest, recognition, resonance. "So, what are you going to do?"

Noah looked at me, his smile uncertain but determined. "I'm going to finish this hike. And then I'm going to figure it out. For the first time in my life, I'm going to figure out what I want."

"That's brave," I said softly.

"Or stupid," Noah countered.

"No," I said firmly. "It's brave. It takes courage to choose yourself."

As the words left my mouth, I realized I was talking to myself as much as to him. Because I'd spent two years not choosing myself.

Maybe this hike was about that for me too. Learning to choose myself again. Learning to be brave enough to want things.

"You know what?" Becca announced. "I think you're both overthinking this. You're on a gorgeous hike, you're making new friends, you're getting epic trail legs. This is the good stuff. The figuring-out-your-life stuff can wait until you're not actively trying not to die from blisters."

I laughed, the tension breaking. "Fair point."

"Although," Becca continued, "I do think Emma should consider a career change to professional hiker. Haven't complained about her feet in at least twenty minutes."

"That's because my feet have transcended pain and entered a realm of pure numbness," I retorted.

"See? Growth," Becca declared.

As we continued down the trail, I felt lighter somehow. The conversation had been heavy, but it had also been real. Honest. And I realized I felt comfortable with Noah; truly comfortable, in a way I hadn't felt with anyone new in years.

That should terrify me. Part of me was terrified.

But another part, a part I'd thought Scott had destroyed, was hopeful.

And hope, I was learning, was both the scariest and the bravest thing of all.

***

We'd been hiking for about an hour when I heard footsteps approaching from behind. My heart did that stupid skip when I turned to see Noah's familiar smile. With him were Elijah and a woman I didn't recognize.

The woman was unexpected. While everyone else wore functional gear, this woman stood out in a flowing tie-dye skirt, loose blouse, and multiple strands of crystal necklaces. Her gray-streaked hair was pulled back with a colorful scarf, and her face was warm and open, creased with smile lines.

"Morning!" Noah called out as they caught up.

"Hey," I replied, trying to sound casual.

The woman stepped forward. "Hi there, I'm Maggie. Mind if we join you?"

"Of course not," Becca said. "The more, the merrier."

As we fell into step together, Maggie explained she'd been hiking sections of the AT for almost two decades. She had a store in Vermont where she sold tarot cards and herbal remedies.

Oh boy, I thought. *We've got a full-on hippie on our hands.*

"The mountains called to me," Maggie said simply. "There's an energy here, a healing power in these ancient hills."

I caught Noah's eye, saw the hint of amusement there, the slight raise of his eyebrows that said *Is she for real?* I had to bite back a smile.

The group naturally spread out along the narrow trail. Elijah moved ahead with his steady pace. Becca started chatting with Maggie. And somehow, whether by accident or design, I found myself walking beside Noah.

"So," Noah said quietly. "Maggie's... interesting."

"That's one word for it," I whispered back. "I'm trying to figure out how she hikes in a skirt."

"Very carefully?" Noah suggested, and we both laughed.

It felt easy, this lightness between us. Different from yesterday's heavy revelations, but no less comfortable.

"How'd you sleep?" Noah asked.

"Terribly," I admitted. "The mosquitoes decided I was an all-you-can-eat buffet. You?"

"Not great either," Noah said, and something flickered across his face, that shadow I was learning to recognize. "Had a lot on my mind."

I waited, sensing he had more to say.

"I actually just got out of a relationship a few months ago," Noah said, his voice careful. "It ended pretty badly. That's part of why I'm out here. Needed to clear my head."

My chest tightened. "I'm sorry. That must be hard."

"It was overdue, honestly," Noah said with a wry smile. "I found out she'd been seeing someone else. And when I confronted her, instead of apologizing, she blamed me for not being there enough. For focusing too much on school."

"That's not fair," I said firmly. The psychology student in me recognized the manipulation.

"Maybe. I mean, I wasn't perfect. I was pretty consumed with medical school. But I was trying." He paused. "Anyway, I spent so long trying to be what everyone else wanted, my dad, my girlfriend, my professors. And then it all fell apart anyway. So now I'm here, trying to figure out what I actually want for once."

I felt that recognition again, that resonance between our experiences. "That's why you're doing this hike solo. Not just to get away, but to find yourself."

"Yeah," Noah said, glancing at me with relief. "Exactly. Most people don't get that."

"I get it," I said softly.

We walked in comfortable silence for a moment.

Up ahead, Maggie had stopped to point out wildflowers to Becca. The group paused, and Maggie turned to look at Noah and me with an expression that was far too knowing.

"You two have a lovely energy together," Maggie said, her eyes twinkling. "Complementary vibrations."

I felt heat rush to my cheeks. "Oh, we're not...we just met..."

"The universe doesn't care about timelines, dear," Maggie said serenely. "It cares about connections."

Becca was grinning. Noah looked somewhere between amused and embarrassed. And I wanted to disappear into the forest floor.

"We should keep moving," Elijah said, clearly taking mercy on me.

As we continued hiking, Elijah gradually opened up about himself. His years in the military, the difficulty of returning home, his PTSD diagnosis.

"I tried everything to find peace," Elijah said quietly. "Therapy, medications. Then someone suggested hiking. This trail became my therapy."

"Does it help?" I asked gently. "Being out here?"

Elijah nodded. "More than anything else I've tried. There's something about the simplicity of it, just you, the trail, one foot in front of the other."

"That makes sense."

"Most folks think that those of us that do this hike are running away from something. It's more than that though. I think we're also running toward something. Tough part is figuring out what that something is."

I found myself thinking about what he'd said. About running toward something, not just away from it. Not just away from Scott, from my fear, but toward... what? Myself? The person I used to be? The person I could become?

I glanced at Noah, found him already looking at me. Something passed between us, recognition, understanding, possibility.

"Speaking of healing," Maggie said, interrupting my thoughts. "I noticed you scratching earlier. Mosquito bites?"

"Yeah," I said. "They ate me alive last night."

"I have something for that." Maggie pulled out a small tin. "Herbal salve I make myself. Should help with the itching."

I took the tin skeptically. It smelled nice, earthy and floral. I dabbed some on one of the worst bites.

To my surprise, the relief was almost immediate.

"Wow," I said, genuinely impressed. "That actually works."

Maggie's smile was knowing. "Not all old remedies are nonsense, dear."

Becca caught my eye and made a subtle gesture, casting a spell, and I had to stifle a laugh. But I pocketed the tin, reconsidering my quick judgment of Maggie.

Maybe the woman was a little out there. But there was something genuine about her, something kind. And if her weird herbal remedies actually worked, who was I to judge?

As we continued hiking, the miles seemed to pass more easily with company and conversation. I found myself relaxing into the rhythm of it. The physical challenge, the mental space it created, the unexpected connections forming.

Noah and I kept gravitating toward each other, our conversations flowing easily between light and serious. And if Maggie kept giving us knowing looks, well, I tried to ignore it.

But I couldn't ignore the feeling growing in my chest. That sense of possibility, of something shifting. I was running toward something, I realized. Not just away from my past, but toward... this. Whatever this was becoming.

And for the first time in two years, that thought didn't terrify me quite as much as it should have.

Chapter 13

That night, we built a fire that sent sparks spiraling up toward the stars. I sat between Becca and Noah, watching Maggie coax the flames higher with practiced ease. Liam and Sophia huddled close on a log across from them, while Elijah poked at the embers with a stick, his face thoughtful in the firelight.

They felt like family to Emma, even though I'd known them only a few days. Something about the trail accelerated intimacy in a way normal life never did. The shared exhaustion, the vulnerability of sleeping in shelters together, the way everyone helped carry each other's burdens.

"You know what I love about being out here?" Maggie said, her voice carrying over the crackling wood. "Everything's connected. The trees, the rocks, the water, us—it's all part of the same system. You can't see it as clearly in the regular world, but out here? It's obvious."

I found myself leaning forward, listening.

"Nature teaches you to slow down," Maggie continued, her gaze on the flames. "To actually observe. You start hearing things you'd miss otherwise: the way leaves sound different depending on what's walking through them, how water changes pitch over different rocks. You learn to listen with your whole body, not just your ears."

Becca shifted beside me. "That's kind of beautiful, actually."

"Out here, everything serves a purpose," Maggie said. "Every creature, every plant, even the decay and death, it all feeds back into the system. Nothing's wasted. And it makes you think about your own life differently. About how your choices ripple outward, how you're part of something bigger whether you realize it or not."

I felt something shift in my chest. I'd spent two years trying to wall myself off, to be self-contained and safe. But maybe that wasn't how life actually worked. Maybe Maggie was right, maybe isolation was just an illusion.

Noah leaned closer, his shoulder warm against mine. "She's got a point," he said quietly. "About the interconnectedness thing."

I glanced at him, caught the reflection of firelight in his eyes. "Yeah," I said. "Maybe she does."

The fire popped and settled. For a moment, we sat in companionable silence, each lost in our own thoughts.

Then Becca sat up straighter, her eyes suddenly bright with mischief. "Okay, but can we talk about what Maggie left out?"

"What's that?" Liam asked, grinning as if he knew something ridiculous was coming.

"The reality of this whole 'interconnected with nature' thing." Becca gestured dramatically at the darkness beyond the fire. "Tomorrow, Emma and I will gracefully glide through those lush forests, our hair flowing in the wind like we're in a shampoo commercial. Birds will serenade us with harmonious tunes as we navigate the trail with the grace of ballet dancers."

I felt a laugh bubbling up.

"And when the trail gets steep and rocky?" Becca swept her arm across the air like she was revealing a grand vision. "That's when our true ninja skills will shine. We'll somersault up those inclines, executing flawless cartwheels while fending off aggressive squirrels with our impressive kung fu moves. Hi-yah!" She made a karate chop motion that nearly knocked over her water bottle.

Sophia was already giggling. Noah pressed his lips together, trying not to laugh.

"What about bears?" Elijah asked, his eyes twinkling. "You've got a plan for those?"

Becca leaned forward, her voice dropping to a mock-serious whisper. "Fear not, for we shall have mastered the ancient art of bear whispering. With a single glance, we will communicate our peaceful intentions to the mighty creatures. They will recognize us as fellow warriors of the forest and politely step aside, perhaps even offering us berries and directions to the nearest shelter."

"Bear whispering," I repeated, wiping tears of laughter from my eyes. "That's your survival plan?"

"It's foolproof," Becca insisted, her face completely straight for about two seconds before she cracked up. "And that's not all. We'll cross rivers using our impeccable balance, outwit thunderstorms with our uncanny meteorological instincts, and befriend every woodland creature like Disney princesses. We'll do it all while retaining our perfectly coiffed hair and manicured nails, remaining completely impervious to bug bites, and somehow still smelling like roses."

The entire group dissolved into laughter. Even Maggie was chuckling, shaking her head with fond amusement.

"I love it," Sophia said, wiping her eyes. "Can I join this fantasy version of the hike? Because the real one has way too many blisters."

"Membership is open to all who believe in the power of bear whispering," Becca declared solemnly, then ruined it by snorting with laughter.

I laughed so hard her stomach hurt, the tension of the day finally releasing. This was why I loved Becca. This absurdity, this refusal to let fear or heavy philosophy dampen her enthusiasm. Becca didn't just see the glass as half full, she saw it overflowing with champagne and confetti and ridiculous ninja moves.

As the laughter died down and the conversation drifted to easier topics, favorite meals we were craving, the worst blisters we'd seen, I felt something warm settle in my chest.

I'd come on this hike to prove I could do hard things alone. But sitting here with these people, watching the fire, feeling Noah's presence beside me, still smiling from Becca's ridiculousness, maybe the harder thing was learning to let people in again.

Maybe that was the real challenge. Not the miles or the mountains, but this. Opening myself up to connection, to caring, to the possibility of being hurt.

And maybe, just maybe, that was worth the risk.

***

I woke to cramping in her lower abdomen and a familiar wetness that made my stomach drop.

No.

I lay still in my sleeping bag for a moment, as if not moving might somehow change the reality. But the cramping intensified, and I knew.

My period. Two days early. And I was in a tent in the Pennsylvania woods.

I unzipped my sleeping bag carefully and felt the confirmation I'd been dreading. I'd bled through my underwear, probably onto my sleeping bag liner too.

Think. I forced herself into problem-solving mode. I had...what? Maybe some toilet paper left. No tampons. I'd checked my supply list twice, but somehow, they hadn't made it into my pack.

Outside, I could hear Becca moving around, the clink of her cooking pot. I pulled on my pants, thankfully dark, and crawled out of the tent.

Becca looked up and immediately read something in my face. "What's wrong?"

"Do you have any tampons?" I kept her voice low, acutely aware that Noah was somewhere nearby.

Becca's expression shifted to sympathy. "Oh no. Em, I'm on Depo. I don't get periods anymore."

"Shit." I pressed my hand against my cramping abdomen. "Okay. I can figure this out."

"There's a town today, right? Boonsboro? We can get there by afternoon—"

"That's hours from now, Bec." My voice came out sharper than I intended.

I grabbed the small roll of toilet paper from my pack and headed into the woods, my face hot. This was exactly the kind of thing that made me feel out of control, vulnerable in a way I hated. I'd planned everything, every mile, every resupply, every contingency, and somehow, I'd forgotten something this basic.

Behind a cluster of trees, I did my best to clean up and fashion something workable from the toilet paper. It wouldn't last long. An hour, maybe two if I was lucky.

When I returned to camp, Noah had emerged from his tent and was heating water for coffee. He glanced up and smiled, and I felt my mortification deepen.

"Morning," he said. "Sleep okay?"

"Fine." I busied herself with rolling up my sleeping bag, avoiding eye contact.

Becca shot me a concerned look but didn't say anything.

We broke camp in relative silence. My cramps were getting worse, the kind that made me want to curl up with a heating pad, not hike twelve miles with a thirty-pound pack. But what choice did I have?

As we started up the trail, each step jarred my entire body. The makeshift padding was already shifting uncomfortably. I tried to focus on my breathing, on putting one foot in front of the other, but my mind kept circling back to the same thought: *I can't do this.*

"You okay?" Noah had fallen back to walk beside me. "You seem quiet."

"Just tired." It wasn't entirely a lie.

An hour in, I had to stop and disappear into the woods again. When I returned, Becca was waiting with a granola bar.

"Eat something. It'll help with the cramping."

"I'm fine."

"Em." Becca's voice was gentle but firm. "You don't have to be fine all the time."

I took the granola bar, blinking back sudden tears that had nothing to do with cramps and everything to do with feeling exposed and helpless and angry at my own body.

By midday, I was exhausted and running through my toilet paper supply at an alarming rate. The town couldn't come fast enough.

When we finally reached Boonsboro in the late afternoon, I made a beeline for the small convenience store. I grabbed tampons, ibuprofen, and chocolate without even looking at prices.

At the register, the clerk, an older woman with kind eyes, smiled knowingly. "Rough day on the trail, honey?"

"Something like that."

In the store's tiny bathroom, I finally got myself properly sorted. The relief was physical and emotional; I could handle this now. I could keep going.

When I emerged, Becca and Noah were waiting outside with bottles of cold water. Noah handed me one without comment, and I was grateful he didn't ask questions.

"Better?" Becca asked quietly.

"Yeah." I took a long drink. "Sorry I was—"

"Don't." Becca cut her off. "You don't have to apologize for being human."

We found a spot in the shade to rest. I swallowed two ibuprofen and let myself lean back against a tree, my pack beside her.

I'd wanted this hike to prove I could handle anything. But maybe part of getting stronger wasn't about handling everything alone. Maybe it was about accepting help when you needed it, about being human and imperfect and still moving forward anyway.

The cramps were already easing. The town had what I needed. I'd made it.

"Ready to keep going?" Noah asked after a while.

I stood, shouldering my pack. "Yeah. Let's go."

***

The others had already headed out, eager to beat the heat. It was just Becca, Noah, and me left at camp.

The rain started just after dawn, a few drops at first, then a steady downpour that turned the trail into a slick, muddy obstacle course. By mid-morning, I was soaked through despite my rain jacket, water running down my neck and pooling in my boots with every step.

I hated this. Hated the cold wetness, the way my pack seemed to gain ten pounds with absorbed moisture, the treacherous footing. But mostly I hated the feeling of being out of control, at the mercy of weather I couldn't change or manage.

"This is ridiculous," I muttered, wiping rain from my face. "It's supposed to be summer."

Becca, somehow still in decent spirits, splashed through a puddle beside me. "Come on, Em. It's kind of fun, right? Like being a kid again."

"Fun?" My voice came out sharp. "My feet are literally swimming in my boots. Nothing about this is fun."

Noah had been quiet for the last mile, focused on his footing. Now he glanced back. "We could find somewhere to wait it out. There's no point pushing through if it's just going to make us miserable."

"We're already miserable," I said. But even as I said it, I knew he was right. My hands were shaking, from cold or stress, I wasn't sure, and the familiar tightness was building in my chest. The kind that came before panic attacks.

Breathe. In for four, hold for seven, out for eight.

"Em." Becca's voice was gentler now. "Hey. Let's just stop, okay?"

I wanted to argue, wanted to push through because that's what I did. I pushed through pain and discomfort and fear because stopping felt like giving up. But my body was betraying me, the shaking spreading from my hands to my core.

"Okay," I said quietly. "Let's stop."

We found a spot where the tree canopy was thickest, offering some shelter. Noah helped string up a tarp between two trees while Becca got me out of my wet jacket.

"You're freezing," Becca said, alarmed. "Em, why didn't you say something?"

"I'm fine." But my teeth were chattering.

"You're not fine." Becca dug through her pack for a dry fleece. "Put this on. Now."

I stripped off my wet layers with numb fingers, acutely aware of Noah working a few yards away, trying to give us privacy. The dry fleece helped, and Becca wrapped me in her emergency blanket too.

"Sorry," I managed. "I just...I couldn't..."

"Stop apologizing." Becca sat beside me under the tarp. "You don't have to be invincible, you know."

Noah joined us, water dripping from his hood. "I've got the stove going. Hot tea in a few minutes."

We sat in silence, listening to the rain drum against the tarp. My shaking was easing, but the tightness in my chest remained. I'd pushed too hard again, ignored my body's signals because admitting I needed to stop felt like admitting weakness.

"You know what I remember about playing in the rain when we were kids?" Becca said after a while. "You always wanted to keep playing longer than anyone else. Even when you were so cold your lips turned blue, you didn't want to go inside."

I managed a weak smile. "I was stubborn."

"Are stubborn," Becca corrected. "Present tense."

Noah handed me a mug of hot tea, and I wrapped her hands around it gratefully. The warmth seeped into my palms.

"My dad used to say that wisdom isn't knowing how to endure everything," Noah said quietly. "It's knowing when to stop and take shelter."

I looked at him. His hair was plastered to his forehead, his clothes soaked, but his expression was calm. Not judging me for falling apart, not frustrated by the delay. Just present.

"I'm not very good at that," I admitted. "The stopping part."

"I've noticed." He smiled, and there was warmth in it that made my chest tighten in a different way. "But you're learning."

The rain continued, but under the tarp with hot tea and dry clothes, it felt less overwhelming. I leaned against my pack and let myself rest, let myself stop pushing for once.

Maybe Noah was right. Maybe I was learning.

The storm would pass. And when it did, we'd keep going. But for now, this was enough, shelter and warmth and people who understood when I needed to stop, even when I couldn't admit it myself.

Chapter 14

E arly July brought heat that shimmered off the trail, and I was grateful when the path dipped into shade. Becca had pulled ahead, her pace energetic despite the temperature, leaving Noah and me walking together.

We'd fallen into this pattern over the past few days, Becca ranging ahead or falling back, giving us space without making it obvious.

"I've been meaning to ask," I said, breaking the comfortable silence. "What made you decide to do this hike?"

Noah glanced at me, something shifting in his expression. "Long story."

"We've got time." I gestured at the endless trail ahead.

He was quiet for a moment. "My dad's a podiatrist. Has his own practice in Indiana. He's always assumed I'd take it over after residency."

"But you don't want to be a podiatrist."

"I don't want to be a podiatrist." Noah smiled, but there was tension behind it. "I went to medical school because I love medicine. But my dad, he's had this vision of 'Clark and Son' since I was a kid. And I just kept going along with it because it was easier than fighting him."

I understood that instinct intimately, the path of least resistance, avoiding conflict at all costs. I'd done the same thing with Scott for far too long.

"So what do you actually want?" I asked.

"Psychiatry, I think." His voice gained energy. "The brain fascinates me. How trauma rewires neural pathways, how medication shifts brain chemistry, how talk therapy actually creates physical changes in brain structure. It's incredible."

I felt something warm bloom in her chest. "It is pretty incredible."

"But my dad doesn't see it that way. To him, it's not 'real' medicine. Not practical." Noah shook his head. "I tried to tell him at Christmas. Had this whole conversation planned out. Chickened out completely."

"What happened?"

"I told him I wanted to take this hike instead. Solo trip before residency. We got into it. Big argument. He couldn't understand why I'd waste time hiking when I should be preparing to join the practice. Eventually he backed down. Said fine, go, get it out of my system."

"But you haven't told him the real reason you needed to clear your head."

"No." Noah was quiet. "I'm terrified it'll destroy our relationship. That he'll see it as a rejection of everything he's worked for."

I recognized it, that weight of carrying someone else's expectations. Of living inside a story someone else wrote for you.

"What about your mom?" I asked. "Does she know how you feel?"

Noah sighed. "Mom's a peacekeeper. She goes along with whatever Dad wants. I think she learned a long time ago that it's easier not to rock the boat."

"That must be lonely," I said. "Not having anyone in your corner."

Noah looked at me, something vulnerable in his expression. "Yeah. It is."

We walked in silence for a while, the only sounds our footsteps and the rustle of leaves overhead.

"You know what scares me most?" Noah said quietly. "I've spent my whole life trying to make him proud. Straight A's, medical school, saying yes to everything he wanted. And I'm not sure he actually knows who I am. The real me, not the version I perform for him."

My chest tightened. I understood that fear, the terror of being truly seen and found lacking. I'd felt it with Scott, constantly shape-shifting to avoid his anger.

"Do you think he'd try?" I asked. "To know the real you, if you gave him the chance?"

"I don't know." Noah's voice was raw. "Maybe. Or maybe he'd just be disappointed that I'm not who he thought I was."

We emerged from the shade into bright sunlight, and I squinted against the glare. Up ahead, Becca had stopped to wait for us.

"Thanks for telling me all this," I said. "I know it's not easy."

Noah met my eyes. "Thanks for listening. And for not telling me I'm being ridiculous or that I should just suck it up."

"You're not being ridiculous." I meant it. "You deserve to live your own life. Not the one someone else planned for you."

Even as I said it, I felt the weight of my own words. I was still learning that lesson myself. I was still figuring out how to separate my own wants from the wreckage of what Scott had made me believe I wanted.

"What about you?" Noah asked. "What made you say yes to this hike?"

My stomach tightened. There it was, the inevitable question. He'd been honest with me. I should return the favor.

But the words stuck in my throat. How did you tell someone about Scott? About the abuse, the pregnancy, the suicide?

"Becca signed me up," I said, which was true but not the whole truth. "Thought I needed to get out of my head for a while."

Noah waited, clearly sensing there was more. But he didn't push.

"Long story," I added, echoing his earlier words.

"We've got time," he said gently.

I looked ahead at Becca, who was pretending to examine something on the trail. The sun was hot on my shoulders. My legs ached. And Noah was looking at me with those deep brown eyes that saw too much.

"Maybe," I said. "Maybe I'll tell you sometime."

"I'd like that." Noah smiled, sad and understanding. "Whenever you're ready."

We caught up to Becca, who launched into a story about a snake she'd nearly stepped on, and the moment passed. But I felt it lingering, that quiet offer, that patience. Noah had shared his truth, and he was willing to wait for mine.

The question was: would I ever be brave enough to give it to him?

***

I woke to sunlight filtering through the trees, my breath already settled into its familiar pattern: in for four, hold for seven, out for eight. I didn't need the technique this morning, but my body had memorized it anyway, the way muscles remember old injuries. Becca and the others had pushed ahead after breakfast, and somehow Noah and I had fallen into step together again.

I noticed things about him now. The way he adjusted his pack straps without breaking stride. How he'd pause before speaking, as if testing his words first. It made me hyperaware of my own gestures, the space between us on the narrow trail.

We'd been talking about medical school, safe territory, when Noah mentioned his residency applications.

"So you've applied?" I asked, stepping over a root that had heaved up through the packed dirt.

"Yeah. Four programs." He paused to let me navigate around a boulder. "All podiatry. My father's really hoping for Kent; that's where he went."

Something in his voice snagged my attention. Not quite resignation, but close. I knew that tone. Had used it myself, once, explaining to Becca why I was moving in with Scott. *It makes sense. He's worried about me after what happened. It's practical.*

"And that's it?" The question came out sharper than I intended. "Just podiatry?"

Noah's jaw tightened almost imperceptibly. "That's what I went to medical school for."

"But you didn't go to medical school for podiatry." I stopped walking, and he turned back to face me. "Every time you talk about psychiatry, you light up. Your whole face changes. And when you talk about podiatry..." I trailed off, unsure how to finish without overstepping.

He looked away, toward the trees. "It's complicated."

It's complicated. How many times had I said those exact words about Scott? To Becca, to her professors, to myself in the mirror at three in the morning.

"Complicated because you don't want it?" I asked carefully. "Or complicated because your father does?"

Noah's exhale was audible. "Both. Neither. I don't know." He adjusted his pack straps again, a nervous gesture. "I thought about applying to psychiatry programs, but the deadline's in a week and a half, and I haven't even started. It feels too late."

I felt something shift in my chest, a recognition I couldn't quite name. Here was someone else trapped between what they knew was right and what everyone expected of them. Someone else who'd spent so long accommodating other people's needs that their own had become background noise.

"When's the actual deadline?" I heard herself ask.

"Next Friday."

"That's ten days." I was doing the calculation before I could stop myself, my mind clicking into problem-solving mode. "That's enough time."

Noah shook his head, starting to walk again. "Emma, it's not just filling out forms. I'd need a personal statement, letters of recommendation, program research..."

"You've already done the research." I caught up to him. "You told me about that study on neural plasticity and trauma processing. You didn't look that up yesterday."

He glanced at me, surprised. "You remember that?"

"Of course I remember."

We walked in silence for a moment, and I felt my pulse quicken with something I recognized as dangerous: investment. I was getting involved, pushing, and a voice in my head asked: *Is this about him, or is this about you?*

Because it was easier, wasn't it, to champion someone else's choices than to face your own stalled life. I'd spent two years explaining Scott's behavior, rationalizing his needs, making myself smaller to accommodate his moods. And when that ended, I'd simply... stopped. Stopped making plans. Stopped wanting things. Now here I was, mapping out Noah's future like I had any right.

"I'm sorry," I said quietly. "I'm being pushy. It's your decision."

Noah stopped walking and turned to face me fully. His eyes held something I couldn't quite read, not irritation, but not gratitude either. Something more complicated.

"You're not being pushy," he said. "You're being honest. That's different."

"Is it?" The question escaped before I could censor it. "I don't want to be one more person telling you what to do with your life."

"You're not telling me what to do." His voice was gentle but firm. "You're asking me what I want. No one else has done that."

The words settled between us, and I felt my throat tighten. When was the last time someone had asked me what I wanted? When was the last time I'd known how to answer?

"So what do you want?" I asked.

Noah's expression shifted, and for a moment I saw past the careful exterior to something raw underneath. "I want to apply. I'm terrified of applying. I want my father to understand. I want to not care if he understands." He laughed, a short, frustrated sound. "I want to want something without apologizing for it."

"Yeah," I said softly. "I know that feeling."

We stood there on the trail, and I became aware of how close we were standing, how the dappled sunlight caught the brown of his eyes and turned them amber at the edges. How my heart was doing something complicated in my chest that had nothing to do with altitude or exertion.

"The next town's not far," I said. "Maybe six miles? There might be a library." I paused, choosing my words carefully. "If you wanted to work on it, I could... I don't know. Buy you coffee? Moral support?"

Noah studied my face for a long moment. "You don't have to do that."

"I know I don't have to. I want to." And then, because honesty seemed to be the currency we were trading in: "Also, it's possible I'm projecting. Fair warning."

A smile tugged at the corner of his mouth. "Projecting what?"

"The desperate wish that someone had pushed me to make my own choices instead of just going along with everyone else's." The admission caught in my throat. I'd had people who pushed; Becca had pushed. Becca had begged me to leave Scott. But I had been so busy protecting him, explaining him, justifying him, that I couldn't hear it. Maybe what I really wished was that I'd been strong enough to listen.

Noah's expression softened. "Okay," he said. "Coffee and moral support. But only if you let me buy lunch after."

"Deal."

***

The town materialized around us in the early afternoon: brick buildings with painted shutters, American flags limp in the humid air, a hardware store with rocking chairs out front. Becca texted that she and the others were at a diner two blocks over, but I barely glanced at the message.

The library was small, tucked between a post office and a real estate agency. Inside, it smelled like old paper and air conditioning, and I felt something in her shoulders relax. Libraries had always been safe spaces, quiet and ordered, places where everything had a system.

Noah claimed a computer station near the back, and I took the chair beside him, close enough to see the screen but not hovering. His hands hesitated over the keyboard, then began to move as he navigated to the residency application portal.

"Okay," he said quietly. "Personal statement. This is the part I've been avoiding."

"What's the prompt?"

He read it aloud: "Describe why you want to pursue this specialty and what experiences have shaped your interest."

I thought about all the things I couldn't say about my own life. All the experiences that had shaped me that sI'd learned to describe in neat, clinical terms so I wouldn't have to feel them. *History of domestic violence. Complicated grief. Avoidant attachment patterns.* Words that created distance, that turned pain into data.

"Start with what's true," I said. "What made you interested in psychiatry in the first place?"

Noah leaned back in his chair, eyes on the ceiling tiles. "My mother," he said finally. "She's been on antidepressants for twenty years, and no one talks about it. My father acts like it's shameful. Like she's broken." He paused. "I wanted to understand how the brain could make someone hurt that much. And how it could heal."

I felt something tighten in her chest. "That's beautiful, Noah. Write that."

His fingers moved across the keyboard, and I watched words appear on the screen. Watched him delete sentences, rework them, his brow furrowed in concentration. I found myself noticing things I shouldn't: the way his shoulders curved forward when he was thinking, the small scar near his left eyebrow, how his presence beside me felt both comfortable and electrically charged.

I looked away, focusing on a display of new releases across the room.

When I glanced back at the screen, Noah had written three paragraphs. They were good, honest and clinical without being distant. Personal without being maudlin. I could see him in the words, the person who noticed when I was pushing too hard, who sat with Elijah's silences without trying to fill them.

"This is really good," I said.

"You think?" He sounded uncertain.

"I know." And I did. This was easier, seeing clearly for someone else. Recognizing their value, their potential. Why was it so impossible to do for myself?

"I need to list programs now," Noah said. "Rankings, research interests, geographic preferences." He pulled up a new tab and began scrolling through options. "There's one in Providence. Rhode Island."

Something in his voice made me look up. Our eyes met, and I felt my pulse kick.

"That would be... convenient," I said carefully. "For coordinating hiking schedules."

A smile ghosted across his face. "Very convenient."

We worked for another hour, Noah typing and researching while I provided commentary, pushed back when he undersold himself, insisted he include the volunteer work with veterans he'd mentioned days ago. The library began to empty around us, afternoon stretching toward evening.

Finally, Noah pulled up the submission page. His cursor hovered over the button.

"This is insane," he said. "I'm really doing this."

"You're really doing this."

He looked at me, and his expression was so open, so vulnerable, that I had to resist the urge to reach for his hand.

"Thank you," he said. "For pushing. For not letting me make excuses."

"Thank you for not resenting me for it."

"I could never resent you, Emma."

The way he said my name made my breath catch. The air between us felt charged, heavy with things unsaid. I became acutely aware of my heartbeat, of how easy it would be to lean forward, to close the space between us.

Instead, I stood up abruptly, my chair scraping against the floor.

"You should submit it," I said, my voice coming out rougher than intended. "Before you overthink it."

Noah studied me for a moment, and I wondered what he saw. Then he turned back to the computer and clicked submit.

"Done," he said quietly.

We walked out of the library into the golden late-afternoon light, and I felt strangely unmoored, like something had shifted that couldn't be shifted back. Noah had taken a step toward his own future, had chosen himself over his father's expectations, and I'd been part of that.

It felt significant in a way I couldn't quite articulate.

"So," Noah said as they headed toward the diner. "You promised moral support. Does that extend to celebrating with pie?"

I laughed, and it felt good, natural. "It definitely extends to pie."

"Good. Because I'm buying you the biggest slice they have."

As we walked side by side down the small-town sidewalk, I let myself feel something I hadn't allowed in two years: possibility. Not certainty, not commitment, just the simple recognition that something was happening between us. Something real and complicated and terrifying.

And for the first time, I didn't immediately push it away.

I just walked beside him toward pie and friends and whatever came next.

Chapter 15

Three weeks later, the trail had led us deeper into Pennsylvania, where the forests grew dense and the hills rolled endlessly toward distant ridgelines. I had fallen into the rhythm of hiking, the morning ache in my muscles that gave way to fluid motion, the weight of my pack becoming part of my body, the way hours could pass in conversation or comfortable silence.

I'd fallen into other rhythms too. The way my pulse quickened when Noah's hand brushed mine passing a water bottle. How I found myself watching for him at rest stops, disappointed when he'd gone ahead or fallen behind. The strange gravity that kept pulling us together on the trail, day after day.

We hadn't talked about it. Hadn't defined it. It existed in the space between friendship and something more, and I told myself I was fine with that ambiguity even as it made my chest tight with uncertainty.

The clearing appeared without warning, a break in the trees where someone had carved out a small overlook years ago. Maggie reached it first and let out a whoop.

"Cell service!" She held her phone aloft like a trophy. "Actual bars!"

The group converged on the spot where the signal presumably bounced off some distant tower. I pulled out my phone and watched notifications cascade across the screen. Text messages from my mother, emails from my university, a voicemail from my dentist's office.

The normal world, intruding.

I glanced at Noah, who stood slightly apart from the group, his phone pressed to his ear. Even from a distance, I could see the change in his posture. His shoulders were rigid, jaw tight. He was listening to something, and whatever it was had turned his body into a line of tension.

My stomach dropped. I looked away, tried to focus on my own messages, but my attention kept sliding back to him.

Noah lowered the phone, stared at it for a moment, then turned away from the group. His fingers moved across the screen, placing a call.

"That doesn't look good," Becca said quietly, appearing at my elbow.

"No." I kept my voice neutral, but my heart was beating too fast.

We stood there pretending not to watch as Noah paced a small circle, phone pressed to his ear. The conversation was brief. I could see his mouth moving, could see the way he ran his free hand through his hair, a gesture I'd learned meant he was stressed. Then he was lowering the phone again, standing very still, staring out at the trees.

When he finally turned back toward the group, his face had gone into that mask of fine. I recognized it. It was one I'd worn so many times myself. My chest constricted.

He walked back slowly, and I found myself taking an involuntary step toward him before stopping myself. I didn't have the right to go to him. We weren't... whatever we were, it didn't give me that right.

"Everything okay?" I asked when he got close enough.

Noah's eyes met mine briefly, then slid away. "Yeah. Fine." He paused, and I could see him wrestling with something. "Actually, no. Not really."

The group had gone quiet, everyone sensing the shift in energy.

"An envelope came from Brown," Noah said, his voice flat. "My mom opened it. They want to interview me for the psychiatry program."

My heart leapt. "Noah, that's..."

"I told her to send a decline letter." He said it quickly, like ripping off a bandage.

The words hit me like cold water. For a moment I just stood there, my hands gripping my pack straps too tightly.

"You what?"

"I told her to decline the interview." Noah still wasn't quite looking at me. "It was a mistake to apply. I shouldn't have..." He stopped, shook his head. "It doesn't matter. It's done."

I felt something sharp and hot rise in her chest. Not anger exactly, but something close to it. Disappointment that felt disproportionate, inappropriate.

"Done?" The word came out harder than I intended. "You haven't even gone to the interview yet."

"Emma." His voice held a warning she'd never heard before. "Please don't."

But I couldn't seem to stop herself. "Don't what? Don't point out that you're giving up before you even try?"

"Three weeks ago, I wasn't thinking clearly." His jaw was tight now, defensive. "I got caught up in... it doesn't matter. My father's been planning this for years. I can't just..."

"Can't just choose what you actually want?"

"It's not that simple."

"Isn't it?" I heard my voice rising slightly and tried to pull it back, but the words kept coming. "You got an interview. They want you. And you're throwing it away because it's easier than having a difficult conversation."

Noah's expression hardened. "You don't understand."

"Then help me understand."

"I can't explain it to you when you've already decided what I should do." He finally met my eyes fully, and what I saw there made my breath catch. Frustration, yes, but also something like hurt. "You decided weeks ago in that library."

The words landed like a slap. I felt heat flood her face.

"That's not fair," I said quietly.

"Isn't it?" Noah's voice was still controlled, but there was an edge to it now. "You sat there and helped me write the whole thing. And now you're angry that I'm making a different choice."

"I'm not angry..." I started, but even as I said it, I knew it wasn't true. I was angry. Or hurt. Or some complicated combination of both that I didn't have the right to feel.

"I appreciate what you did," Noah continued, his tone softening slightly. "I do. But this is my life. My family. My decision." He paused, and I saw something flicker across his face. Regret, maybe. "I'm sorry if that's disappointing."

The clearing felt very quiet. I was aware of the rough bark of a tree trunk pressing into her back and of Becca standing nearby, of Maggie and Elijah pretending not to listen. My hands were trembling.

"You're right," I said, forcing the words out past the tightness in her throat. "It's your decision. I shouldn't have pushed."

Noah opened his mouth like he might say something else, but then seemed to think better of it. "I'm going to keep walking," he said instead. "I'll see you guys at the shelter."

And then he was turning away, shouldering his pack, heading down the trail with long strides that put distance between them.

I stood there watching him go, her chest tight and aching.

"Em." Becca's hand found my shoulder. "You okay?"

"No." The admission came out small. "No, I don't think I am."

"Come on." Becca guided me away from the clearing, away from where Maggie and Elijah were quietly packing up. "Let's walk."

We moved down the trail in the opposite direction from Noah, and I felt tears prick at my eyes.

"I did it again," I said quietly. "I pushed too hard. I tried to control something that wasn't mine to control."

"You were trying to help."

"Was I?" My voice cracked. "Or was I trying to fix him because it felt easier than dealing with my own mess?"

Becca was quiet for a moment. "Maybe both. That's allowed, Em."

"He's right to be upset. We barely know each other, and I'm acting like I have some claim on his decisions." I wiped at my eyes roughly. "What am I doing?"

"You're letting yourself care about someone. That's not a crime."

"It feels like one." My laugh was bitter. "It feels like I'm repeating every pattern I swore I'd never repeat. Getting too invested too fast. Thinking I know what's best. Pushing until they have to push back."

"Emma, no." Becca stopped walking, turned to face me. "You're not Scott. You disagreed with Noah. You expressed your opinion. That's what people do."

"But I don't have the right—"

"You have the right to care. You have the right to be disappointed." Becca's voice was firm. "What you don't have is the right to make the decision for him. And you didn't. You said what you thought, and now you both need space."

I felt something loosen slightly in her chest. "I don't know how to do this. I don't know how to care about someone without being terrified I'm doing it wrong."

"Nobody does, Em. That's the whole point." Becca squeezed her shoulder. "But for what it's worth? I think you showed up for someone you care about, and it didn't go the way you hoped. That's all."

I nodded, not quite believing it but wanting to. We stood there on the trail, and I tried to do my breathing. In for four, hold for seven, out for eight. But it kept hitching in my chest.

"I really like him, Becca." The admission felt both terrifying and necessary.

"I know you do."

"And I don't know if I'm ready for that."

"You're doing it right now," Becca said gently. "Messy and scared and uncertain. That's what it looks like."

"It's awful."

"Yeah. It really is." Becca smiled slightly. "But also, kind of wonderful, right? The fact that you can feel this much?"

I thought about that. About the way my chest had felt light when Noah smiled at me. About the easy conversations and comfortable silences and how I'd started to look forward to each day because it meant more time near him.

About how much it hurt now, standing here in his absence.

"Yeah," I said quietly. "Wonderful and terrible. Both."

"Welcome back to the land of the living, Em."

We started walking again, and I tried to focus on the physical sensations: my feet on the trail, the weight of my pack, the dappled sunlight through the trees. Tried not to think about Noah walking somewhere ahead of us, alone.

Tried not to think about the careful distance he'd put in his voice when he said *this is my life.*

Because he was right. It was his life. His decision.

And I had to find a way to be okay with that, even if watching him walk away from what he wanted felt like watching him walk away from himself.

Chapter 16

*Y*ou need to calm down, Emma. You're being dramatic.

Scott's voice, so reasonable. Always so reasonable when he was explaining why my feelings were wrong.

I'm trying to help you. Why do you always make this so difficult?

The wedding dress hung in his apartment like a ghost, white satin gleaming in the darkness. I reached for it but my hands wouldn't work right, wouldn't close around the fabric. Behind me, I could hear the creak of rope, that awful sound from the basement, and I needed to get to it, needed to stop it, but my legs were moving through water, through concrete, not moving at all.

This is your fault, Emma. You know that, right? All of this is because of you.

I tried to speak, tried to say no, but my throat closed around the words. The dress was closer now, or I was closer to it, I couldn't tell. When I reached for it again, it dissolved between my fingers, and underneath...

I woke gasping, my sleeping bag twisted around my legs like a trap. My heart slammed against my ribs, too fast, irregular, and some distant clinical part of my brain started cataloguing: *Tachycardia. Hyperventilation. Patient presents with...*

I clamped down on that voice, that stupid detached voice that tried to make everything a case study instead of something I actually had to feel.

My hands were shaking. I pressed them against my face, trying to ground myself. Tent fabric above me. Sleeping bag beneath me. The smell of earth and pine and my own sweat. Real things. Present things.

In for four. Hold for seven. Out for eight.

Except I couldn't hold for seven because my breath kept hitching, breaking apart in my chest.

I became aware of sounds outside my tent. Footsteps, soft but deliberate. Someone moving nearby. My stomach dropped. Had I cried out? Made noise?

The zipper of my tent began to lower, and my first instinct was to pretend to be asleep, to avoid the mortification of being seen like this. But the sound stopped halfway, and a voice came through the gap.

"Emma?" Maggie's voice, quiet and careful. "Are you all right?"

My throat was too tight to answer immediately. I managed, "I'm fine," but even I could hear how unconvincing it sounded.

A pause. Then: "May I come in? Or would you rather come out?"

The careful offer of choice made something in my chest loosen slightly. I didn't want Maggie in my tent, in my small contained space where the nightmare still felt too close. "I'll come out," I said.

I untangled myself from the sleeping bag with clumsy fingers and crawled out into the night. The air was cool against my overheated skin, and I became acutely aware of how I must look: hair wild, face probably blotchy, hands still trembling.

Maggie sat on the ground a respectful distance from my tent, her sleeping bag spread out beneath her. She didn't ask what the nightmare was about. Didn't offer empty reassurances. She just patted the ground beside her.

I sat, hugging my knees to my chest. I glanced around the campsite: three other tents in a loose circle. Becca's was to my left, still and quiet. Thank God she was a heavy sleeper. And Noah's tent was...

My eyes found it almost against her will. Twenty feet away, maybe. Close enough that he might have heard. The thought made my face burn.

"I get them too sometimes," Maggie said quietly. "Nightmares."

I looked at her. In the dim moonlight filtering through the trees, Maggie's face was more lined than I usually noticed. Older. Tired in a way that spoke of experience.

"The trail helps," Maggie continued. "But they don't just disappear because you're sleeping under the stars. That's not how trauma works."

The word, trauma, sat between us. I felt my defenses rise automatically. "I know how trauma works," I said, more sharply than I intended. "I studied psychology. I know about PTSD, about nightmare interruption protocols, exposure therapy, cognitive behavioral interventions." I heard my voice getting clinical, detached. "I know all of it. Knowing doesn't make it go away."

"No," Maggie agreed gently. "It doesn't."

I pressed my palms against my eyes. "Sorry. I didn't mean to snap."

"You're allowed to snap. You just woke up terrified." Maggie shifted slightly. "Do you want to try something that might help? Or would you rather just sit?"

My first instinct was to refuse. I was tired of trying things that didn't work. Tired of failing at techniques I could teach to someone else but couldn't seem to apply to myself. But the residual terror from the dream still clung to my skin, and the thought of going back into that tent made my chest tighten.

"What kind of something?" I asked warily.

"Mindfulness meditation. Very simple. Not magical, not a cure. Just something to bring you back into your body instead of stuck in your head."

I almost laughed. "I've tried meditation. Multiple times. I'm terrible at it."

"Most people are, at first. And most people judge themselves for being terrible at it, which makes it harder." Maggie's tone was matter-of-fact, not preachy. "But you don't have to be good at it for it to help a little. You just have to be willing to try."

I hesitated, every reason this wouldn't work lining up in my mind. My racing thoughts, my inability to quiet my mind, my tendency to analyze everything. I was doing it again. Intellectualizing instead of just making a choice.

"Okay," I said finally. "But if I'm bad at it, I don't want commentary."

A smile ghosted across Maggie's face. "Deal. No commentary."

Maggie settled more comfortably on her sleeping bag and gestured for me to do the same. "Close your eyes if that feels okay. If it doesn't, keep them open and find a soft focus on something neutral. The trees, the ground."

I closed her eyes, then immediately opened them again. Too dark. Too much like the dream. I focused on a patch of moonlight on the ground instead, where a small fern caught the light.

"Good," Maggie said. "Now just breathe. You don't have to control it or count it. Just notice it. Notice the inhale. Notice the exhale."

I tried. My breath was still uneven, still catching. I noticed that, and immediately started critiquing myself for noticing. *Stop analyzing. Just breathe. Just...*

"Your mind's going to wander," Maggie said, as if reading her thoughts. "That's what minds do. They wander, you notice, you bring your attention back. Over and over. That's the practice."

My mind was doing more than wandering. It was sprinting through the confrontation with Noah, through fragments of the nightmare, through a mental list of everything I was doing wrong in this moment.

"Now notice your body," Maggie continued, her voice low and unhurried. "Not judging it, not trying to change it. Just notice. Where are you tense? Where are you touching the ground?"

My shoulders were up near my ears. My jaw was clenched. My fingers were digging into my knees. The sleeping bag beneath me was damp with dew. I tried to relax, but it felt performative.

"Imagine you're in a place that feels safe," Maggie said. "Don't force it. Just let an image come if it wants to."

My mind went to the trail. Not here, but a section we'd hiked a week ago. Open meadow, wildflowers, the sun warm on my shoulders. Noah had been walking beside me, talking about nothing important, easy conversation that didn't require me to be anything other than myself.

The memory made my chest ache. I'd ruined that.

"Thoughts are going to come," Maggie said softly. "Worries, memories, judgments. Let them pass like clouds. You don't have to grab onto them."

But I was already grabbing onto them, clutching them. This wasn't working. I was doing it wrong...

A sound from Noah's tent made my eyes fly open. Just the rustle of fabric, someone shifting in sleep. But my heart rate kicked up again.

"Emma." Maggie's voice pulled her back. "You're here. Right now. On the trail. Under the stars. Safe."

I forced myself to look at the moonlight again. To feel the ground beneath me. To hear the night sounds: wind in the trees, some small animal moving through the underbrush, the distant sound of water.

Safe. I was safe.

Except I didn't feel safe. I felt exposed and raw.

"I can't do this," I whispered.

"You're doing it right now," Maggie said. "It doesn't have to feel good to be working."

We sat in silence for several minutes. My breathing didn't become calm exactly, but it became more even. The nightmare images didn't disappear, but they lost some of their sharp edges. My body stayed tense, but the worst of the trembling eased.

It wasn't peace. It wasn't healing. It was just slightly less awful than it had been ten minutes ago.

"The thing about mindfulness," Maggie said eventually, "is that it's not about feeling better. It's about feeling what you feel without adding extra suffering on top. Without the voice in your head telling you you're doing it wrong, or you should be over this by now, or you're broken because you can't just breathe your way through trauma."

I felt tears prick at her eyes. "That's a terrible sales pitch."

Maggie's laugh was quiet. "Maybe. But it's honest. You're going to have nightmares, Emma. Maybe for a long time. The best we can do is make the aftermath a little less overwhelming. Not fix it. Just... soften it."

"I'm so tired of softening things," I said. "I'm tired of managing symptoms and using techniques and just trying to survive each day without falling apart."

"I know." Maggie's voice held something that wasn't pity, understanding, maybe. "But you're here. You showed up for this hike even though it's hard. You let me sit with you even though you wanted to handle it alone. That's not just surviving. That's brave."

I wiped at her eyes roughly. "It doesn't feel brave."

"Those two things aren't mutually exclusive."

Despite myself, I huffed out something almost like a laugh. We sat together in the darkness, and I felt genuine tiredness settling over me. It wasn't the panicked adrenaline from the nightmare, but exhaustion.

"Thank you," I said quietly. "For coming over. For not making me explain."

"You don't owe me explanations." Maggie stood, gathering her sleeping bag. "But if you want to talk sometime, about whatever haunts you at night, I'm here. No judgment. No advice unless you want it."

I nodded, not trusting my voice.

Maggie started back toward her own tent, then paused. "Emma? That man in the tent over there." She nodded toward Noah's tent. "He's not sleeping either. I can tell by his breathing. Whatever happened between you two today, it's weighing on him too."

My stomach twisted. "I don't know how to fix it."

"Maybe it doesn't need fixing. Maybe it just needs time." Maggie smiled slightly. "Get some sleep if you can. Tomorrow's a new day on the trail."

After Maggie disappeared into her tent, I sat for a few more minutes, looking at the dark outline of Noah's tent. I wondered if he really was awake. Wondered what he was thinking.

Finally, I crawled back into my own tent. The sleeping bag still smelled like fear-sweat, and the space felt claustrophobic, but I forced myself to lie down. To close my eyes. To try the breathing again.

In for four. Hold for seven. Out for eight.

The nightmare would probably come back. Tomorrow night or the night after. I knew enough about PTSD to know that one meditation session wasn't going to cure me. That healing wasn't linear.

But for now, in this moment, I was okay.

And maybe that was enough.

Chapter 17

Pennsylvania was beautiful, but it was also relentless in its challenges. Mud caked our boots, earth and sweat stained their clothes, and the seemingly never-ending rocky terrain tested their spirits.

A week had passed since the cell service clearing. A week since Noah had shut down my opinions about the Brown interview. A week of careful politeness that felt worse than outright conflict.

We still hiked together sometimes, the group dynamics made it inevitable, but everything felt calibrated now. Measured. Noah would offer me a hand over difficult terrain with the same courtesy he'd offer anyone, and I would accept with a thank you that sounded hollow even to my own ears. We talked about safe things: the weather, the next shelter, whether we'd see a bear. Nothing that mattered.

I hated it.

I also didn't know how to fix it, so I just kept walking, one foot in front of the other, pretending the careful distance between us didn't make my chest ache.

We were all exhausted and dirty; a shared burden of filth and fatigue. Becca was somehow still smiling despite not having showered in over a week, still cracking jokes about our collective smell. I watched her and felt a spike of something like envy. What would it be like to not replay every awkward interaction on a loop? To just exist without constantly analyzing whether I'd said the wrong thing, done the wrong thing, been too much or not enough?

But today, there was hope on the horizon: Boiling Springs, Pennsylvania.

The name alone held promises of respite: a chance to wash away the accumulated grime and indulge in the simple pleasures of civilization. Shower, real food, and then back to the woods.

"Only three more miles," Becca announced, checking her map. "Three miles to running water and real bathrooms."

"And a tavern," Maggie added. "Don't forget the tavern."

My stomach flipped. A tavern meant sitting together around a table with nowhere to look but at each other. No forward motion to hide behind. I glanced at Noah, walking a few yards ahead with Elijah, and wondered if he was dreading it too.

As if sensing my gaze, Noah looked back over his shoulder. Our eyes met for a brief second before I looked away, heat rising in my face. Even that, a simple glance, felt loaded now.

When did a look become something to overthink?

The miles stretched on, and I found myself falling into step with Noah as the trail narrowed. It happened naturally, inevitably, the way it had for weeks before everything got weird. For a moment, neither of us spoke, and my mind raced through possible conversation starters, discarding each one as too loaded or too trivial.

"You know," Noah said finally, his tone light, "there's something strangely liberating about being this dirty and exhausted."

I glanced at him, surprised he'd spoken first. "Yeah?"

"Yeah. It's like... we've all shed layers of pretense. Nobody's trying to impress anyone when we all smell like a locker room."

Despite myself, I felt a smile tug at my lips. "Well, if that's the case, then I think I've achieved peak authenticity. 'Eau de Forest' isn't exactly my signature scent."

Noah's laugh sounded genuine, unguarded, and something in my chest loosened slightly. "I don't know. It has a certain... earthiness."

"That's a diplomatic word for it."

We walked in silence for a moment, but it felt different than the brittle quiet of the past week. Less like walking on eggshells. I found myself stealing glances at him. The way his hair was getting longer, curling slightly at his neck, the shadow of stubble on his jaw. When had I started cataloguing these details?

Don't, I told myself. *Don't do this. Don't get invested again.*

But my heart was already doing that complicated flutter thing it did when he was near, and I couldn't seem to stop it.

***

We arrived at the campground with sunlight still clinging to the afternoon. Setting up camp took on a hurried quality, everyone eager for showers and the promise of clean clothes. I grabbed my carefully hoarded clean outfit from the bottom of my pack (jeans that probably wouldn't fit right after weeks of hiking, a clean t-shirt, underwear that didn't have holes) and headed for the shower facilities.

The warm water felt like absolution. I stood under the spray longer than necessary, watching weeks of trail dirt swirl down the drain. My muscles loosened under the heat, but my chest stayed tight. That knot had been there since the hostel, since I'd pushed Noah away with my unsolicited advice about his father. Since I'd watched something shift in his face and realized too late that I'd crossed some invisible line.

I'd done it again. Treated someone like a patient instead of a person. Used clinical distance as a shield when things got too close, too real.

When I finally emerged, wrapped in a towel with my wet hair dripping down my back, Becca was waiting by the sinks.

"You okay?" Becca asked, leaning into the mirror to apply mascara with the concentration of a surgeon.

"Why wouldn't I be okay?"

"Oh, I don't know. Maybe because you've been radiating emotional constipation for a week?" Becca swept the mascara wand through her lashes with a flourish. "You and Noah are doing this whole tragic period drama thing. Lots of longing looks. Heavy sighs. Zero actual conversation."

I pulled on my clean clothes; the cotton foreign against my trail-roughened skin. "I don't know how to fix it."

"Revolutionary concept: have you tried talking to him?"

"About what?" The jeans felt loose around my waist. I tugged at the waistband, oddly disoriented by how my own clothes fit. "Sorry I overstepped boundaries we never actually defined? Sorry I psychoanalyzed your relationship with your father like you're some interesting case study instead of..." I stopped, my throat closing around the rest of the sentence.

"Instead of what?"

Instead of someone who matters. Instead of someone who made me feel things I'd sworn I wouldn't feel again.

"We're not anything," I said finally, dragging a comb through my tangled hair. It caught on a knot and I pulled harder, welcoming the sting. "I don't have standing to make things weird between us. But I did anyway."

"Em." Becca turned from the mirror, mascara wand still in hand. "You're allowed to have opinions. You're allowed to care about people without it being some kind of professional boundary violation."

The comb snagged again. My eyes watered. "I know."

"Do you? Because from here it looks like you're punishing yourself for being human."

My eyes met Becca's in the mirror. "I just don't want to lose whatever we had," I said quietly. "Even if I'm not sure what that was."

"Then talk to him tonight. Dance with him. Stop overthinking." Becca turned back to the mirror, capping her mascara with a decisive click. "I know it's hard for you. But not everything needs to be analyzed to death."

I looked at my own reflection. My wavy auburn hair was already starting to curl as it dried, wild and untamed as always. My face looked thinner, sharper somehow, my freckles dark against sun-weathered skin. But it was my eyes that I noticed. The way they looked both harder and softer than they had five weeks ago. More uncertain. More open.

The girl who'd started this hike wouldn't have let herself care this much.

That girl had kept everyone at a careful distance, had treated vulnerability like a contagion. And now here I was, chest aching over a guy I'd known for a month, my heart doing complicated things I'd promised myself I wouldn't allow.

My breathing had gone shallow. In for four, hold for seven, out for eight. The technique was supposed to engage the parasympathetic nervous system, interrupt the anxiety response. But knowing the mechanism didn't make the anxiety less real. That was the thing my textbooks had never quite captured; the gap between understanding something and feeling it, between knowing you're safe and believing it.

"Stop it," I said to her reflection.

"Stop what?" Becca looked over.

"Cataloging my own defense mechanisms like I'm my own case study." I dropped the comb into my toiletry bag. "My brain won't shut up."

Becca grinned. "Your brain's kind of an asshole sometimes."

"Yeah." I managed a small smile. "It really is."

***

The local tavern greeted us with warm light spilling from its windows and the muffled thump of live music. My stomach clenched as our group pushed through the door into noise and bodies and the smell of beer and sweat.

Too many people. Too close. I cataloged the exits automatically and hated myself for it. Front door behind us, emergency exit by the bathrooms, kitchen probably had a back way out. Two years and I still couldn't walk into a crowded room without mapping escape routes.

The space was small and rustic, exposed beams overhead, a tiny stage where a band was setting up. Wooden tables scattered throughout, already half-full with locals and other hikers. The smell of fried food cut through my anxiety enough to make my mouth water. After weeks of trail mix and dehydrated meals, anything cooked seemed like luxury.

Maggie claimed a large table near the back. I slid into a seat and found Noah directly across from me, close enough that our knees bumped under the table. I pulled back instinctively, then felt stupid about it. He'd gone still too, careful not to take up too much space.

This was going to be a long night.

"First round's on me," Elijah announced, heading to the bar.

I studied the sticky menu, hyperaware of Noah across from me. He'd showered; his hair still damp, pushed back from his face. Clean-shaven. I'd gotten used to the stubble, the trail version of him. This felt too formal somehow, like we were strangers again.

He was staring at the menu like it held the secrets of the universe.

When Elijah returned with beers, Becca raised hers with theatrical flair. "To making it to Boiling Springs without killing each other, getting murdered by the trail, or dying of emotional repression!"

"Jesus, Becca," I muttered, but I clinked glasses anyway.

The beer was cold and bitter and perfect. I took a long drink, felt it settle in my empty stomach. The band started up with sounds of bluegrass, fiddles and banjos, and gradually the knot in my shoulders loosened a fraction.

Conversation flowed around the table. Trail stories, blisters, weather speculation. I laughed at Becca's jokes, nodded at appropriate moments, but part of my attention stayed fixed on Noah. The way he smiled at something Elijah said. How his fingers tapped against his beer bottle; nervous energy he couldn't quite contain. The careful way he looked at everyone except me.

After we'd ordered (burgers for everyone, salad for Maggie that made Becca announce she'd "literally rather eat her boot") the band shifted into something slower. Couples drifted onto the small dance floor.

Maggie grabbed Elijah's hand. "Come on, soldier. Let's show these youngsters how it's done."

I watched them move onto the floor with a pang I couldn't quite name. They made it look easy, that kind of uncomplicated connection. No baggage. No land mines.

A guy in a cowboy hat materialized at our table, eyes on Becca. "Care to dance?"

"Do I?" Becca practically levitated out of her seat. She shot me a look that clearly said *you're welcome* before letting the cowboy lead her away.

Then it was just Noah and me at the table. The sudden absence of buffer made everything feel exposed.

I drank more beer. Noah did the same. The silence stretched, thick and uncertain.

Say something. Apologize. Fix this.

But my throat had closed up, all the words I'd practiced dissolving into nothing.

"I'm sorry," we both said simultaneously.

I let out a surprised laugh that sounded too high, too nervous. "You're sorry? For what?"

"For last week." Noah finally looked at me directly, and I saw my own anxiety reflected back. "You were trying to help and I shut you down. That wasn't fair."

"I pushed too hard." The words came out clipped, defensive. I made myself continue. "I made your life about me, about what I thought you should do. That wasn't fair either."

Noah shook his head. "You pushed because you saw me giving up on something I wanted. You were right. I was taking the easy path."

"Was?" My heart kicked against my ribs. "Past tense?"

A slight smile, rueful and uncertain. "I called the program. Asked if my interview slot was still available."

The bloom of feeling in my chest was too big, too bright. Joy and pride and something more complicated that I didn't want to name. "When?"

"Two days ago. There was cell service at the last shelter." He ran a hand through his hair, making it stick up. "I've been trying to figure out how to tell you. How to bridge this weird gap."

"I thought you hated me," I heard myself say.

"What? No." Noah leaned forward, earnest and open in a way that made my chest ache. "I thought you were done with me. That I'd proven I was exactly the kind of person you shouldn't waste time on. Someone who can't stand up for themselves."

The irony of it hit me hard. Both of us assuming the worst, both of us convinced we were the problem.

"That's not what I thought," I said quietly. "I thought I'd ruined everything. Whatever this is."

"What is this?" Noah asked, and the vulnerability in his voice made something inside me crack open.

"I don't know." The admission felt like pulling glass from a wound. "I'm not good at knowing. I'm good at analyzing myself into paralysis and sabotaging things before they can hurt me. But I don't know how to just be in something."

The band shifted into a slower song. I watched couples sway on the dance floor and felt the familiar urge to flee rising in my throat.

"Do you want to dance?" Noah asked.

My eyes snapped to his. My pulse spiked, fight-or-flight kicking in hard. "What?"

"Dance. With me." He stood, extending his hand across the table. His hand was trembling slightly. "No pressure. But we've been walking on eggshells for a week and I just...I miss talking to you. I miss you."

I miss you.

The words hit like a fist to the sternum. I stared at his outstretched hand and felt everything in me scream *no*. I wasn't ready. I was broken. This was how it started last time. Someone charming and patient, someone who made me feel special until I was trapped.

But Noah wasn't Scott. I knew that intellectually, had known it from the first conversation. Scott had been charming in a way that demanded something from me. Noah's kindness asked for nothing.

Knowing that didn't make my hand any steadier as I placed it in his.

He led me onto the dance floor and my breath was coming too fast. In for four, hold for seven, out for eight. His hand settled at my waist and I flinched before I could stop myself.

Noah felt it; I saw it in his face, the flicker of concern. "We don't have to..."

"No." I forced myself to stay. "I want to. I'm just..."

"Scared," Noah finished gently.

"Yeah."

We swayed together, finding a rhythm. I kept my gaze fixed on his shoulder, couldn't quite manage eye contact. His hand on my waist was warm through my shirt but not possessive, not demanding. I waited for the other shoe to drop, for the shift from gentle to controlling.

It didn't come.

Gradually, incrementally, my breathing steadied. Not calm, but manageable.

"What's the most surprising thing you've discovered on this hike?" Noah asked softly, and I recognized it for what it was: a lifeline back to safer ground.

I considered the question, hyperaware of every point of contact between us. His hand. My waist. The space I was maintaining between our bodies.

"That I'm stronger than I thought," I said finally. "The trail's been brutal. But I've survived it." I paused, made myself add, "Even when I'm terrified of something that's not the trail."

Noah's hand tightened slightly at my waist. Not a demand, just acknowledgment. "I've seen that strength. Even when you don't see it yourself."

"Working on it," I managed. "The seeing it part."

We swayed in silence for a moment, and I felt the careful distance between us, physical and emotional. We were both so scared of getting this wrong.

"Thank you," I said. "For calling the program."

"Thank you for pushing me to apply in the first place."

"We're a mess," I said, and felt a smile tug at my mouth despite everything. "Both terrible at seeing ourselves clearly."

"Maybe that's why..." Noah started, then stopped. Recalibrated. "Maybe we balance each other out."

The song ended. We stood there, not quite pulling apart, not quite staying together.

"Should we..." Noah gestured vaguely toward the table.

"Yeah."

But neither of us moved, caught in the weight of everything unsaid. My heart was hammering against my ribs, my body still primed to run even as part of me wanted to stay exactly where I was.

Finally, Noah offered his hand again, just to hold this time. I looked at it for a long moment before taking it. My palm was sweating. I was sure he could feel it but he didn't let go as we navigated back through the crowd.

When we slid into our seats, Becca caught my eye and raised her eyebrows in exaggerated delight. I felt my face heat but couldn't quite suppress my smile.

Nothing was fixed. The fear hadn't evaporated. I still had a thousand questions tangled in my chest, still felt the shadow of Scott every time I let myself feel too much. But we'd found their way back to something like solid ground.

And for now, as Noah's knee pressed carefully against mine under the table and conversation flowed around us, that was enough.

Chapter 18

The morning after Boiling Springs felt different. Not fixed, not perfect, but lighter somehow. I woke to find Maggie and Elijah's tents already gone. They must have started early. That left just Becca, Noah and me to break camp together.

Noah caught my eye as we were packing up, and something passed between us. Not quite a smile, but an acknowledgment. We're okay. We're figuring this out.

I felt my chest do that complicated flutter thing again and forced myself to focus on rolling my sleeping bag.

We ate a quick breakfast of granola bars and instant coffee, then hit the trail. The morning started pleasant enough; cool air, dappled sunlight and the usual ache in my legs that I'd learned to ignore. Noah fell into step beside me naturally, and Becca dropped back to give us space, humming something off-key that might have been Taylor Swift.

But as the morning wore on, the trail turned mean. The terrain grew increasingly rocky, studded with loose stones that shifted underfoot. Fallen trees blocked our path, forcing us to scramble over or around. My entire body ached, muscles screaming with each step.

We'd been hiking for maybe three hours when I heard it.

A yelp. A crash. Then Becca's voice: "Shit. Shit shit shit."

I spun around. Becca was on the ground about ten feet back, one leg twisted beneath her at an angle that made my stomach lurch. Her face had gone white, lips pressed together.

"Becca!" I dropped my pack and scrambled back, my heart suddenly slamming against my ribs. Noah was right behind me.

"I'm okay," Becca managed through gritted teeth, but her hands were shaking as she reached for her ankle. "There was a loose rock and I..." She inhaled sharply. "Okay. Not okay."

I crouched beside her and saw the swelling starting, the skin already turning angry red. Becca's foot sat at a slightly wrong angle.

My hands hovered uselessly. Should I touch it? Check for broken bones? Or would that make it worse? Elevate first, or stabilize? My mind raced through half-remembered first aid protocols, but nothing felt certain.

"Should we...do I check if it's broken?" I looked at Noah, hating how uncertain I sounded.

"Let me." Noah's voice was calm as he knelt beside Becca. "I've done this before."

Relief and inadequacy hit me in equal measure. Of course he had. Of course, he knew what to do while I was just kneeling here, second-guessing everything.

"Emma." Noah glanced up at me. "Can you talk to her while I examine this? Keep her focused on something else?"

Right. That I could do. I shifted to Becca's other side, taking her hand. "Hey. Remember that time in college when you convinced me to try hot yoga and I almost passed out?"

"And you blamed me for three days?" Becca's attempt at a laugh came out as a wince. "How is this my fault this time?"

"Gravity. You should have been more careful with gravity."

Noah worked methodically; his hands gentle as he assessed the injury. "Can you wiggle your toes for me, Becca?"

I watched Becca's foot move slightly, saw her face contort with pain. My stomach twisted. What if it was broken? What if we couldn't get her out? What would we do if...

Stop. One thing at a time.

"Good," Noah said. "That's good. Can you tell me where it hurts most?"

"Outside of my ankle. It's bad." Becca's voice was tight. "Eight out of ten. Maybe nine."

Noah sat back on his heels. "Emma, can you get my first aid kit? And my sleeping bag?"

I nodded, grateful for the concrete task. My hands shook slightly as I dug through Noah's pack, and I forced them steady. Focus. Just do the next thing.

Behind me, Noah continued asking Becca questions, his voice steady and professional. I listened as I worked, trying to absorb the information. No numbness in the toes. Good. Swelling contained to the ankle. Also good. No obvious deformity beyond the slight angle.

"Here." I handed Noah the supplies, watching as he spread the sleeping bag on a flatter section just off the trail.

Together, we helped Becca move to it, supporting her weight between us. Becca hissed in pain, her breath coming in sharp bursts, and I found myself mentally cataloging every sound, every change in her expression. Was that normal pain or something worse? Should her face be that pale?

Once Becca was settled with her ankle elevated on Noah's pack, Noah sat back. "I don't think it's broken, but it's a bad sprain. Could be a small fracture. Without an X-ray, I can't be sure."

"So, what's the verdict, Doc?" Becca's attempt at humor came out thin. "Am I going to lose the foot?"

"You're going to be fine." Noah's smile was gentle. "But you can't hike on it."

The words settled over me like a weight. Can't hike. Which meant evacuation. Which meant... what, exactly? My mind immediately started spinning through logistics. We were miles from anywhere. No one was expecting us. What was the protocol for this?

I fumbled for my phone. No signal. Of course, no signal.

"Nothing," I said, and heard the edge in my voice. "No service."

"Hey." Becca reached for my hand. "It's just an ankle. We'll figure it out."

But we were in the middle of nowhere and Becca was hurt and I was supposed to know what to do in situations like this, wasn't I? I'd researched this hike for months. Why hadn't I looked up emergency protocols more carefully? What if the swelling got worse? What if there was internal bleeding we couldn't see?

"Okay." Noah's voice cut through my spiraling thoughts. "Here's what we're going to do. According to my map, there's a road crossing about five miles ahead. From there, it's maybe two miles to a small town. I can get there, find help, come back."

My head snapped up. "You're going alone?"

"Someone needs to stay with Becca. Someone needs to go for help." Noah met my eyes. "I can move faster alone, and you can keep her comfortable here."

The logic made sense. I knew it made sense. But my mind immediately jumped to complications. "What if you get hurt on the way? Or lost? These trails aren't always well-marked and if you're moving fast..." I could hear my voice rising and forced it level. "Sorry. I just...there are a lot of variables."

"I know." Noah's expression was patient. "But it's the best option we have. And I need you to stay here and take care of Becca. Can you do that?"

I looked at Becca, who was watching us both, pain etched in every line of her face. Could I? What if I missed something important? What if the swelling suddenly got worse and I didn't know what to do?

But what other choice did we have?

"Yes," I said, trying to sound more confident than I felt. "I can do that."

"I know you can." Noah squeezed my shoulder before turning to his first aid kit. He pulled out ibuprofen, handing me the bottle. "Give her 600 milligrams now. Three pills. Then another dose in six hours if I'm not back yet. Keep the ankle elevated above her heart if possible. Watch for increased swelling or any numbness in the toes. If you see either, that's concerning, but I'll be back before then."

I took the bottle, mentally repeating his instructions. 600 milligrams. Six hours. Watch for swelling and numbness. I could do that. Those were concrete things I could monitor.

Noah transferred water bottles to my pack, checked his supplies. "I'm going to move fast. Four hours there, maybe less. However long it takes to arrange transport. Four hours back. So maybe nine hours total. Ten at most."

Nine hours. I glanced at the sky. It was barely noon. That meant we'd be waiting until evening, possibly after dark. My mind immediately cataloged concerns: temperature drop at night, wild animals, keeping Becca warm enough, what if the pain medication wasn't enough, what if...

Stop. Cross those bridges when you come to them.

"Okay," I said. "Go. We'll be fine."

Noah looked at me for a long moment, and I could see him assessing whether I was actually fine or just saying I was. Then, before I could process what was happening, he leaned down and pressed a quick kiss to my forehead.

I froze, every muscle locking. The gesture was so gentle, so unexpectedly intimate, that my brain temporarily short-circuited. By the time I'd processed it enough to respond, he was already pulling back.

"I'll be back soon," Noah said, and then he was gone, disappearing down the trail at a near-jog.

I stood there for a moment, my hand drifting up to touch where his lips had been. My heart was doing something complicated in my chest, warmth and surprise and a flutter of worry all tangled together.

"Em." Becca's voice, tight with pain, snapped me back. "Pills. Now."

Right. Pills. I could do pills.

I shook three tablets into my palm, handed them to Becca with a water bottle. Watched as she swallowed them, her face contorting.

"So," Becca said once she'd settled back. "He kissed you."

"It was just... it doesn't..." I busied myself adjusting the sleeping bag under Becca's leg, avoiding eye contact.

"Em. He kissed you goodbye like you're his person. That's not nothing."

I felt my face heat. "Your ankle is possibly fractured. That seems more pressing."

"I can be injured and observant." Becca closed her eyes for a moment, breathing through obvious pain. When she opened them again, her gaze was knowing. "You like him. And that freaks you out a little."

I sank down beside Becca, suddenly exhausted. "I don't know how to do this. The casual dating thing. The trusting someone thing."

"You don't have to figure it all out right now." Becca winced. "Sorry. Hurts to talk."

"Then don't talk. Just rest."

But Becca's hand found mine and squeezed. "He's coming back, Em. Stop worrying."

I nodded, but my mind was already spinning ahead. Five miles to the road, two more to town. That was seven miles, assuming the map was accurate. What if it wasn't? What if the town didn't have a way to send help? What if Noah twisted an ankle too, or what if...

Stop. He's competent. He knows what he's doing. Focus on what you can control.

The afternoon stretched long. I checked Becca's ankle every thirty minutes: swelling stable, no discoloration beyond the initial bruising, toes still moving when I asked. All good signs. I knew they were good signs. But knowing didn't stop me from second-guessing my own assessments. Was that more swelling or was I imagining it? Should the bruise be that color? Was I checking too often or not often enough?

Two hours. Three. The sun moved across the sky in its slow arc.

Becca dozed on and off, the pain medication helping. I was grateful for it. Becca needed rest, and I could focus on keeping watch without having to maintain conversation.

I tried to read, but couldn't focus. Tried to eat some chili that I heated on the camp stove, but my stomach was too tight. Instead, I found myself watching the trail, mentally calculating timelines. He'd said four hours to get there. It had been three. So one more hour until he reached the town, then however long to arrange help, then four hours back. I could handle that. It was just time. Just waiting.

But what if the map distances were wrong? What if it took longer? What if...

Four hours. Five.

I gave Becca another dose of ibuprofen, checked the ankle again. Still stable. Still okay. I was probably checking too often, but doing something felt better than just sitting here, letting my mind spiral through worst-case scenarios.

The rational part of my brain knew Noah was fine. The trail had been well-marked. He was experienced and careful. But the anxious part, the part that had learned to expect things to go wrong, to expect that moment when control slipped away, kept whispering doubts.

What if he got hurt and no one found him? What if I'd made the wrong call letting him go alone? Should I have gone instead? Should we have both gone and carried Becca somehow?

"Em." Becca's voice, groggy with pain meds. "I can hear you overthinking from here."

"Sorry. I'm just... running through scenarios."

"Well, stop. You're doing fine. I'm fine. Everything's fine." Becca's eyes were half-closed. "He's coming back."

"I know." And I did know, logically. But logic and anxiety didn't always speak the same language.

Six hours. Seven.

The sun was lower now, casting long shadows through the trees. My shoulders were tight with tension, my jaw aching from clenching. I forced myself through a breathing exercise and felt marginally better. Four counts in, seven hold, eight out.

It was fine. Everything was fine. This was taking exactly as long as Noah had said it would take.

Eight hours.

I heard voices on the trail before I saw anything. Multiple people. I scrambled to my feet, my heart jumping into my throat, and then Noah came around the bend followed by two EMTs with a stretcher.

The relief that hit me was physical; my shoulders dropped, my breath released in a rush, and I felt suddenly, intensely tired. He'd come back. Of course he'd come back. But actually seeing him, solid and real and here, made something unclench in my chest.

Noah's eyes found mine immediately. "Told you I'd come back."

"You did." My voice came out a little unsteady, but I managed a smile. "How was the run?"

"Long." He crossed to me, his hand finding my arm in that now-familiar gesture. "You okay?"

"Yeah. Becca's stable. I checked every half hour like you said." I realized I was talking too fast and made myself slow down. "No increased swelling, no numbness, toes still moving fine."

"You did good." Noah squeezed my arm gently, and something in his expression made me believe it.

The EMTs moved in, professional and efficient, asking Becca questions as they examined her ankle. I watched as they carefully loaded Becca onto the stretcher, my mind already jumping ahead to next steps. Hospital, X-rays, treatment plan...

One of the EMTs turned to us. "We're taking her to the hospital in Carlisle for X-rays. You two want to come, or continue hiking?"

I looked at Becca, who was already shaking her head. "You guys keep going. I'll be fine. They'll probably just give me crutches and tell me to ice it."

"Becca, I can come with you..."

"Em. We planned this hike for months. Don't stop because of me." Becca's expression was firm despite the pain. "Besides, someone needs to finish it for both of us."

I felt torn. There wasn't much I could actually do at the hospital. I'd just be sitting in a waiting room. But leaving Becca felt wrong somehow, like I was abandoning my post.

"I'll be okay," Becca said more gently. "I promise. And I'll call you when I have service. But you need to keep hiking. For both of us."

I looked at Noah, who was watching me with that patient expression. "Your call," he said quietly. "Whatever you want to do."

The fact that he meant it, that he was actually leaving the choice to me without pressure, made the decision easier.

"Okay," I said to Becca. "But you call me the second you know anything."

"I will. Now get out of here before I start crying and ruin my tough girl image."

The EMTs started down the trail with the stretcher. Becca gave us a thumbs up that was probably more for my benefit than anything else.

And then Noah and I were alone in the forest, the evening shadows lengthening around us, and I felt the full weight of the last eight hours settle over me.

I sat down heavily on a nearby log, suddenly boneless with exhaustion. My hands were shaking slightly, adrenaline finally draining out of my system.

Noah sat beside me, not touching, just present. "That was intense."

"Yeah." I let out a long breath. "I kept second-guessing everything. Every time I checked her ankle, I wasn't sure if I was seeing it right. If I was missing something."

"You weren't. You did exactly what I would have done."

"But you would have been more confident about it." I rubbed my face with both hands. "I hate not knowing if I'm making the right call."

"Nobody knows for sure. We just do our best with what we have." Noah was quiet for a moment. "For what it's worth, you handled it really well. Becca was safe, comfortable, and you kept it together even though I know you were worried."

"I was worried you'd get hurt," I admitted. "Or that the map was wrong and you'd get lost. Or that I'd miss something with Becca and make it worse." I glanced at him. "Basically, I worried about everything possible."

"That sounds exhausting."

"It really is." I felt myself smile despite everything. "But we're okay. Becca's okay. You made it back."

"I told you I would." Noah's hand found mine, his fingers warm around mine. "I meant it when I said it. I meant it when I kissed you goodbye..." He paused. "Sorry, that probably freaked you out."

"Only a little," I said honestly. "I'm not great with... unexpected physical contact. But it was nice. Just... surprising."

"I'll try to be less surprising."

"Don't." The word came out before I could think about it. "I mean...I'm working on being okay with surprises. With not needing to control everything." I looked at our joined hands. "You can kiss me goodbye if you want. I'll try to actually respond next time instead of freezing like a startled deer."

Noah laughed, and the sound eased something in my chest. "Deal."

We sat there as the light faded, my hand in his, and I let myself feel the relief without questioning it. Let myself believe that sometimes things worked out. That sometimes people came back when they said they would.

That maybe, just maybe, I could learn to trust this.

***

I didn't know how long we sat there on that log, but eventually the shadows deepened enough that Noah glanced at the sky.

"We should make camp," he said. "It's getting dark."

I nodded and stood, my legs protesting after sitting still for so long. Every muscle in my body felt like I'd hiked twice the distance we actually had. Adrenaline crash, I recognized distantly. My body had been running on stress hormones for eight hours and now it was sending me the bill.

"I've got my tent," I said, pulling my pack over. "I can get it set up."

I managed to get the tent bag open and the poles out before my hands started shaking again. Not panic this time, just exhaustion making my fingers clumsy. I fumbled with the shock cord connections, and then Noah's hands were there.

"I've got this part," he said. "Why don't you clear some rocks from the tent site?"

I wanted to argue that I could do it myself, but honestly, I was grateful. I kicked aside some larger stones and pine cones while Noah assembled the poles with the easy efficiency of someone who'd done this hundreds of times.

"You're good at that," I said.

"Lots of practice." He glanced up with a slight smile. "I've set up tents in worse conditions than this. Rain, wind, once in nearly complete darkness when my headlamp died."

"How'd that go?"

"Tent ended up backwards. Didn't realize until morning." He threaded the poles through the fabric. "Still kept me dry, though."

I found myself smiling despite my exhaustion. By the time both tents were up, full darkness had settled over the forest. Noah pulled out his camp stove and started heating water.

"Tea?" he offered.

"That sounds perfect."

I sank into my camp chair and watched him work. There was something calming about the familiar routine of making camp, the small domestic rituals of outdoor life. Noah handed me a steaming cup and I wrapped my hands around it, letting the warmth seep into my palms.

We sat in comfortable silence for a while. My body was starting to feel less like it might vibrate apart, more like it might actually be able to sleep eventually.

"I should eat something," I said, though the thought of food made my stomach uncertain.

"You made chili earlier, right?" Noah asked. "I saw the container when I was looking for the first aid kit."

"Yeah. It's probably cold now."

"Cold chili is still chili." Noah stood and found the container in my pack. "And you need to eat."

He was right. I knew he was right. I watched him heat it on the stove, portion it into two bowls. When he handed me one, I managed several bites before my stomach decided that was enough.

"Thanks," I said, setting the bowl aside. "I'm just not very hungry."

"That's okay. You ate something." Noah took a few more bites of his own, then set his bowl down too. "Long day."

"That's an understatement." I pulled my knees up to my chest, wrapping my arms around them. "I keep thinking about Becca. Wondering if she's okay, what the X-rays showed."

"She'll call when she can," Noah said. "But she's in good hands now. Professional medical care, pain management, probably a comfortable bed."

"Better than a sleeping pad in the woods."

"Definitely better than a sleeping pad." Noah smiled. "Though she'd probably argue the company's not as good."

I felt a small laugh escape despite everything. Then the quiet settled again, and with it, the weight of the question I'd been avoiding all evening.

"I don't know if I can do this without her," I heard myself say.

Noah looked at me, patient and curious. "Do what?"

"Finish the hike. Keep going." I pressed my forehead against my knees. "Becca's the one who convinced me to do this trail in the first place. And now she's gone and I'm just... I don't know if I can do it alone."

"You wouldn't be alone," Noah said quietly.

I looked up at him. "I know. But that's not... I mean, you have your own hike. Your own plans. I can't just attach myself to you because my friend got hurt."

"You're not attaching yourself to me. We've been hiking together for weeks now." Noah leaned forward slightly, his expression earnest. "Emma, I've watched you tackle some of the hardest sections of this trail. You're stronger than you think you are."

I shook my head. "I'm not, though. Today proved that. I was second-guessing everything, couldn't even properly assess Becca's injury without your help..."

"You kept her stable and comfortable for eight hours. You followed instructions perfectly. You managed your own anxiety well enough to take care of someone else." Noah's voice was firm but kind. "That's not weakness. And it's definitely not incompetence."

"Scott used to say I couldn't handle things on my own. That I'd fall apart without him to..." I stopped, realizing what I'd said. "Sorry. I don't know why I brought that up."

"Because he got in your head," Noah said simply. "And you're still fighting against what he told you about yourself." He paused. "But Emma, I've hiked with you for a month now. I've seen you navigate in fog, handle difficult terrain, problem-solve when things went wrong. You're capable. You just don't always see it."

I felt something loosen slightly in my chest. I wanted to believe him. Part of me even did believe him. But there was still that nagging doubt, that voice that sounded suspiciously like Scott telling me I was in over my head.

"What if I quit?" I said quietly. "What if I just... call it here and go home?"

"Then you go home." Noah shrugged. "There's no shame in that. But I don't think that's what you want."

He was right. The thought of quitting, of going home without finishing, made something in me rebel. Becca had looked me in the eye and told me to keep going, to finish for both of them. And beyond that...

I glanced at Noah in the dim light of the camp stove. If I quit, I'd head home tomorrow. He'd continue on. And I'd never see him again.

The thought landed with unexpected weight. I pushed it aside quickly, not ready to examine what that meant.

"I want to finish," I admitted. "I'm just scared I'm not strong enough."

"You are," Noah said with quiet certainty. "You've already proven that. Today, you proved it again."

I met his eyes and saw no doubt there, only steady belief. It was unsettling and comforting all at once.

"Okay," I said finally. "I'll keep going. One day at a time."

"That's all any of us can do."

I felt exhaustion pulling at me now, my body finally ready to give up and sleep. I stood, swaying slightly, and Noah stood too.

"Get some rest," he said. "Tomorrow will be easier. Just hiking. No medical emergencies."

"From your mouth to the universe's ears." I managed a tired smile. "Thank you, Noah. For everything today."

"Anytime." He said it simply, like it was a fact. Like he'd always come back, always help, always be there. I didn't know what to do with that level of steadiness.

I headed for my tent, then paused and looked back. "I'm glad you're here."

Something warm crossed Noah's face. "I'm glad I'm here too."

I crawled into my tent and burrowed into my sleeping bag, my body finally giving in to the exhaustion. I could hear Noah moving around outside, the quiet sounds of him settling in for the night. The sounds were oddly comforting, a reminder that I wasn't alone out here.

My mind drifted over the day: Becca's fall, the waiting, the relief when Noah returned. The way he'd believed I could handle staying with Becca. The way he believed I could finish this hike.

The way I didn't want to say goodbye to him yet.

I pushed that thought away, too tired to untangle what it meant.

Tomorrow I'd keep hiking. That was enough of a decision for tonight.

Just before sleep pulled me under, I heard Becca's voice in my memory, fierce and certain: Don't you dare quit on me.

I won't, I thought. I'm going to finish this.

And somewhere in the back of my mind, a quieter thought: Not just for Becca.

But I was asleep before I could examine that any further.

Chapter 19

I woke to sunlight filtering through my tent fabric, my body still aching from yesterday's stress. For a moment I just lay there, listening to the forest waking up around me. Then I heard Noah moving around outside, the quiet sounds of him starting to break camp.

I sat up slowly and unzipped my tent. Noah glanced over and gave me a small smile.

"Morning. How'd you sleep?"

"Better than I expected," I admitted. Which was true. Exhaustion had pulled me under fast and kept me there.

We made quick work of breakfast and packing up. My body was sore and my mind still worried about Becca, but I'd made my decision last night. I was going to keep going. For Becca. For myself. And, though I wasn't quite ready to examine it too closely, because I wasn't ready to say goodbye to Noah yet.

We shouldered our packs and started down the trail together. The morning was cool and clear, and despite everything, I felt something like hope stirring in my chest.

Maybe I could do this after all.

***

Three days into hiking without Becca, I was starting to believe I actually could finish this trail.

The first day had been quiet, both of us processing what had happened. But by the second day, Noah had coaxed me into conversation about my master's program, and I'd found myself actually laughing when he told me about a disastrous camping trip in college where he'd managed to set up his tent directly over an anthill.

"You didn't notice?" I'd asked, incredulous.

"Not until two in the morning when I woke up covered in ants." He'd shuddered at the memory. "Worst night of my life. I had to sleep in my friend's car."

"That's what you get for not checking your campsite."

"Yeah, yeah. Rookie mistake."

By day three, we'd fallen into an easy rhythm. We'd hike for a few hours, stop for lunch, hike some more. Sometimes we talked, sometimes we didn't. The silences were comfortable, not loaded with tension like I'd feared they might be.

This morning, Noah had woken me up by lobbing a pinecone at my tent.

"Rise and shine, we're burning daylight!"

"It's barely dawn," I'd groaned.

"Exactly. Daylight. Which we are burning."

I'd emerged from my tent to find him grinning at me, holding out a cup of coffee like a peace offering. I'd tried to glare at him but couldn't quite manage it.

Now, several hours into the day's hike, I was feeling the accumulated weight of the miles. My pack dug into my shoulders, the straps cutting into spots that had finally started to callous over. My lower back throbbed with each step. I'd thought I was getting stronger, that my body was adapting, but today felt harder than it should.

I tried to adjust my shoulder straps for the hundredth time, looking for relief that didn't exist.

"You okay?" Noah glanced back at me. "You've been messing with those straps for the last mile."

"Yeah, just trying to find a comfortable position." I forced a smile. "One of those days, I guess."

We kept walking, but I could feel Noah's attention on me. That quiet observation he did, noticing things. It should have made me self-conscious, but mostly it just made me feel seen.

After another half mile, Noah stopped and shrugged off his pack.

"What are you doing?" I asked.

"Your pack is killing you. Let me take some weight."

My first instinct was to refuse. I'm fine, I can handle this, I don't need help. The automatic responses lined up in my mind, ready to deploy.

But my shoulders were screaming, and I was tired, and hadn't I just decided I needed to learn to trust people more?

Still. The offer made something uncomfortable twist in my chest. Scott's voice whispered in the back of my mind: This is how it starts. Small favors. Until you need them. Until you can't manage without them.

"I don't want to slow you down," I said carefully.

"You're not." Noah was already reaching for my pack. "Come on. What's the heaviest thing in here?"

"The tent, probably."

"Perfect. I'll take the tent. You keep everything else."

I hesitated, and Noah must have seen something in my face because his expression softened.

"Emma. It's just a tent. I'm not trying to take over your hike or prove you can't handle it. I'm just offering to help because we're hiking together and that's what people do." He paused. "And you can take it back literally whenever you want. If it feels weird, just say the word."

The way he said it, so straightforward and uncomplicated, made something loosen in my chest. This wasn't Scott making me dependent. This was just someone being kind.

I could accept kindness. I could let someone help me without losing myself.

"Okay," I said. "Just the tent."

My hands only shook a little as I helped him extract it from my pack. When I shouldered the pack again, the difference was immediate. My shoulders could straighten. I could breathe more deeply.

"Better?" Noah asked.

"Yeah." I managed a real smile this time. "Thank you."

"Anytime."

We started walking again, and I waited for the anxiety to kick in. For the feeling that I'd made a mistake, that I'd given up too much control, that this was the beginning of something dangerous.

But it didn't come. Instead, I just felt lighter. And grateful. And maybe, just maybe, like I could trust this.

Noah wasn't Scott. He'd proven that over and over in the past month. He gave me space when I needed it. He listened when I talked. He helped without making me feel weak. He was just genuinely kind, with no ulterior motives, no strings attached.

I needed to stop waiting for the other shoe to drop and just accept that some people were exactly who they appeared to be.

"So," Noah said after a while, breaking the comfortable silence. "Tell me more about your thesis. You said it's on anxiety disorders, right?"

And just like that, we were talking again. Easy conversation as we hiked, my pack lighter, my steps easier. The Pennsylvania forest stretched ahead, and for the first time since Becca's accident, I felt like I could actually enjoy it.

Maybe I was stronger than I thought. Maybe I could do hard things. Maybe I could even let people help me sometimes without it meaning I was weak.

By the time we stopped for lunch, I was actually laughing at one of Noah's stories about his emergency medicine rotation. We sat on a fallen log, passing trail mix back and forth, and I realized I was happy.

Despite everything, despite Becca being gone and my body aching and all my fears about not being enough, I was actually happy in this moment.

"Thanks for carrying the tent," I said.

"No problem." Noah smiled at me, warm and genuine. "Thanks for letting me."

I smiled back, and it felt like something had shifted. Not fixed, not perfect. But better.

I was learning. Slowly, maybe, but I was learning.

And that felt like enough for today.

***

When we arrived at Cove Mountain Shelter that evening, I spotted the familiar navy blue tent with an American flag sewn to the door. Beside it stood Maggie's purple tent.

"Well, look who it is!" Maggie called out, emerging from her tent with theatrical flair. "We were wondering if you guys would catch up."

Relief washed over me. It was good to see familiar faces, to have more than just Noah for company. Not that Noah wasn't good company, but there was something comforting about the trail family expanding again.

Elijah appeared from behind his tent, and they both looked happy to see us. We dropped our packs and I sank gratefully into my camp chair.

"Where's Becca?" Maggie asked, looking around. "Don't tell me she's finally faster than you."

My chest tightened. "She got hurt three days ago. Sprained her ankle pretty badly. They took her to the hospital."

"Oh no!" Maggie's face fell. "Is she okay?"

"Yeah, she'll be fine. But she couldn't keep hiking." I managed a smile. "She told me to finish for both of us."

"And you're actually doing it," Elijah said, looking impressed. "That's not easy."

"She's not doing it alone," Noah said, and there was something warm in his voice that made me glance over at him.

Maggie's eyes lit up with obvious delight. "Oh really? So you two are hiking together now?"

I felt my face heat. "We're going the same direction. It made sense."

"Uh huh." Maggie grinned. "Sure. That's the only reason."

"Maggie," I protested, but I was smiling despite myself.

"I'm just saying, when we left you guys at Boiling Springs, there was definitely something happening."

"There was not..." I started, but Noah cut me off.

"There was definitely something happening," he said calmly, and my heart did a little flip in my chest.

Maggie looked absolutely delighted. Elijah just smiled and shook his head. "Good for you guys."

I didn't know what to say to that, so I just ducked my head and tried not to grin too obviously.

Maggie enlisted my help with dinner, and we fell into easy conversation while we cooked. She told me about the shelters they'd stayed at, the people they'd met, a black bear that had wandered through their campsite two nights ago.

"It was just walking through like it owned the place," Maggie said. "Didn't even look at us. Elijah nearly had a heart attack."

"I did not," Elijah protested. "I was just being cautious."

"You climbed on top of the picnic table."

"Strategic positioning."

I laughed, and it felt good. Natural. Like maybe I was still capable of normal human interaction after all.

We ate together as darkness fell, the four of us passing food around and swapping trail stories. Noah told them about my superior chili-making skills, which made me roll my eyes.

"It was one meal," I said.

"Best meal I've had on the trail," Noah insisted.

"You're easy to impress."

"Or you're better at cooking than you think you are." He smiled at me, and there was something in his expression that made my stomach flutter.

Maggie caught my eye and waggled her eyebrows. I tried to glare at her but couldn't quite manage it.

After dinner, Maggie and Elijah retreated to their tents, and Noah and I stayed by the dying campfire. The night was cool and clear, stars visible through the canopy above us.

"Thanks for today," I said quietly. "For carrying the tent. I know I was weird about it at first."

"You weren't weird. You were careful." Noah poked at the fire with a stick. "There's a difference."

"Still. It helped. A lot."

"Good." He glanced over at me. "You doing okay? With Becca being gone?"

I considered the question honestly. "Yeah, actually. I mean, I miss her. But it's not as scary as I thought it would be. Hiking without her." I paused. "Maybe because I'm not really alone."

"You're not," Noah said, and the certainty in his voice made something warm bloom in my chest.

We sat in comfortable silence for a while, watching the fire burn down to embers. I felt tired in a good way, the kind of tired that comes from a full day of hiking and good company and laughter around a campfire.

"I should get some sleep," I said eventually, but I didn't move right away.

"Yeah, me too." Noah stood and offered me his hand to help me up.

I took it without hesitation, and he pulled me to my feet. For a moment we stood there, hands still linked, and I felt my breath catch.

"Goodnight, Emma," Noah said softly.

"Goodnight."

I headed for my tent, and as I crawled into my sleeping bag, I realized I was smiling. My body ached from the day's miles, but it was a good ache. An earned ache.

I thought about Maggie's teasing, about Noah saying "there was definitely something happening" like it was a fact he wasn't afraid to acknowledge. About his hand in mine and the way he'd looked at me by the firelight.

Maybe I was building something new out here. Not just completing a hike, but figuring out who I could be when I wasn't defined by fear. When I let people in just a little. When I accepted help and kindness without waiting for it to turn into something else.

I closed my eyes and felt sleep pulling at me, gentle and welcome. No anxiety about nightmares, no spiraling about tomorrow's decisions. Just contentment and the knowledge that I had people who cared about me, who believed in me.

For tonight, that was more than enough.

***

The rain had been relentless all day, turning the trail into a muddy gauntlet. By late afternoon, when we realized we'd missed a turn and added an extra hour to our day, I felt panic starting to claw up her throat.

Cold. Soaked through. Exhausted. And now lost.

This is your fault. You weren't paying attention. You slowed everyone down and now look what happened.

The voice in my head sounded like mine but the words were Scott's. They always were.

When Elijah sheepishly admitted he'd misread the trail markers, I braced myself. Waited for the explosion. The blame. The cold anger that would settle over everything and make the air feel poisonous.

Noah laughed.

Actually laughed.

"Well, at least we're getting our money's worth out of this section," he said, pulling out the map.

I stared at him, waiting. Any second now. The patience would crack. The real response would come; the heavy sigh, the pointed silence, the way Scott used to make his disappointment a physical thing I could feel pressing against my skin.

But Noah just helped Elijah figure out where we'd gone wrong and led us back without a single harsh word.

My hands were shaking. I told herself it was from the cold.

***

As evening wore on, the hostel filled with warmth and voices and laughter. I sat near the wood stove, finally feeling the cold leach out of my bones. My body ached in that satisfying way that came from a hard day's hike, and I was content to just sit and listen to the conversations flowing around me.

Maggie pulled out her tarot deck and started offering readings. I watched hikers take their turns, saw how Maggie asked questions more than gave answers, how she made people smile and think. It seemed like fun, a nice way to pass the evening.

"Emma?" Maggie's eyes found mine across the room. "Want to see what the cards have to say?"

My first instinct was a flicker of anxiety. Being the center of attention, being seen that closely. But I recognized the feeling for what it was, an old habit, not a real threat.

"Sure," I said, and meant it.

I settled across from Maggie, cross legged on the floor. She handed me the deck to shuffle, and the cards felt smooth and worn under my fingers.

"Just think about where you are right now," Maggie said. "What you're moving through."

I shuffled, handed the deck back. Maggie laid out three cards in a neat row.

"Past, present, future," she said, and turned over the first card.

Five of Cups. A figure in a black cloak standing before three spilled cups, two still standing behind them unnoticed.

"The past," Maggie said gently. "Loss and grief. But see these?" She pointed to the two cups still standing. "What remains. What you didn't lose, even when it felt like you lost everything."

I felt my throat tighten, but not in a bad way. It was accurate. I had lost something, or maybe let go of something that was hurting me. But I'd kept myself. I'd kept Becca. I'd kept moving forward.

The second card turned over. Four of Swords. A figure lying in rest, swords mounted on the wall nearby.

"The present. Taking time to heal. Recovering from battle." Maggie looked up at me with warm understanding. "The trail isn't just physical for you, is it?"

I shook my head, managed a small smile. "No. It's not."

"That's okay. That's what it's here for. Space to figure things out."

The third card flipped over, and I felt my breath catch. Two of Cups. Two figures facing each other, cups raised between them, a connection forming.

"The future," Maggie said, and her smile was knowing. "Partnership. Connection built on mutual respect and genuine care. Someone who sees you clearly and chooses to walk beside you anyway."

My eyes flicked to Noah before I could stop myself. He was across the room talking to Elijah, but as if he felt my gaze, he looked over. Our eyes met and he smiled, warm and genuine.

I looked back at Maggie, felt my face heat.

Her grin was delighted but gentle. "Or maybe they're just cards. The real magic is in what we choose to do with the possibilities they show us."

"Thank you," I said, and meant it. "That was really nice."

"Anytime, honey."

I moved back to my spot by the stove, but this time the flutter in my chest wasn't anxiety. It was something else. Something that felt almost like hope.

I thought about the cards. Past, present, future. Loss, healing, connection. It made sense in a way I hadn't expected. I was healing out here. Learning to trust again, learning to accept help, learning that not everyone who offered kindness wanted something in return.

Learning that maybe I could let someone walk beside me without losing myself.

Noah caught my eye again from across the room and raised his eyebrows in question. You okay?

I nodded and smiled. Yeah. I'm okay.

And for once, I actually meant it.

***

By late afternoon, we arrived at Crystal Mountain Campsite. My arms had been itching for the last few miles, and when I finally looked down at them in the fading light, my stomach dropped.

Red welts. Spreading up my forearms.

"Hey Noah?" I called out as I dropped my pack. "Can you look at something?"

He came over immediately, and I held out my arms. His expression shifted to concern.

"Poison ivy," he said, examining the rash without touching it. "Bad case. You remember that overgrown section yesterday afternoon?"

I did remember. I'd been so focused on the trail ahead that I hadn't paid attention to what I was pushing through. "Yeah. I didn't even notice."

"It happens. I've got hydrocortisone cream and Benadryl. That should help."

Maggie emerged from setting up her tent and came over to look. "Oh honey, that looks miserable."

"I have jewelweed salve if you want to try a natural remedy first," she offered.

"Thanks, Maggie. I'll try that."

We tried the jewelweed salve first, but after an hour, the itching was still intense. Noah quietly handed me the hydrocortisone cream and Benadryl at our next break.

"Thanks," I said, taking them gratefully.

Within thirty minutes, the itching subsided significantly. But the Benadryl brought a drowsiness that made my limbs feel heavy and my thoughts fuzzy. I kept stumbling over roots I normally would have stepped over easily.

By early afternoon, I was struggling. Every step felt like pushing through molasses.

"I need to slow down," I admitted. "The Benadryl is hitting me pretty hard."

"My sister's meeting me at the overlook in about five miles," Elijah said. "She's doing a day hike in and we planned to have lunch together. We should probably keep our pace up to meet her on time."

"You guys go ahead," I said. "I'll catch up tomorrow when this wears off."

"I'll stay back with you," Noah offered. "No point in you hiking alone when you're drowsy."

I felt a flicker of my old instinct to refuse, to insist I'd be fine alone. But honestly, hiking while this medicated wasn't the safest idea. And I was learning to accept help without making it complicated.

"Okay," I said. "Thanks."

"We'll see you two up the trail," Maggie said warmly. "Hope you feel better, Emma."

They gathered their gear and headed out, and soon it was just Noah and me in the quiet clearing.

"Why don't you rest?" Noah suggested. "The Benadryl will probably knock you out for a few hours. When you wake up, we can figure out dinner."

"That sounds perfect."

I crawled into my tent, grateful for the excuse to lie down. The relief of being horizontal was immediate. My body was exhausted, my arms still itched despite the cream, and the drowsiness was pulling me under.

But as I drifted off, I felt surprisingly calm. Noah was outside setting up camp. I was safe. This was okay.

Sleep came quickly, heavy and dreamless.

***

I slept for hours, pulled under by exhaustion and Benadryl into a heavy, dreamless void. When I finally woke, disoriented and groggy, the light filtering through my tent was golden and slanted. Late afternoon, maybe early evening.

I lay there for a moment, listening to Noah moving around outside. The quiet sounds of camp tasks being done. Part of me felt safer knowing he was there. That feeling scared me, but not as much as it would have a few weeks ago.

I unzipped my tent and emerged into the cooling air. Noah had set up both our tents properly, arranged the camp chairs, and was now tending something on the camp stove.

"Hey," he said, looking up with a smile. "How are you feeling?"

I looked down at my arms. The rash was still angry and red, but the itching had dulled to a manageable level. "Better. Still looks terrible, but better."

"Good. You should probably reapply the hydrocortisone before dinner."

I nodded and ducked back into my tent to do just that. When I emerged again, Noah had plated up beans and rice.

"Thank you," I said, taking the bowl. "For all of this. For staying."

"Of course."

We ate in comfortable silence for a while. I watched the way the evening light filtered through the trees, the way Noah seemed completely at ease out here. There was something I'd been thinking about since the tarot reading, since Maggie had looked at me with such knowing encouragement.

I set down my bowl, my heart starting to race. "Noah, can I tell you something?"

He looked at me, patient and open. "Of course."

I pressed my palms against my thighs, trying to ground myself. "Two years ago, I was in a relationship. With someone named Scott."

I watched his face, but found only quiet attention.

"It was bad." The words felt inadequate, too small. "He seemed great at first. Really great. But then things changed. Or maybe they didn't change, maybe I just finally saw who he really was." I stopped, tried again. "He was controlling. Manipulative. He'd twist things until I didn't know what was real anymore, until I thought everything was my fault."

My hands were shaking. I gripped my thighs to steady them. "And then he got violent."

I heard Noah's sharp intake of breath but kept going, needing to get it all out.

"I stayed longer than I should have. I kept thinking if I just tried harder, if I just didn't make him angry..." My voice cracked. "But it kept getting worse. And I finally left."

The silence that followed felt heavy but not uncomfortable. I forced myself to look at Noah.

His expression was full of compassion. "Emma. I'm so sorry that happened to you."

I nodded, feeling tears prick at my eyes. "I thought I was past it. I thought I'd dealt with it, moved on. But being out here, I've realized I've just been existing. Going through the motions. Too afraid to let anyone in." I managed a shaky smile. "That's why I'm like this. Why I panic when people help me. Why I keep waiting for kindness to turn into something else."

"Thank you for telling me," Noah said quietly. "I know that wasn't easy."

I let out a breath I didn't know I'd been holding. "It wasn't. And part of me is panicking right now that I told you. That you're going to think I'm broken or too much work or..."

"I don't think that," Noah said firmly. "Emma, you survived something awful. That doesn't make you damaged. It makes you strong."

"I don't feel strong."

"You hiked hundreds of miles. You kept going when Becca got hurt. You're sitting here telling me something that clearly terrifies you to talk about." He leaned forward slightly. "That's strength."

I felt more tears slip down my cheeks and wiped at them. "I like spending time with you," I whispered, feeling vulnerable saying it out loud. "I just needed you to understand why I'm so complicated about it."

"I like spending time with you too," Noah said simply. "And nothing you just told me changes that."

The simplicity of it hit me hard. Not pity. Not a mission to fix me. Just genuine care.

We sat as the light faded, and I felt something shift in my chest. I'd told him, and he hadn't run. He was still here, still looking at me the same way.

Maybe I could trust this. Maybe I could trust him.

As darkness settled over the clearing, I noticed something at the edge of the trees. Tiny points of light, appearing and disappearing in slow, graceful patterns.

"Fireflies," I breathed.

Noah followed my gaze. "I haven't seen them in years."

They emerged from the tree line in clusters, their bioluminescence creating a soft, pulsing glow against the darkness. I watched, transfixed, as they danced through the air. Appearing, disappearing, appearing again.

"They're beautiful," I said softly.

I thought about what Maggie had said during the tarot reading. About healing, about connection, about walking beside someone. And watching the fireflies, I had a thought that felt both profound and freeing.

The fireflies didn't fight the darkness. They existed within it. They carried their own light, created beauty precisely because of the contrast. They didn't wait for perfect conditions. They just glowed anyway.

Maybe that's what I'm supposed to do. Not wait until I'm completely healed to live. Just carry my own light through the dark.

"What are you thinking?" Noah asked quietly.

I considered deflecting, but I'd already chosen vulnerability tonight. Already taken the risk of letting him in.

"I'm thinking the fireflies have it right," I said slowly. "They don't wait for perfect conditions. They just glow anyway. Even in the dark." I paused. "Maybe I don't have to wait until I'm not scared anymore to try. To live. To let people in."

The words felt like a promise. One I wasn't entirely sure I could keep, but that I wanted to try.

"You don't," Noah agreed softly. "You really don't."

"That terrifies me," I admitted.

"I know. But maybe that's okay."

We sat in silence, watching the fireflies dance. My old instinct was to spiral, to catalog all the ways this could go wrong. But I recognized the pattern now, and I chose to let it go. Chose to just sit here in this moment, watching something beautiful with someone I was learning to trust.

My exhaustion returned, settling deep into my bones. I stood, stretching carefully.

"I should get some sleep. Long day tomorrow if this rash cooperates."

"Hopefully you'll feel better in the morning." Noah stood too.

I paused before heading to my tent. "Thank you. For listening. For staying. For just being you."

"Anytime," Noah said, and I believed him.

I crawled into my tent and lay in my sleeping bag, and felt something unexpected. Not peace exactly, but something close to it. I'd told Noah about Scott, and he was still here. Still kind. Still genuine.

I could still see the faint glow of fireflies through the tent fabric, dancing their patient dance outside. I closed my eyes and held onto that image. Light in the darkness. Not fighting it, just glowing anyway.

I felt a flicker of anxiety, that old familiar fear trying to take hold. What if you're wrong about him? What if this is a mistake?

But I recognized it for what it was now. Just fear. Just old patterns trying to protect me in ways I didn't need anymore.

Noah wasn't Scott. I knew that. And maybe, just maybe, I was ready to believe it too.

I thought about the fireflies, how they glowed even though darkness surrounded them. How they didn't wait for safety to show their light.

I could do that too. I was doing it. Scared but moving forward anyway.

Sleep came easier than it had in days. And in my dreams, fireflies danced at the edges. Small points of light that refused to go out.

Even in the darkness. Especially in the darkness.

Chapter 20

I woke to the sound of Noah rustling near his tent. I lay still for a moment, eyes closed, and felt last night come rushing back. I'd told him about Scott. About the abuse. I'd cried in front of him.

But as I replayed it, I realized it didn't feel as terrifying as I'd expected. He'd listened. He'd stayed. And I'd slept peacefully for the first time in days.

Through the mesh window, I could see Noah crouched by his pack, moving quietly. Trying not to wake me.

He caught me watching.

"You're awake," he said softly.

"Hard to sleep past dawn out here." I unzipped my sleeping bag and reached for my fleece. The morning air had a bite to it. "What are you doing up so early?"

"Couldn't sleep." He smiled, and there was something shy in it. "Happy birthday."

The words landed strangely. I'd almost forgotten what day it was. Out here, time moved differently.

"How did you know?" I started, then remembered. "The license photo."

"The terrible license photo," he corrected, grinning. "Which isn't terrible, by the way."

I crawled out of the tent, my body stiff from yesterday's hiking. "I made coffee," Noah said, gesturing to his camp stove. "Well, instant coffee. But it's hot."

"Thanks." I accepted the metal cup, wrapping both hands around it. The warmth felt good.

We sat on a fallen log, and I tried to settle into the moment. Birthdays had become complicated over the past few years, but this one felt different. Quieter. Like maybe it could just be a day.

"You okay?" Noah asked.

"Yeah. Just, birthdays are kind of weird for me."

"We don't have to make it a thing," he said immediately. "I just wanted you to know I remembered."

The relief was instant. "Thank you. I appreciate that."

"Want to hike to the Vermont border? That can be the whole event."

"That sounds perfect."

We broke camp efficiently, and I felt surprisingly normal. Not anxious, not overthinking. Just ready to hike.

***

The trail to the Vermont border was easy, relatively flat, with morning sun slanting through the trees. I let myself fall into the rhythm of walking, grateful for the movement and the quiet companionship.

When we reached the sign, "VERMONT" carved into weathered wood, I let my pack slide to the ground.

"Another state," Noah said. "Number five."

"Five down, two to go." I touched the sign, the wood smooth under my fingers. It felt good to mark the progress. To see how far I'd come.

"We should get a photo," Noah said, pulling out his phone.

We took the obligatory pictures, both of us grinning at the timer. The kind of photos I'd show Becca later. Proof I was actually doing this.

When we settled on a flat rock for a snack, Noah reached into his pocket.

"So, I do have something for you," he said. "It's not much."

He held out his hand. In his palm was a smooth gray stone, about the size of a quarter. When I took it, I saw he'd scratched a word into the surface: Brave.

My throat went tight. I stared at the stone, turning it over in my fingers.

"I found it a few days ago near that stream," Noah said. "And I kept thinking about how you show up every day. Even when you're scared. That's brave."

I felt tears prick at my eyes. For a split second, my old instinct kicked in. Gifts mean expectations. But I recognized the thought for what it was: an old pattern, not the truth. Noah wasn't Scott. This stone wasn't manipulation. It was just kindness.

"Thank you," I managed, my voice rough. "This is really special. The best birthday gift I've gotten in years."

I meant it. I slipped the stone into my pocket, feeling its weight settle there. A reminder. A talisman.

We sat quietly, sharing trail mix. The morning was peaceful, the kind of quiet that felt comfortable rather than loaded.

"Can I ask you something?" Noah said eventually.

"Sure."

"You said birthdays are weird for you. Is that because of your ex?"

I hesitated, then nodded. "Scott used to make a big deal out of my birthday. Expensive dinners, elaborate gifts. It seemed sweet at first, but it was always about the performance. About showing everyone what a great boyfriend he was." I paused. "And if I didn't react the right way, if I seemed tired or ungrateful, he'd get hurt. Or angry. He'd pout for days, or drink, and eventually I'd apologize for ruining my own birthday."

"That sounds like manipulation," Noah said quietly.

Hearing someone else name it felt validating. "He was very good at making me feel like everything was my fault. Like I was too sensitive, too demanding. I spent so much energy trying to be easier. Smaller. Less."

The words came more easily than I expected. "I'd analyze my own reactions, watch myself from outside my body. I used all my psychology training against myself. Pathologized my own responses instead of questioning his behavior."

"How long were you together?" Noah asked.

"A year and a half. Maybe a little more." It felt both endless and impossibly short. "It took me so long to leave. The red flags were there, but I kept thinking I could understand it away. Fix it."

"You're not responsible for fixing someone else," Noah said.

"I know that. Intellectually." I rubbed my thumb over the stone in my hand, feeling the word carved into it. "But knowing something and feeling it are different."

"Yeah," Noah said. "They really are."

There was something in his voice, a recognition. I glanced at him, saw the shadow cross his face.

"Your ex," I said. "Susan. You said she cheated."

Noah nodded. "Found out in February. The worst part wasn't even the cheating. It was realizing how long I'd ignored the signs because I didn't want to deal with my dad's reaction."

"Your dad liked her?"

"Loved her. She was 'appropriate.'" He said it with audible quotes. "And I just went along with it. Even when I knew it wasn't right. I tried to fix it instead of accepting we weren't supposed to be together."

I heard the parallel. Both of us contorting ourselves for other people's expectations.

"The interview at Brown," I said carefully. "That's something."

Noah's expression shifted, hope and dread mixing together. "One month after we finish this hike. If we finish." He paused. "My dad doesn't know about it."

"You haven't told him?"

"No. I'm still officially starting at Kent in July. The podiatry residency. Everything he wants." His voice went flat. "I don't even know why I'm doing the Brown interview. It's not like I can actually choose it."

I heard what he wasn't saying: I'm twenty-six and I still can't tell my father no.

"What do you want?" I asked.

He met my eyes. "I want to show up to that interview. To not let him talk me out of it." His voice was quiet. "And part of me still wants to just make him happy. Even though I know it would make me miserable."

The vulnerability in that admission made my chest ache. I understood it completely, that weight of wanting to be good enough.

"The interview is a start," I said quietly. "Even if you don't know what comes after."

"Maybe." Noah didn't sound convinced. "Or maybe I'm just going through the motions so I can tell myself I tried."

"For what it's worth," I said, "I think you'd be an incredible psychiatrist."

Noah's smile was small but genuine. "Thanks. That means a lot."

We sat in comfortable silence. I turned the stone over in my hands, feeling its weight. Brave. Maybe I was. Maybe showing up every day, even scared, even uncertain, was enough.

I thought about the fireflies from last night. About carrying your own light through the darkness. It still felt true in the morning light.

"We should probably keep moving," Noah said eventually. "Unless you want to camp here all day."

I laughed. "No, let's go. Vermont isn't going to hike itself."

As I stood and shouldered my pack, I felt the stone settle in my pocket, close where I could reach it. A reminder that I was braver than I thought. That I was making progress, even when it didn't feel like it.

We crossed into Vermont together, and I felt something shift. Not healed, not fixed. But maybe, just maybe, moving in the right direction.

I was still walking forward. And today, that felt like enough.

Chapter 21

The day had been brutal. Not in any single dramatic way, but in the grinding accumulation of small difficulties: steep climbs, rocky descents, heat that pressed down like a weight. By the time we reached the shelter, a three-sided wooden structure with a tin roof, my legs were shaking with exhaustion.

Noah dropped his pack with a grunt. "I vote we stay here tonight. I know it's only four o'clock, but I'm done."

"God, yes." I let my own pack slide to the ground, then sat heavily on the shelter's wooden floor. Every muscle ached. "I don't think I could walk another mile if you paid me."

We set about our evening routine with the efficiency of practice: filtering water, setting up sleeping pads, hanging our food bags. The shelter was empty except for us, unusual for late August, but I was grateful for the solitude.

As the sun lowered and the forest softened into shadow, we sat side by side on the edge of the shelter, legs dangling, sharing a bag of trail mix. The silence between them was comfortable. Easy. That itself felt remarkable, that quiet could feel safe instead of tense.

"Can I ask you something?" Noah said eventually.

"Sure."

"Your ex. Scott." He paused, choosing words carefully. "You said he was controlling. Manipulative. But you don't really talk about how it ended. How you got out."

My chest tightened. I'd known this conversation was coming. Had been both dreading it and needing it. My fingers found the stone in my pocket, Brave, and I held it like a talisman.

"Why are you asking now?"

"Because I'm falling for you," Noah said simply. "And I want to know you. All of you. Not just the parts you think are safe to share."

The honesty of it made my throat hurt. I looked at him, his profile against the darkening sky, and felt the weight of what I'd been holding back.

"It's not a good story," I said quietly.

"I didn't think it would be."

I took a breath. Let it out slowly. "Can I tell you something first?" Noah said. "About my dad. About why I'm really out here."

I looked at him, surprised by the shift.

"Last Christmas, we had a huge fight. About my future, about the practice, all of it. And at one point he said I was wasting my potential. That I was disappointing him. That if I didn't take over the practice, I was essentially throwing away everything he'd worked for. And my mom just sat there. Silent. Like she always does."

"That must have been awful."

"The worst part was that I almost caved. Right there, I almost just said, 'Okay, fine, I'll do podiatry, I'll take over the practice, I'll be exactly who you want me to be.' Because that would have been easier than living with his disappointment." Noah picked at the wood grain of the shelter floor. "I'm twenty-six years old and I still can't stand up to him. Even now, with the Brown interview coming up, I haven't told him. I'm just hiding. Hoping I can figure out what to do before I have to actually face him."

I heard the shame in his voice. The self-judgment. I recognized it intimately.

"You're not hiding," I said. "You're giving yourself time to get strong enough."

Noah looked at me. "Is that what you did? With Scott?"

And there it was. The opening I both wanted and feared.

I stared out at the forest, at the trees blurring into darkness. My fingers tightened around the stone.

"I left him," I said. "Eventually. But it took something really bad to make me do it."

Noah waited. Didn't push.

"He got me pregnant." The words came out flat, clinical. "I didn't want to be. I was on birth control, but it happened. And when I told him, he was angry. He wanted me to end it. Started drinking more. Getting angrier. And one night he tried to throw me down the stairs."

I heard Noah's sharp intake of breath but didn't look at him. Couldn't.

"He was drunk. Screaming at me. And I realized he was trying to make me miscarry. That he didn't think I would actually go through with an abortion. He wanted control. And I had an abortion a week later. Because I knew if I was pregnant, I'd never be able to leave him. He'd use it to keep me tied to him forever."

"Emma," Noah said softly.

"I'm not done." I needed to get it all out now, before I lost my nerve. "After I left, he wouldn't stop calling. Showing up at my apartment. I reported him to the police and they warned him to stay away. And then he called me one night, late. Said he'd tried to hang himself. That he'd put the noose around his neck but the rope broke. That he needed me, that he'd die without me."

The shame of what came next was thick in my throat. "And I went to his apartment. Took him to the psychiatric hospital."

"The social worker there was really kind. She told me the suicide attempt was manipulation. That the noose wasn't even tied properly. She helped me set boundaries. Told me not to see him again." I clasped my hands together to still their shaking. "His mother called me. Told me Scott was sick. That he had a history of this, prior attempts, prior hospitalizations I didn't know about. She told me I deserved better, that I should move on. And I tried. I went back to my life. Started therapy. And for a few weeks, there was nothing. Silence. And I thought maybe it was over."

I closed my eyes.

"And then Officer Turner called me. The cop who'd warned Scott to stay away. He said Scott was dead. That he'd hanged himself. That his mother found him."

The words hung in the air between us. I felt like I was falling.

"I'm sorry," Noah said quietly. "Emma, I'm so sorry."

"That was two years ago." I forced myself to continue. "Two years, and I still don't know how to feel about it. Because I'm relieved he's gone. Relieved I don't have to be afraid anymore. But I also feel responsible. Like if I'd just tried harder, been better, maybe..."

"No." Noah's voice was firm. "No, Emma. You are not responsible for his choices. You know that, right?"

"Intellectually, yes." I finally looked at him, tears blurring my vision. "But knowing something and feeling it are different things."

He reached for my hand, and I let him take it.

"I keep thinking about the baby," I whispered. "The one I didn't have. And I know having the abortion was the right choice. The only choice. But I still grieve it sometimes. This whole alternate life I didn't live."

"That's allowed," Noah said. "All of it's allowed. The relief and the grief and the guilt that doesn't make logical sense. You don't have to have it all figured out."

I wiped at my eyes with my free hand. "I haven't told anyone the whole story. Becca knows most of it, but not all the details. My therapist knows. And now you."

"Thank you for telling me."

I laughed, but it came out broken. "You might want to run now. I'm a mess, Noah. I have nightmares. Panic attacks. I don't know if I'm ready for this. For you. For someone being kind to me without it being a trap."

"I can't promise I'll never hurt you," Noah said carefully. "I can't promise I'm perfect. But I can promise I'm not him. And I can promise that if I do something that scares you or triggers you, you can tell me. And I'll listen."

I searched his face in the near darkness. Looking for pity, horror, discomfort. But all I saw was steadiness. Compassion.

"I'm still falling for you," Noah said quietly. "If you're worried that this changes things. It doesn't. Not in the way you think."

"How can it not?"

"Because this is part of who you are. What you survived. And Emma, you're incredible. You left an abusive relationship. You had the strength to choose yourself. You're hiking the Appalachian Trail. You're out here doing something hard because you wanted to prove to yourself you could. That's not a mess. That's courage."

I shook my head. "I don't feel courageous. I feel broken."

"You can be both." He squeezed my hand. "And for what it's worth, I don't think you're broken. I think you're healing. There's a difference."

I wanted to believe him. And sitting here, his hand warm in mine, his eyes steady on my face, maybe I could start to.

"I'm scared," I admitted. "Of wanting this. Of letting myself fall for you and then losing you. Or worse, of it turning into something like what I had before."

"I'm scared too," Noah said. "I'm scared I'm going to disappoint you. That I'll go back to Indiana and cave to my father's pressure and become someone you don't recognize. I'm scared that I'm not brave enough to choose what I want instead of what's expected of me."

I heard the vulnerability in that admission. The fear that mirrored my own.

"I think you're braver than you give yourself credit for," I said softly.

"Same to you."

We sat in the darkness, hands clasped, both of us trembling a little from the weight of what we'd shared. The night sounds of the forest filled the silence: crickets, the rustle of leaves, something small moving through the underbrush.

"Can I ask you something?" Noah said after a while.

"Yeah."

"Is there anything I should know? Things that might trigger you? I don't want to accidentally..."

I appreciated the thoughtfulness of it. "Raised voices. Sudden movements when I'm not expecting them. Being grabbed, even playfully." I thought about it. "Drinking. Heavy drinking, I mean. I know you have a beer sometimes in town, and that's fine. But if you got drunk, I don't think I could handle that."

"I won't," Noah said immediately. "I don't really drink much anyway, but I won't. Not around you."

"You don't have to change who you are..."

"I'm not. I'm just telling you what I can do. To make you feel safe." He shifted slightly, his shoulder brushing mine. "What else?"

"I don't know. I'm still figuring it out." I laughed, but there were still tears on my cheeks. "I'm a work in progress."

"Aren't we all."

We sat quietly for a while longer. I felt wrung out, exhausted in a way that had nothing to do with the miles we'd hiked. But alongside the exhaustion was something else. Relief, maybe. The weight of secrets I'd been carrying was lighter now that I'd shared them.

For a moment, my old instinct kicked in. What if you just ruined everything? What if he's only being nice and tomorrow he'll be different?

But I recognized the thought for what it was: fear, not truth. Noah had listened without judgment. He'd shared his own vulnerabilities. He'd said he was still falling for me, even knowing all of this.

I could choose to believe him. I could choose to trust this.

"I should probably try to sleep," I said finally. "Today was long."

"Yeah." Noah squeezed my hand once more before letting go. "Thank you for trusting me with all of that."

We set up our sleeping bags in the shelter. I lay down, feeling raw but not regretful. Vulnerable but not destroyed.

I pulled the stone from my pocket, ran my thumb over the word etched into its surface. Brave.

Maybe it was brave to tell the truth. Maybe it was brave to let someone in, even when it terrified me.

I thought about the fireflies, about carrying light through darkness. About not waiting for perfect conditions to try.

I'd told Noah everything, and he was still here. Still kind. Still falling for me.

That had to mean something.

My eyes grew heavy, and for once, sleep came without a fight. I was exhausted, yes. Emotionally spent. But I also felt something I hadn't expected.

Peace. Or at least the beginning of it.

I closed my eyes and let myself rest, the stone warm in my hand, Noah's steady breathing a comfort in the darkness.

***

Morning came slowly, the shelter gradually filling with pale gray light. I woke to find Noah already up, sitting at the edge of the shelter with his camp stove, making coffee.

He looked over when he heard me stirring. "Morning."

"Morning." My voice came out rough. I sat up, and immediately felt last night settle over me. The weight of everything I'd told him.

Noah poured coffee into my mug and brought it over. He sat down beside me, not quite as close as usual, and I felt a flutter of anxiety.

"Thanks," I said, wrapping my hands around the mug.

We were quiet for a moment. The silence felt different from yesterday, more careful, and I didn't know if that was coming from him or from me.

"How'd you sleep?" Noah asked.

"Okay. You?"

"Not great." He paused, then looked at me directly. "I kept thinking about everything you told me."

My stomach clenched. Here it comes. "Noah, if you need to—"

"Let me finish." His voice was gentle but firm. "I kept thinking about it because I wanted to make sure I said this right. Emma, thank you for trusting me with all of that. I know it wasn't easy to tell me."

I nodded, not trusting my voice.

"And I want you to know that nothing you said changes how I feel about you. I meant what I said last night. I'm still falling for you."

Relief washed over me, but alongside it came confusion. "Then why does it feel weird this morning?"

Noah let out a breath. "Honestly? Because I'm trying to figure out how to be here for you without making you feel like I'm treating you differently. But maybe I am treating you a little differently. You told me things that trigger you, things that scare you. I'm trying to be aware of that."

"But I don't want you to be afraid of me," I said quietly.

"I'm not afraid of you. I'm afraid of hurting you accidentally." He set down his coffee. "Emma, what you went through with Scott, it was really bad. And I'm still processing that. Not because I think less of you, but because I care about you and I want to understand."

The honesty of it made my throat tight. "I'm scared I told you too much. That now you see me as this broken thing you have to be careful around."

"You're not broken." Noah turned to face me more fully. "But you did go through something traumatic. And yeah, that's part of who you are now. That doesn't make you less. It just means I need to be thoughtful. Is that okay?"

I thought about it. Really thought about it, instead of just spiraling. "I think I'm scared that thoughtful turns into pity. Or that you'll start seeing me as a victim instead of just... me."

"I see you," Noah said simply. "All of you. The parts that are healing and the parts that are healed and the parts that are still figuring it out. And I like all of it."

I felt tears prick at my eyes. "I'm sorry if I'm being weird about this. I just don't know how to do this. How to be vulnerable with someone and not immediately panic about it."

"You don't have to have it figured out." Noah reached for my hand, and I let him take it. "We'll figure it out together. But Emma, you have to talk to me. If I do something that bothers you or scares you, tell me. Don't just spiral about it."

"How did you know I was spiraling?"

He smiled slightly. "Because I've been hiking with you for weeks. I know your faces."

Despite everything, I felt myself smile back. "Okay. I can do that. Talk to you instead of spiraling."

"And I'll try not to overthink everything I do around you. Deal?"

"Deal."

We sat there for a moment, hands linked, and I felt something settle. It wasn't perfect, and I was still scared, but it was honest. We were being honest with each other.

"For what it's worth," I said, "I'm glad I told you. Even if it's a little scary now."

"Me too."

We finished our coffee and started breaking camp. The awkwardness from earlier had lifted, replaced by something more comfortable. Not quite back to where we'd been before, but somewhere new. Somewhere that felt like it might actually be okay.

As we shouldered our packs and started down the trail, Noah fell into step beside me.

"So," he said, "ready to hike into Maine?"

"Maine?" I blinked. "How close are we?"

"We could cross the border in a couple days if we keep up the pace."

The realization hit me. We were actually going to finish this. After everything, all the miles and the fears and the growth, we were almost there.

"Yeah," I said, and meant it. "I'm ready."

We walked together into the morning, and for the first time since the confession, I felt like we were actually walking toward something instead of away from it.

***

The next two weeks passed in a rhythm I'd never quite found before on the trail. The miles accumulated, the terrain grew more challenging as we pushed into Maine, but something had shifted. I'd stopped waiting for the other shoe to drop.

Noah and I fell into an easy partnership. We'd hike side by side when the trail allowed, or single file when it didn't, but always together. We talked about everything: his nervousness about the Brown interview, my plans to start my master's program in the fall, the books we'd read, the places we wanted to see. And sometimes we didn't talk at all, just walked in comfortable silence broken only by birdsong and the crunch of our boots on the trail.

One afternoon, crossing a rocky stream, my foot slipped on a moss-covered stone. I windmilled my arms, about to go down hard, when Noah's hand shot out and caught my elbow.

"I've got you," he said, steadying me until I found my footing.

"Thanks." I squeezed his hand before letting go, and the moment passed without anxiety, without spiraling. Just gratitude.

That night, camped on a ridge with a view of mountains stretching endlessly north, Noah pointed out constellations while I leaned against his shoulder. The contact felt natural now. Safe.

"I can't believe we're almost done," I said.

"You sound disappointed."

"Maybe a little." I looked up at the stars. "Out here, everything feels simple. I'm worried about what happens when we go back to real life."

"Real life doesn't have to be scary," Noah said quietly. "We'll figure it out."

I wanted to believe him. And sitting there under the stars, with his warmth beside me and Maine stretched out ahead, I almost did.

The trail grew steeper as we approached the final stretch. The terrain turned wild and beautiful, all granite peaks and alpine lakes. My body was stronger than it had ever been. I could hike twenty miles without the bone-deep exhaustion I'd felt in Pennsylvania. I could carry my full pack without my shoulders screaming. I'd earned this strength, step by step, mile by mile.

And somewhere along the way, I'd stopped thinking of myself as broken. Started thinking of myself as someone who'd survived. Someone who was still here, still choosing to show up, still learning how to be brave.

The stone Noah had given me stayed in my pocket, a quiet reminder. I didn't need to hold it anymore to remember what it said. I was starting to believe it.

We were two days from Katahdin when we ran into Maggie and Elijah at a shelter, their familiar tents a welcome sight.

"Look who made it!" Maggie called out, pulling me into a hug. "I knew you would."

"We're almost there," I said, and felt the truth of it settle in my chest. "We're actually going to finish."

That evening, the four of us sat around a small campfire, swapping stories from the miles we'd hiked separately. Elijah told us about a moose encounter that had him climbing a tree. Maggie described a thunderstorm so fierce she'd thought her tent might blow away. Noah recounted the time I'd mistaken a boulder for a bear and nearly given myself a heart attack.

"In my defense," I protested, laughing, "it was dusk and the boulder was moving."

"It was not moving," Noah said.

"The shadows made it look like it was moving!"

Maggie grinned at us. "You two are good together."

I felt my face heat but didn't deny it. Because we were good together. Whatever happened after the trail ended, that much was true.

"Tomorrow we tackle Katahdin," Elijah said. "You ready for the final push?"

I looked at Noah, who smiled at me. Then at Maggie and Elijah, this trail family that had become so important. And finally at the darkening sky above us, stars beginning to emerge.

"Yeah," I said. "I'm ready."

***

The day began in darkness, all four of us gathering outside the hostel at 4:30 AM. The air was cold enough that I could see my breath, and I wrapped my hands around the travel mug of coffee the hostel owner had pressed into my palm.

"You sure about this?" he'd asked when we'd told him our plan yesterday. "Katahdin's no joke. And that route you're talking about, the Knife Edge, that's expert level."

"We're sure," Noah had said, and I'd nodded, even though my stomach was churning with nerves.

Now, standing in the predawn darkness with headlamps cutting through the gloom, I felt the weight of what we were about to do.

This was it. The final push. The mountain that had been our goal for months.

"Everyone good?" Elijah asked, adjusting his pack straps.

A chorus of affirmatives. I caught Noah's eye and he smiled at me, and some of the nerves settled. We were doing this together.

The trail started gently enough, a gradual ascent through thick forest, our headlamps bobbing like fireflies in the dark. I fell into the rhythm of it: step, breathe, step, breathe. My legs were strong now, months of hiking having built muscle and endurance I'd never had before. I thought about the first day on the trail, how I'd doubted I could make it a week. And here I was, climbing the final mountain.

As dawn broke, the forest began to thin, and we emerged above the tree line. The world opened up around us, vast and rocky and breathtaking. I stopped, turning to take it in: mountains rolling away in every direction, the sky shifting from deep blue to pink to gold.

"Holy shit," Noah breathed beside me.

"Yeah," I agreed.

We climbed higher, the terrain growing steeper and more rugged. Around mid-morning, we reached a junction where the trail split.

Maggie studied the map, then looked up at the two routes ahead. "Okay, so the main trail continues along the ridge. It's longer but more gradual. And then there's the Knife Edge." She pointed to a narrow ridge of rock that looked impossibly steep, impossibly exposed. "That's the direct route to the summit, but it's technical. Scrambling, some exposure."

"By exposure, you mean..." I started.

"Drop-offs on both sides," Elijah said. "Not for the faint of heart."

I felt my pulse quicken. But beneath the nerves was something else: a pull. A desire to do the hard thing.

"I want to try it," I heard myself say. "The Knife Edge."

Noah looked at me, surprised. "You sure?"

"No. But I want to do it anyway." I met his eyes. "If you'll come with me."

His smile was slow and warm. "Always."

Maggie looked between us, then at Elijah. "We old folks will take the easier route. Meet you at the summit?"

"You sure?" I felt a flicker of doubt.

"We're sure," Maggie said firmly. She pulled me into a quick hug. "You've got this, honey. Trust yourself. Trust each other."

I nodded against her shoulder, breathing in her familiar scent: sunscreen and sage and something earthy. When I pulled back, Elijah gave me a solemn nod.

"See you at the top," he said.

And then it was just Noah and me, standing at the base of the Knife Edge, looking up at the impossible rocky spine stretching toward the sky.

"Ready?" Noah asked.

I took a breath. Let it out. "Ready."

The climb was immediately more challenging than anything we'd done before. The Knife Edge was exactly what it sounded like: a narrow ridge of granite with steep drop-offs on both sides. I had to use my hands as much as my feet, scrambling over boulders, testing each handhold before trusting it with my weight.

The exposure was dizzying. When I made the mistake of looking down, I could see hundreds of feet of empty air before the ground. My stomach lurched, but I pulled my focus back to the rock in front of me.

"You okay?" Noah called from just ahead.

"Yeah. Just taking it slow."

"Good. No rush."

We climbed in silence for a while, all our concentration focused on the physical challenge. My world narrowed to the rock under my hands, the next foothold, the way my muscles engaged and released.

There was something almost meditative about it, the absolute presence it required.

But as we climbed higher, the wind picked up. I felt it buffet against me, strong enough to make me sway.

"Em?" Noah had stopped, was looking back at me. "You good?"

"Wind's getting strong."

"I know. We can turn back if you want. Take the other route."

I looked up at the summit, so close now. Then back down at the path we'd climbed.

"I want to keep going," I said.

Noah studied my face. "Okay. But we go careful. And if it gets worse, we reassess."

"Deal."

We continued upward. The terrain grew even more technical, larger boulders to navigate, sections where I had to stretch my legs wide to reach the next foothold. My arms were shaking with effort, my legs burning.

And then, without warning, my foot slipped.

One moment I was reaching for a handhold, the next my boot skidded on loose rock and I was falling, sliding, my fingers scrabbling for purchase on the smooth granite.

I screamed, a sound of pure terror, and then I was over the edge, the world tilting sickeningly, nothing but air beneath me.

My body slammed against the rock face about six feet down. I managed to grab onto a narrow ledge, my fingers digging into the stone with desperate strength. My heart hammered so hard I thought it might burst.

"EMMA!" Noah's voice, sharp with panic. "Don't move! I've got you!"

I couldn't have moved if I wanted to. Every muscle was locked in terror, my entire body rigid against the rock. I could feel the void beneath me, all that empty space.

"Emma, listen to me." Noah's voice was closer now, steadier. I could hear him moving above me. "You're okay. I can see you. You're on a ledge."

"I can't..." My voice came out thin and strangled.

"I know. I know you're scared. But I need you to stay calm. Can you do that for me?"

I tried the breathing technique. In for four, hold for seven, out for eight. My chest was tight, but I focused on the pattern.

"I've got rope in my pack," Noah was saying. "I'm going to lower it down to you, and you're going to secure it around your waist. And then I'm going to pull you up. Okay?"

"Okay."

"Emma, look at me."

I tilted my head back carefully and met his eyes. He was leaning over the edge, his face pale but determined.

"I've got you," he said. "I'm not going to let you fall. Do you trust me?"

The question hung in the air between us. This was different from the stream crossing, from accepting his help with my tent, from telling him about Scott. This was my life, literally in his hands.

But I knew the answer.

"Yes," I said. "I trust you."

Relief flickered across his face. "Okay. Hold on. I'm getting the rope."

He disappeared from view, and I focused on my breathing, on the stone under my fingers, on staying present.

The rope came snaking down the rock face, and I grabbed it with my right hand, still keeping my left hand locked on the ledge.

"Got it!" I called up.

"Good! Now I need you to tie it around your waist. Can you do that?"

I looked at the rope, then at my precarious position. To tie the rope properly, I'd need to use both hands. Which meant letting go of the ledge.

My body tensed, but I recognized the fear for what it was. Just fear. Not truth.

"I have to let go," I said.

A pause. Then: "I know. I know that's terrifying. But Emma, I've got the other end secured. Even if you slip while you're tying it, you won't fall more than a few feet. I won't let you fall."

This was it. The moment. I could keep clinging to the ledge, frozen in fear. Or I could choose to trust him, choose to believe that he meant what he said, choose to let go of the safety I could see for the safety I had to believe in.

I took a breath. And made the choice.

I let go of the ledge with my left hand and grabbed the rope with both hands, working quickly to loop it around my waist and tie the knot Becca had taught me weeks ago. My fingers shook, but I got it secure.

"Done!" I shouted up.

"Okay! Now I need you to hold onto the rope and use your feet against the rock face. I'm going to pull you up, but you need to help by walking up the wall. Can you do that?"

"Yes."

"You can do this, Emma. I know you can."

I gripped the rope with both hands and felt it go taut as Noah began to pull. My feet found purchase on the rock, and I started walking backwards up the face, using my legs to push while the rope took most of my weight.

It was slow. Every muscle in my body screamed with effort, and the rope cut into my waist. I could hear Noah grunting with exertion above me.

One step. Another step. Keep going.

My fingers crested the edge, and then Noah's hand was there, gripping my wrist, pulling me the last few feet. I scrambled over the top and collapsed onto the solid rock of the ridge, gasping for air, my entire body shaking.

Noah pulled me away from the edge, into the safer center of the ridge, and then his arms were around me and I was sobbing into his shoulder, all the terror releasing at once.

"I've got you," he murmured into my hair. "You're okay. You're safe. I've got you."

I clung to him, my face pressed against his chest. I could hear his heart racing as fast as my own.

"I thought..." I couldn't finish the sentence.

"I know. Me too." His voice was rough. "But you didn't. You're okay."

We stayed like that for a long time, wrapped around each other on the narrow ridge, neither of us willing to let go. I felt the adrenaline slowly drain from my system, leaving me exhausted and shaky but alive. So completely alive.

When the shaking finally subsided, I pulled back just enough to look at Noah. His face was streaked with sweat and dirt, his eyes still wide.

"You saved my life," I whispered.

"You saved yourself," Noah said. "You let go of the ledge. You tied the rope. You climbed back up. I just held the other end."

"That's everything." My voice cracked. "You were everything."

I kissed him then, desperate and grateful and full of all the things I couldn't find words for. He kissed me back, his hands cupping my face, and for a moment the mountain and the danger and everything else fell away.

When we pulled apart, both breathing hard, I rested my forehead against his.

"I love you," I said. The words came without hesitation. "I'm in love with you, Noah."

His expression transformed, relief and joy breaking through the fear. "I love you too. God, Emma, I love you so much."

We sat there, foreheads touching, hands clasped, both of us still trembling. I felt something settle in my chest. Not the absence of fear, but the presence of something stronger. Trust. Love. The knowledge that I'd chosen to let go, and he'd caught me.

"We should probably finish this climb," Noah said finally.

I looked up at the summit, so close now. "Yeah. Let's finish this."

They untied the rope and coiled it back into Noah's pack. My hands were still trembling slightly, scraped and raw from the rock, but I felt present. Alive. Like something fundamental had shifted.

The rest of the climb was careful and slow, but we made it. And when we finally pulled ourselves up onto the broad, rocky summit of Mount Katahdin, I felt tears spring to my eyes.

We'd done it. I'd done it.

Maggie and Elijah were already there, sitting on a flat boulder. When they saw us emerge, Maggie stood up with a whoop of celebration.

"You made it!" She was already hurrying over, pulling me into a fierce hug. "Oh honey, you did it!"

"We had a moment," Noah said, and I heard the lingering strain in his voice. "Emma fell. Had to do a rope rescue."

Maggie pulled back, her face going pale. "Are you okay?"

"I'm okay." I was surprised to find it was true. Shaken, scraped up, but whole. "Scary as hell, but I'm okay."

Elijah had joined us now, his expression serious. "That's the mountain. She tests you." He looked at me with something like respect in his eyes. "But you're here. That's what matters."

I looked around at the summit: the weathered wooden sign marking the northern terminus of the Appalachian Trail, the endless expanse of wilderness stretching in every direction, the sky impossibly blue above us. Maggie and Elijah, my trail family. Noah, the man I loved.

I'd started this hike broken and scared, unsure if I could trust anyone, including myself. And here I was: standing on top of a mountain, scraped and exhausted and absolutely alive.

Not healed. Not perfect. But stronger than I'd ever imagined I could be.

"We should take a picture," Maggie said, pulling out her phone. "All of us together."

We crowded around the summit sign, arms around each other, grinning at the camera despite the exhaustion, despite the fear still lingering at the edges. Evidence that we'd made it. That we'd done the impossible thing.

As Maggie set up the timer and ran to join us, I leaned into Noah's side. He pulled me closer, and I felt the solid warmth of him, the steady presence that had caught me when I fell.

"We did it," I whispered.

"We did it," he agreed.

The camera clicked, capturing the moment: four people on a mountaintop, windblown and tired and absolutely triumphant.

I looked out at the wilderness we'd walked through, at the long trail stretching behind us, all those miles, all those moments of doubt and fear and slowly-built trust. Not an ending, I realized. A beginning.

I pulled the stone from my pocket one last time. Brave. I ran my thumb over the word, and this time I knew, really knew, it was true.

I was brave. Not fearless. Not unbroken. But brave enough to keep choosing trust, keep choosing love, keep choosing to let go of the ledge even when every instinct screamed to hold on.

That was enough. That was everything.

I slipped the stone back into my pocket and reached for Noah's hand. He laced his fingers through hers and squeezed.

Ready for whatever came next.

***

The restaurant was a small, wood-paneled place that smelled like grilled meat and beer. The four of us claimed a corner booth with cracked vinyl seats and a wobbly table. I'd changed into the one clean shirt I had left, a soft gray henley, and attempted to do something with my hair beyond just pulling it back in a ponytail.

"You look nice," Noah said, and the way he looked at me made my cheeks warm.

Maggie arrived in a flowing purple tunic and Elijah in a flannel shirt that had definitely seen better days. I bit back a laugh when I remembered he'd said he was going full hiker trash.

"There they are," Maggie said warmly, sliding into the booth across from us. "Our mountain conquerors."

We ordered quickly: steaks for everyone except Maggie, who got the grilled salmon. And a bottle of wine to share, because we were celebrating.

"To Katahdin," Elijah said when the wine arrived, raising his glass. "And to the crazy people who climb her."

"To trail family," Maggie added, her eyes shining.

"To making it," Noah said, looking at me.

I raised my glass, feeling the weight of the moment. "To new beginnings."

We clinked glasses, and I took a sip. The wine was cheap and slightly sour, but it didn't matter. Nothing could diminish this: the four of us gathered around this wobbly table, tired and triumphant and together.

The food arrived, and for a few minutes we were all silent, devouring our meals with the single-minded focus of people who'd been eating dehydrated rations for months.

"God," Noah groaned around a mouthful of steak. "I'm never eating ramen again."

"You say that now," Elijah said. "Give it a month. You'll be craving it."

We laughed, and I felt a pang at the thought of a month from now. Where would we all be? Back to our separate lives, this trail family scattered.

"What's the first thing you're going to do when you get back?" Maggie asked, looking around the table.

Elijah answered first. "Sleep in my own bed for approximately three days straight. Then maybe make an actual cooked meal."

"I'm going to hug my dog," Maggie said. "God, I miss that ridiculous animal."

"I'm going to see Becca," I said. "And then figure out what comes next, I guess."

I felt Noah's eyes on me but didn't look at him. The question of what came next felt too big.

"What about you, Noah?" Maggie asked.

Noah was quiet for a moment, turning his wine glass in his hands. "I'm going back to Indiana. I have an interview at Brown in a month, the psychiatry program. And I need to tell my father about it before then."

"That's wonderful!" Maggie's face lit up. "In Providence, right? That's perfect!"

"If I get in," Noah said carefully. "It's just an interview. Nothing's certain yet."

"But you're going to tell your father anyway?" Elijah asked.

"I have to." Noah's jaw tightened. "He's been planning my life for years. Expects me to take over his podiatry practice. And I need to tell him that's not what I want, even if I don't get into Brown. Even if I have to figure out another path."

Maggie's expression softened. "That takes courage."

"It takes something," Noah said, but he didn't sound convinced.

We traded stories as we ate, favorite moments from the trail, close calls, the funniest things we'd seen. I laughed until my stomach hurt, listening to Elijah describe the time he'd gotten his pack stuck in a tree.

"What about you two?" Maggie asked, gesturing between Noah and me with her fork. "Favorite trail moment?"

Noah and I looked at each other.

"The fireflies," I said at the same time Noah said, "The stone."

We laughed.

"There was a night a few weeks ago," I said. "We were camped in a clearing, and fireflies came out. Hundreds of them. And I realized that even in darkness, there's still light. You just have to look for it."

Maggie's eyes had gone soft. "That's beautiful, honey."

"Your turn," I said to Noah.

"Emma's birthday. Vermont border. I gave her a stone with 'Brave' carved into it." Noah smiled. "Watching her realize she actually was brave, that was everything."

I reached into my pocket and felt the stone's smooth surface. "I still carry it. Every day."

Under the table, Noah reached for my hand, and I laced my fingers through his. Solid. Real. Here.

As we waited for dessert, Elijah cleared his throat. "I want to say something. If that's okay."

Everyone turned to look at him.

"I've been hiking trails for ten years," he said. "Since I got back from Afghanistan. And I've met a lot of people out here. But this was special. You three made this hike more than just miles. You made it mean something."

I felt my eyes fill with tears.

"I came out here to deal with my own demons," Elijah continued. "The PTSD, the anxiety, all of it. And I thought I had to do it alone. But you showed me that healing doesn't have to be solitary. That it's okay to let people in."

Maggie reached over and took his hand.

"So thank you," Elijah said, looking at each of us in turn. "For being my trail family. For making me remember that I'm not alone in this."

"Oh, you old softie," Maggie said, but her voice was thick with emotion. "Now you've got me crying into my wine."

I couldn't speak. Couldn't get words past the lump in my throat. I just nodded, squeezing Noah's hand under the table.

Eventually, inevitably, the bill came. We split it four ways, and then we were standing outside the restaurant in the cool evening air, delaying the goodbye.

"So," Maggie said, pulling her cardigan tighter. "I guess this is it."

"Don't," I said, my voice breaking. "Don't say goodbye. Not yet."

Maggie pulled me into a fierce hug. I buried my face in her shoulder and let myself cry for the end of the trail, for the parting of this family.

"You are so strong," Maggie whispered in her ear. "Stronger than you know. Don't forget that when you go back to the real world. Don't let anyone make you small again."

"I won't," I managed.

"And you," Maggie pulled back and pointed at Noah. "You be brave. Tell your father the truth. Whatever happens with Brown, you deserve to live your own life."

"I'm trying," Noah said, his voice rough.

Maggie hugged him too, and then Elijah was there, pulling me into a surprisingly strong embrace.

"You're going to be okay, kid," he said. "You've got this."

"Thank you," I whispered. "For everything."

We exchanged more hugs, promises to stay in touch, even though we all knew that trail friendships rarely survived the transition back to regular life.

Finally, Maggie and Elijah headed toward their rental car. Noah and I stood on the sidewalk, watching them drive away.

The silence that fell between us was heavy.

"Want to walk?" Noah asked.

"Yeah."

We walked through the small town, past darkened storefronts and quiet houses. The air smelled like pine and wood smoke.

"Tomorrow," I said finally. "We should probably talk about it."

"I know."

We found a bench overlooking a small park and sat down. I could feel the weight of everything unsaid between us.

"I don't know how to do this," I admitted. "I don't know how to say goodbye to you."

Noah turned to face me. "I don't want to say goodbye."

"But you're going back to Indiana. And I'm going back to Providence. And you have the interview in a month, but that doesn't mean..." I couldn't finish.

"Doesn't mean I'll get in," Noah said quietly. "I know. And even if I do, I still have to tell my father. Which could go very badly."

"Are you scared?" I asked.

"Terrified." He let out a shaky laugh. "There's a good chance he won't speak to me after I tell him. My mom will be caught in the middle. And if I don't get into Brown, I'll have burned that bridge for nothing."

I heard the uncertainty in his voice, the fear. This wasn't a sure thing. None of it was.

"But I have to try," Noah continued. "I can't keep living his life instead of mine. Even if it means disappointing him. Even if it means I have to figure out another path."

"What if you do get into Brown?" I asked carefully. "What if you move to Providence?"

Noah looked at me, and I saw hope and fear warring in his expression. "Then I'd be in the same city as you. And we could... we could see what happens. If you wanted to."

"I want to," I said, and felt the truth of it. "But Noah, that's a lot of ifs. If you get in. If you can stand up to your father. If this," I gestured between us, "translates to real life and not just trail life."

"I know." He reached for my hand. "I know it's uncertain. But Emma, whatever happens with Brown, whatever happens with my father, I want to try. Even if it's long distance for a while. Even if it's complicated."

I felt tears prick at my eyes. "I want to try too. But I'm scared. What if you go back and everything changes? What if you decide this was just a trail thing?"

"It's not just a trail thing," Noah said firmly. "Emma, I'm in love with you. That's not going to change when I get on a plane tomorrow."

"You don't know that."

"I do know that." He cupped my face with his hand. "But I can't promise you everything will work out. I can't promise I'll get into Brown or that my father will accept my choice or that long distance won't be hard. All I can promise is that I'm going to try. I'm going to show up for that interview. I'm going to tell my father the truth. And I'm going to call you, text you, visit when I can. That's all I've got."

I looked at him, at the sincerity in his eyes, and felt something settle in my chest. He couldn't promise me certainty. But he was promising to try. And maybe that was enough.

"Okay," I whispered. "Okay, we try."

He kissed me then, soft and tender, and I kissed him back, trying to memorize the feeling: his hand in my hair, the warmth of him, the way my heart felt too big for my chest.

When we pulled apart, we sat in silence for a while, foreheads touching, hands clasped.

"I should probably get back to the hostel," I said eventually. "Early bus tomorrow."

"Yeah. Early flight for me too."

We walked back slowly, neither of us wanting the night to end. At the hostel entrance, we stopped.

"So," Noah said.

"So."

"I'll call you. When I land in Indiana."

"Okay."

"And I'll let you know how it goes with my father. And the interview."

"Okay."

He pulled me into one more hug, holding me tight. "I love you," he whispered into my hair.

"I love you too."

We stood there for a long moment, and then I forced myself to pull away. If I didn't leave now, I wasn't sure I'd be able to.

"Goodbye, Noah."

"Not goodbye," he said. "Just see you later."

I smiled through my tears. "See you later."

I walked into the hostel without looking back, knowing that if I did, I'd fall apart completely. In my room, I sat on the bed and let myself cry, the stone clutched in my hand.

Tomorrow I'd get on a bus back to my real life. And Noah would fly back to his. And we'd figure out if what we had on the trail could survive in the real world.

But tonight, I let myself feel the grief of this ending. And underneath it, the tiny seed of hope for what might come next.

I pulled out my phone and texted Becca: I'm coming home. I have so much to tell you.

Her response came almost immediately: I can't wait to hear everything. I'm so proud of you, Em.

I smiled through my tears and typed back: Me too. I'm proud of me too.

And I meant it. Whatever happened with Noah, whatever came next, I'd done this. I'd hiked the Appalachian Trail. I'd faced my fears. I'd let someone in, even knowing I might get hurt.

I'd been brave.

And that was something no one could take away.

***

I woke to pale morning light filtering through the hostel window and the immediate, crushing awareness that this was the last day.

Noah was in the room next door. We'd left our doors open last night, neither of us wanting to be completely apart. I could hear him moving around, getting ready, and I wanted to memorize every sound.

My bus left at noon. His flight was at two. In a matter of hours, we'd be going in opposite directions: me to Providence, him to Indiana. And everything we'd built over the summer would have to survive on phone calls and texts and hope.

I got up and padded to the bathroom to splash water on my face. The woman in the mirror looked different than she had five months ago. Stronger. More present. But right now, she just looked sad.

When I came back, Noah was in my doorway, leaning against the frame.

"Hey," he said softly.

"Hey."

"How long have you been up?"

"Not long. I didn't want to wake you."

He crossed the space between us and pulled me into his arms. We stood like that for a long time, not talking, just breathing together.

"I don't want to do this," I finally whispered.

"Me neither."

We got ready in a kind of numb silence. Packing the last of our things, checking out of the hostel, walking to the small café down the street for breakfast neither of us really wanted.

I pushed eggs around on my plate, my stomach too tight to eat. Across from me, Noah was doing the same thing with his pancakes.

"This is awful," I said.

"Worst breakfast ever," Noah agreed.

"I meant the leaving. But yeah, also the food."

We laughed, but it was hollow. There was no escaping what was coming.

At eleven thirty, we walked to the bus station. My pack was strapped to my back one last time, and it felt both familiar and strange, like I was wearing someone else's clothes, playing at being a hiker when really, the hiker version of myself was being left behind.

The bus was already there, idling, the driver loading luggage into the cargo hold. I handed over my pack and watched it disappear into the belly of the bus. Going home. Back to real life.

I turned to Noah, and for a moment we just stood there, looking at each other in the harsh sunlight of the parking lot.

"I don't know how to do this," I said, and my voice broke.

"Me neither."

Noah pulled me into his arms, and I clung to him, breathing in the scent of him: trail dust and soap and something uniquely Noah. I tried to memorize everything. The feel of his arms around me, the steady beat of his heart under my palm, the way he fit against me like we were two pieces of the same whole.

"I love you," I said into his chest. "I love you so much."

"I love you too." His voice was rough. "God, Emma, I love you too."

I pulled back just enough to look at him. His eyes were red, and I realized he was crying. It broke something in my chest.

"Four weeks," he said. "The Brown interview is in four weeks. And then I'll know if I got in, if I'm coming to Providence."

"And you'll tell your father before then," I said. Not a question.

"Yeah." Noah nodded. "I will. Whatever happens with Brown, I'm telling him the truth. That I can't take over the practice. That I need to live my own life."

"I'm proud of you," I whispered.

"Don't be proud yet. I haven't done it."

"You will."

The bus driver called out a five-minute warning, and I felt panic claw up my throat. Five minutes. That was all we had left.

"Call me?" I said. "When you land? And after you talk to your dad?"

"I will. And you call me when you get home. When you see Becca. Whenever you want." Noah's thumbs were brushing away my tears. "Emma, I'm a phone call away. Always. You hear me?"

I nodded, not trusting my voice.

"And in four weeks, I'll call you after the interview. Whatever happens, we figure it out together. Okay?"

"Okay."

The bus driver called final boarding, and I knew I couldn't delay any longer. I stood on my toes and kissed Noah, pouring everything I felt into it: all the love and fear and hope and grief. He kissed me back like he was trying to memorize me, his hands in my hair, holding me close.

When we finally broke apart, we were both crying openly.

"I have to go," I whispered.

"I know."

"This isn't goodbye. Right? This is just see you later."

"See you later," Noah agreed. "See you soon."

I forced myself to step back, to let go of his hands. Every instinct screamed at me to stay, to not get on that bus, to hold onto this moment and this man and not let the real world tear us apart.

But I'd learned something on the trail: sometimes the hardest thing and the right thing were the same thing.

I walked to the bus steps, and then turned back one more time. Noah was still standing there, watching me, his face a mixture of love and anguish.

"Choose yourself," I called to him. "When you talk to your dad. Choose yourself."

His smile was small but real. "Only if you promise to do the same."

"Deal."

I climbed onto the bus and found a window seat. As the bus pulled away from the station, I pressed my hand against the glass, watching Noah grow smaller and smaller until he was just a figure in the distance, and then gone.

I pulled the stone from my pocket, Brave, and held it in my palm as the bus carried me away from the mountains and back toward home.

The woman next to me asked if I was okay, and I realized I was crying again.

"I'm fine," I said, and it wasn't entirely a lie. "I just finished a really long hike. And now I have to figure out what comes next."

The woman smiled sympathetically. "That must be hard. Not knowing."

"It is." I looked out the window at the landscape rolling past. "But I guess that's life, right? We never really know what comes next. We just keep walking forward and hope for the best."

The woman nodded and went back to her book, and I leaned my head against the window.

I thought about everything I'd done over the past five months. The miles I'd walked. The mountains I'd climbed. The person I'd been when I started, broken and scared and unsure I'd survive, and the person I was now.

I'd told Noah about Scott. About the pregnancy, the abortion, the suicide. I'd fallen off a mountain and climbed back up. I'd let myself fall in love even though it terrified me. I'd learned to trust again, to open myself to possibility, to believe that maybe I deserved good things.

And now I was going home. Back to Providence. Back to my apartment and my job and my regular life. But I wasn't the same person who'd left. That Emma was gone. This Emma, the one who'd walked five hundred miles, who'd summited Katahdin, who'd learned what she was made of, this Emma was different.

Stronger. Braver. More herself than she'd been in years.

The uncertainty about Noah scared me. The not knowing. The possibility that this beautiful thing we'd built might not survive the distance, or the interview might not go well, or his father might make things impossible.

But I'd survived worse. I'd survived Scott. I'd survived grief and trauma and self-doubt.

I could survive this too. Whatever came next, whether it was Noah coming to Providence for residency or figuring out long distance or, worst case, learning to be okay on my own again, I would handle it.

Because I wasn't the same scared girl who'd gotten on the trail back in May. I was someone who'd proven to herself that she could do hard things. That she was brave, not because she wasn't afraid, but because she kept choosing to move forward even when she was terrified.

I didn't need Noah to be okay. I wanted him, I loved him, I hoped with everything in me that it would work out. But I didn't need him to validate my worth or prove that I was capable of being loved. I already knew those things now. I'd learned them on the trail, one step at a time.

That was the real victory. Not finishing the hike, though that mattered. Not falling in love, though that was beautiful. The victory was knowing, really knowing, that I was enough. Just as I was. Scared and strong and still healing. Still human.

I pulled out my phone and texted Becca: On the bus. Coming home. Can't wait to see you.

Becca's response was immediate: I'm making tacos and opening ALL the wine. Tell me everything.

I smiled through my tears and typed back: Everything. I promise.

Then I pulled up Noah's contact and sent him a message: Made it on the bus. Miss you already. Call me when you land. I love you.

I watched the message deliver, then tucked the phone away and closed my eyes.

The trail was behind me. The future was uncertain. But for now, I was here, on a bus heading home, carrying all the strength I'd built and all the love I'd found and all the hard-won wisdom about who I was and what I deserved.

It wasn't a perfect ending. It was real and uncertain and a little scary.

And maybe real was better than perfect anyway.

Don't miss out!

Visit the website below and you can sign up to receive emails whenever Melissa Ann Palmer publishes a new book. There's no charge and no obligation.

https://books2read.com/r/B-A-JBLME-ISKFI

BOOKS 2 READ

Connecting independent readers to independent writers.

Also by Melissa Ann Palmer

The Emma Series
Dance of the Firefly

About the Author

Melissa Ann Palmer discovered author Judy Blume in fourth grade and immediately saw herself in the pages of Blubber. It was the moment she realized stories could mirror our own lives back to us. She has been writing ever since, crafting tales where she explored the messy, complicated parts of being human.

By day, Melissa is a clinical social worker, doing her small part to enrich lives. By night (and weekends, and any spare moment), she writes novels that do the same, offering hope and understanding to those who need it most. She believes stories help us learn about ourselves because sometimes it's easier to see truth in someone else's journey.

Melissa lives in a small log cabin in the woods of Connecticut with her handy husband and two opinionated dogs: Otis, an elderly pug who makes his royal status known to all, and Owen, a Boston Terrier and certified mama's boy who provides comfort whenever the characters in her head make her cry.

She loves coffee, polka dots, taking naps, and anything sweet. Cheesecake is her weakness. Melissa believes stories have the power to heal, and that every woman is stronger than she realizes.

Melissa loves connecting with readers on Instagram @melissaannpalmer.author